## THE WAR ROOM WAS QUIET AS THE IMPLICATIONS WERE CONSIDERED

"The idea of creating the old Cold War mood doesn't thrill me. On the other hand, I can't say I feel too comfortable having the rest of the world tell me I can't defend myself because it makes them feel insecure. That puts me in a tricky position. Makes me feel I've got my back against the wall, a guy coming at me, and I don't have a thing in my hand to protect myself. By my calculation there's something wrong with that setup. If it gets to that situation, it's too late. If we let ourselves be talked into throwing down our weapons, we deserve what we get."

The big Fed glanced around the table. No one had anything to say.

"Look, maybe I made it too simplistic. Nothing is as black and white as that. Hell, I understand politics and diplomacy. We live in a—"

"Hal, you explained it just fine," Barbara Price said. "The truth is, we get too tangled up in the fancy discussions. Maybe that's what it needed. Someone saying it like it is."

"The Koreans have the Slingshot data, and we have to get it back, no matter what it takes," Schwarz added.

DON PENDLETON'S

# STONY

AMERICA'S ULTRA-COVERT INTELLIGENCE AGENCY

# MAN

## ROGUE
## STATE

## A GOLD EAGLE BOOK FROM
## WORLDWIDE.

TORONTO • NEW YORK • LONDON
AMSTERDAM • PARIS • SYDNEY • HAMBURG
STOCKHOLM • ATHENS • TOKYO • MILAN
MADRID • WARSAW • BUDAPEST • AUCKLAND

First edition October 2002

ISBN 0-373-61945-6

ROGUE STATE

Special thanks and acknowledgment to
Mike Linaker for his contribution to this work.

**Printed in U.S.A.**

# ROGUE STATE

# PROLOGUE

*North Korea*

Carl Lyons knew that morning was going to be different from any of the others. The first indication was when his guard failed to wake him just as it started to get light. Lyons took time to wonder why, waiting to see if he was going to be fed at the usual time. When that didn't happen, either, he began to suspect something was different. As light crept into his cell from the high window over his head, exposing the stone walls and floor, and the sounds of the compound penetrated, Lyons knew for certain that this day was going to be different. He settled with his back to the stone wall, the thin blankets wrapped around his shoulders, and waited. A couple of hours later he heard sound outside his cell door. It was hard to judge time because they had taken his watch away soon after his arrival.

Footsteps approached his cell. Stopped. The bolts were drawn and the door flung open. Lyons remained where he was and watched as two guards stepped inside. He didn't recognize either of them. Both were armed, and they aimed their rifles at him as if they expected him to leap on them from the far side of the cell. Lyons couldn't have done that even if he had wanted. Lack of food and proper sleep had left him weakened. He had already lost weight, and the rough treatment he had received had done nothing to ease his condition. So he remained where he was and let the guards take the initiative.

A third figure appeared. It was Yat Sen Took, the North Korean who had taken Lyons prisoner during the abortive raid on the radar facility in Alaska. Took's left hand was still bandaged and held in a sling against his body. His injury was a legacy of the raid. Took had lost two fingers from the hand. In Lyons's opinion, two fingers weren't enough, but then he was slightly prejudiced.

"No breakfast today," Took said. His tone was soft, emotionless. "Time to go. You are leaving here. We are sending you to another place. I must tell you now that you will not like it. The conditions are far below our standards, the work is hard and the food is unpleasant."

Took said something to the guards. They strode across the cell and hauled Lyons to his feet. One of them wrenched the blankets from his shoulders. They began to shout at him in Korean. He had no idea what they were saying, so he ignored their shouts. One of the guards became enraged and struck Lyons across the back of the shoulders with his rifle, driving the American to the floor.

"These guards are from your new place," Took explained. "They expect obedience."

"Then tell them to speak English, because I don't understand what they're jabbering about," Lyons snapped.

"Then you should learn," Took said. "You are in Korea now. This is our country. You are not in America any longer."

"And don't I know it," Lyons said. "Far as I'm concerned, Took, you can take Korea and shove it."

The Korean snapped an order to the guards. They dragged Lyons out of the cell and down the passage to the outside door. A military truck waited, its engine idling. Thick trails of exhaust fumes hung in the cold air around the rear of the vehicle. The tailgate was down, and Lyons was manhandled into the back of the truck. He was thrown to the floor, boots slamming into his sides as his escort joined him. The Korean guards sat on benches lining either side of the truck.

Took stood at the tailgate, a faint smile on his face.

"You should arrive before dark. It's a long journey. Especially without food or water. And it gets extremely cold where you are going."

The truck started to move. Just before the tailgate was lifted into place, Lyons sat up.

"Hey, Took, how's the hand?" he asked. "Still hurting, I hope."

The expression in the Korean's eyes was worth the hard blow that landed across Lyons's back.

The truck pulled out of the compound, vanishing from sight. Took returned to his office on the upper floor of the building that stood on the side of the compound across from the cell block. He climbed the stairs and pushed open the door. The room he entered was long and spacious. As well as serving as his office, it also provided a high degree of comfort. A log fire was blazing in the stone hearth, and as Took made his way across to the fire a voice rose from one of the large armchairs set before the blaze.

"No last-minute confession?"

Took sat in the chair across from the speaker.

"He might feel more inclined to cooperate after he samples the delights of the camp," he said.

"Have you considered the possibility he might not have anything to tell you?"

"The thought has crossed my mind. But we cannot allow anything to slip by us. This man is part of the American conspiracy against this country. Whatever his role, he could be holding information that could be vital to our struggle."

Nikolai Gagarin inclined his head in mute response.

"During your time you must have come across individuals who carried all kinds of secrets in their heads. Sometimes the smallest piece extracted can open many doors. This American may be nothing more than a paid assassin for the U.S.A. He could also be one of their key agents. Until I establish one or the other, we must maintain the pressure on him."

Gagarin, late of the KGB and now in the service of one of Russia's hard-line parties, took a drink from his cup of coffee. He didn't share Took's belief that the American captive had valuable information in his head. Gagarin's interest went further than that. He needed the American as bait, a hook to draw in the rest of the covert commando team that had caused problems for him in the past—and that was doing exactly the same now. Gagarin was convinced the commandos would come after their colleague. The Americans were a sentimental breed. They carried a need to rescue missing colleagues. They refused to abandon them. To let them lie where they had fallen. They would come after the captive. And when they did, Gagarin would be waiting for them. He needed the kudos of a victory over the Americans after the fiasco of the Alaskan venture. The whole thing had gone wrong, and he had been dragged into the mess. He had used his influence to call up a Russian strike fighter from one of the Siberian bases in an attempt to take out the American helicopter stalking the Russian combat team. The American craft had destroyed the MiG fighter. The loss hadn't been accepted well, and Gagarin had been held to account, which was why he had decided to join Took in Korea and do what he could to make amends.

They had subjected the American captive to a hard regime, alternating between sympathy and straightforward brutality. The man, to his credit, had taken all they threw at him without a murmur. Gagarin, often on the sidelines, had seen a toughness in the man that would keep him sane and in control no matter what. Took had a personal agenda to follow, Gagarin saw. The Korean wasn't a good loser. He held the American totally responsible for what had happened in Alaska and throughout the whole of the planned strike against the U.S. Slingshot program.

Took's masters, the ruling North Korean regime,

were determined to destroy the Slingshot system. They wanted to be the dominating force in Asia, even over the Chinese themselves, and had a firm basis in the arms market with their superior range of missiles. The thorn in their sides was Slingshot. If it became active, presenting an unbreachable shield against incoming missiles, then the North Koreans would lose face with their buyers. What would be the point of purchasing long-range missiles if it was known from the start that the Americans had a workable defense shield? So the Koreans had decided that if they wanted to remain top dog, then the only way would be to put Slingshot on the scrap heap.

Gagarin saw the logic in terms of self-preservation. He simply doubted the Koreans had the foresight to realize that the Americans weren't going to stand aside and let it happen. Twice now attempts had been made to interfere with Slingshot, and on both those occasions the Americans had blocked those attempts. Once they became aware that Korea was still trying, they would put up another robust defense.

As far as Gagarin was concerned, any strike made by the Americans would draw them out into the open. When that happened, he wanted to be in the know. Certainly his intention would be to prevent them from interfering with any campaign against Slingshot. But he would also be following his own agenda—which was the destruction of the American commando team. The Russian was aware of his own mortality. If he could at least stand up and face these Americans, even take them out of the picture once and for all, then he could die—perhaps not a happy man, but at least with a sense of accomplishment. That part of his policy Gagarin kept to himself. It was something for him alone. No one else.

THE TRIP WAS BAD. Lyons, cold and wet from the rain that fell for most of the ride, was made to lie on the floor of the truck. His guards moved to the front of the vehicle, where a canvas was draped over a metal frame. They sat on wooden benches, protected from the downpour, and watched him, grinning and chatting to one another. The extremes of the weather were bad enough. The hard ride, caused by the poor suspension on the lurching truck, jolted Lyons continuously. Stiff from lying in his cold cell, Lyons's starved and battered body protested at the new torture it was having to endure. Lyons did his best to move away from the physical discomfort. He forced his mind to other things, bringing himself to other times and places. He thought of the crashing Pacific waves off Topanga Beach; the sand and the blue sky of California; balmy days, cool nights; past pleasures and remembered experiences. Anything to draw him out of his cocoon of cold and wet. Away from his aching body and the empty, gnawing sensation in his stomach. He had been denied a decent meal for so long he was beginning to forget what food was like. They hadn't allowed him to shave since his capture, and the beard he wore still itched, and his skin was sore from being hit.

He told himself he could survive. He was Carl Lyons, the Ironman, and his philosophy was never to let the bastards grind him down. Ever. So it was time to put that into practice. He thought of the two guards sitting behind him. They weren't so far off his condition themselves. What did they really have? Perched on hard wooden benches in the back of a smoking truck, being bounced around like sacks of potatoes. Maybe not wet, but they would be cold, sitting there in those rough, crude uniforms. He didn't think they would be moving on to relax in warm, modern houses when they had delivered him. Their lives were on a pretty low level compared to what Lyons had back home.

Lyons found he was grinning to himself. It was a slack, crooked grin since his bruised mouth wasn't working properly, but nevertheless it was a grin. Here he was lying in the back of a truck in the freezing rain, half-starved, beaten and on his way to who knew where—and all he could think of was the condition of his guards. It struck Lyons as funny. He didn't quite make it to an outright laugh, but for a short time he did feel pretty good.

That light moment in his dark mood kept his spirits up when the truck reached its destination and the light began to fade. Lyons felt the vehicle slow as it reached the gates of the camp. It jerked into motion again, and as they passed through the gates Lyons caught a glimpse of a high perimeter fence that was constructed of thick wooden poles and heavy layers of barbed wire. He also spotted guard towers. Each one he saw held a pair of uniformed men and a machine gun, the barrel pointing in toward the camp that was encircled by the wire and guns. There were searchlights, too, sweeping back and forth across the darkened compound. He heard dogs, as well, snapping and snarling somewhere in the gloom. He could only count the defenses he was able to see within his limited field of vision. Lyons realized that there were probably more of the towers, armed guards and dogs taking in the whole of the camp.

"Always wanted to do the Universal Tour," Lyons said softly to himself.

One of the guards had to have heard Lyons speak. Out of the shadows a hard boot administered a savage kick to his side. The pain snapped Lyons out of his semidoze and he reared up, eyes wild and hot, teeth bared in his unshaved face. He stared at the guard who had kicked him and refused to look away. The Korean spit out a torrent of abuse, and it was obvious he wanted to hand out more punishment, but his companion said something that held him back. Lyons figured they were under orders to deliver him alive and keep him that way. It gave him some satisfaction, though nowhere near enough to compensate for his present situation.

The truck came to a stop, swaying dangerously. Lyons slid across the floor and slammed against the side. His guards stood and approached. They caught his arms and dragged him to the rear. Someone on the outside lowered the tailgate. Lyons felt himself being propelled over the edge, and he hit the ground hard. Some of the impact was absorbed by the wet, muddy earth. There was still a layer of semifrozen soil beneath. Lyons lay stunned by the fall. He spit cold, gritty mud from his mouth. Rough hands hauled him upright, and his guard escort dragged him across the compound. One of them kicked open the door of a crude hut. Lyons was shoved bodily into the gloom. He lost his balance and went down on the filthy floor of the hut. The door was closed, and he was left alone.

The interior smelled foul, a mix of damp and excrement. Lyons dragged himself into a sitting position. As his eyes adjusted to the gloom, he was able to make out shapes. No furniture. The floor was littered with discarded blankets and broken clay pots. There was a larger clay pot suspended from one of the rafters. There was a metal ladle hanging by a cord from the larger pot.

Water?

Lyons stood, staying motionless for a while as a wave of dizziness swept over him. When he felt steady, he crossed to the hanging pot and tilted it. The gleam of water showed inside. He took the ladle and dipped it into the water. Lifting it out, he sniffed the water. No odor. He tilted the ladle to his lips and tasted a little of the liquid. It was cold. Not the freshest he'd ever tasted, but he wasn't in any position to be too choosy. Lyons was careful not to drink too much. He took enough to moisten his throat and mouth.

A faint sound caught his attention. Lyons stayed where he was, still drinking slowly. He was listening, though, trying to gauge where the noise had come from. Somewhere behind him was the closest he could manage. He was shaking the ladle dry when he heard the sound again. This time it was closer, on his left side, only a couple of feet away. He finished at the water pot, cleared his throat and began to turn away. Now he could sense someone behind him. More than anything, Lyons could smell the man. He turned suddenly, bringing up both hands to protect himself—and came face-to-face with a wreck of a man who looked more scared than Lyons might have expected. He was staring at the Ironman with the incredulous expectation of a man who had just come face-to-face with an alien. The man reached out with a skinny, dirt-engrained hand, almost touching Lyons's face before he drew back, his expression turning to one of surprise.

"Jesus, are you real?" He gave a soft moan, pulling back into the shadows, muttering to himself. "Hey, friend, I hope you ain't been sent by that son of a bitch, Captain Yun. I thought they stopped fuckin' around with my head."

"I don't know any Captain Yun," Lyons said. "They just brought me in by truck from the last place I was locked up. Right now I don't have any idea where I am. Or what happens here. I can't even understand what these assholes say when they speak."

The other man moved closer again, pale light falling across his face. It showed him to be emaciated, his cheekbones hard against his skin. He was unshaved and the flesh remaining exposed was bruised and covered in half-healed cuts. His left eye was swollen and puffy.

"No shit?"

"I've been in better shape but I'm real. And I'm no plant. Do I look like a damn Korean?"

The man stared at him, still unsure. He shook his

head, muttering as he held some kind of internal argument.

"Where you from?"

"West Coast. L.A. But I move around a lot with my work these days."

"You can say that again. This place is a hell of a step from California."

"Tell me about it," Lyons grumbled.

"What year is it? These bastards won't tell me a damn thing."

Lyons told him and saw the shock in his face.

"Sweet Jesus, it can't be."

"How long have they had you here?"

"You told me the truth?"

"About the year? I told you the truth."

"Then they've had me here for three years."

"Why?"

The man attempted a smile. It seemed to be an effort. Lyons thought about the three years the man had spent here, and it didn't seem the man had anything to smile about.

"I guess they had cause. I was making a flyover. Pretty high until one of my engines decided to quit. I tried to make it back to my base, but they sent up a couple of jets and forced me down. Right then I was figuring it can't get any worse than this. Was I wrong."

"Air Force?"

"Yeah. Based in South Korea."

Lyons stared around the hut. It was pretty bad. He glanced at the man.

"You been in here the whole time?"

"Yeah. They won't let me sleep with the Korean prisoners. Guess they're scared I might corrupt them with my Yankee lies."

Pressing his face to the front wall of the hut, Lyons peered through the gaps in the rough timber. He couldn't see a great deal. What he did see didn't fill him with much enthusiasm. There were plenty of bright lights shining down on the compound from the high guard towers. He could also see more of the armed guards, some with hungry-looking dogs on leashes.

"If you're thinking about getting out, forget it. This place is tight. You'll see better in the morning when they wake us for breakfast. Pal, this place would have made Alcatraz look like a fuckin' nursery."

Lyons scouted out a place to sit down. He helped himself to one of the dirty blankets and pulled it around his body. He watched the other man wander around and do the same, moving to what was plainly *his* spot. There was silence for a while.

"How did you land up in this place?"

The question had been bound to come. Lyons considered his answer, unable to come up with anything that would explain the long and convoluted route that had brought him here.

"Just lucky," he said. He was too tired to go into a long explanation. "Maybe I'll tell you over breakfast."

BREAKFAST WAS some kind of watery soup containing cabbagelike vegetable and rice. The meal was served from large cans placed on a crude trestle table. The prisoners shuffled along in a ragged line, heads down so they were unable to make eye contact with the numerous armed and belligerent guards. The dogs were still around, too, snapping and snarling at the prisoners. Sometimes a handler would deliberately provoke his dog to lunge at a prisoner. If the unfortunate one was unable to avoid the attack, there would be a few seconds of agony as canine fangs tore at flesh, leaving the prisoner bleeding while the guards laughed and jeered at him.

Lyons took all this in as he stood behind his fellow captive at the end of the shivering, stumbling line. They were the last to be fed. He took the opportunity to check out the camp. The sight was depressing. About a dozen long huts stretched into the misty chill of the morning. Set apart were the huts for the guards. The first thing Lyons noticed were the chimneys on these huts, with smoke issuing from them. None of the prisoners' huts had any kind of heating. He spotted a motor pool, where trucks and smaller jeeps were parked. The perimeter fence, with its barbed wire and guard towers, was larger than he had realized from his restricted view the previous night.

"Great place, huh?" Lyons's American companion said. "Just think about it. Waking up to this for three fuckin' years."

The prospect had little appeal for Carl Lyons. A week in this place would drive him crazy. Somehow, some way, he had to get out.

They finally reached the trestle table. Lyons followed his companion's moves and helped himself to a wooden bowl. His soup was ladled into his bowl by a bland-faced Korean. He moved on and picked up a wooden spoon and a tin cup of water. The food was eaten outside. The prisoners simply squatted on the ground and ate quickly. Lyons caught on and did the same. He soon saw why. The guards began to move in on the squatting prisoners, urging them to hurry, knocking against some so that the food was spilled. He downed his soup quickly, ignoring the fact that it was hot, then drained the cup of water. He felt his stomach grumble in protest at the unhealthy way the food had been consumed. He was going to have to get used to that. On his feet, Lyons stayed close to his American companion. He needed to find out the rules of the camp, and staying close was the best way.

The prisoners were being herded into a large open space in the center of the compound, surrounded by the guards and dogs.

"Hey, you're lucky. This morning we get a speech from Captain Yun."

Before Lyons could ask anything about Captain Yun, there was a sudden disturbance around his American companion. A number of the Korean prisoners were closing in on him. Lyons saw one of them raise a hand and club the American across the back of the neck, driving him to his knees. Lyons could have made the decision to look the other way and leave the man to his fate. He knew little about him. The American might have done something to offend the Koreans and they were meting out their own punishment. That made no difference. Right now the American was Lyons's only friend in the camp.

Two strides and Lyons was behind the Korean who had struck the blow. He reached up and grabbed a handful of the Korean's thick black hair and yanked his head back. Lyons powerful right fist sledged into the Korean's side, over the ribs. He hit hard and fast, delivering a number of crippling blows that drew a pained groan from the Korean. The man sagged. Lyons kept hold of his hair, and as the man swung around, his face registering his pain, Lyons drove his right forearm into the man's face. Blood spurted. He released his hold and the Korean fell to the ground. His companions closed around him, hiding his plight from the guards, and strangely they ignored Lyons.

Lyons stepped away from the spot and moved in behind the stunned American, grabbing him by the shoulders and moving him through the milling prisoners. His retaliation had been so swift and deadly that it had gone practically unnoticed by the prisoners. Lyons moved them both as far from the scene as possible, letting them be swallowed up by the bulk of the crowd.

"You okay?" Lyons asked.

The other nodded. "I guess. Hey, whatever you did, thanks. Time we were introduced. I'm Chuck Rinaldi."

"Carl Lyons, but don't go spreading it around."

Rinaldi nodded. "No problem, pal."

"Why the attack?"

Rinaldi seemed reluctant, so Lyons let it go for the moment.

"So tell me what this Captain Yun is all about."

"Oh, he's a beauty. You'll love him. The guy is a certifiable nut. Hates his job. Hates the camp. But most of all he hates us. The prisoners. Does anything he can to humiliate us. Hurt us. Deprive us. Those things he loves. I don't like having to tell you this, but next to Korean prisoners the thing he hates most are American prisoners."

Lyons was able to see over heads of the other prisoners. A wooden platform had been placed in the open space. Two armed guards stood by. Lyons's attention was drawn to a lone figure walking toward the platform. This had to be Captain Yun. The man was dressed in a uniform that was far superior to that of any of the guards, and he was heavily decorated. Medals and ribbons covered the front of his uniform. He was also a big man for a Korean. Tall and powerfully built, he was an imposing figure.

Yun stepped up onto the platform and raised a hand. The assembled prisoners fell silent, save for one man who was unable to contain the hacking cough riddling his chest. One of the guards moved quickly to where the man was hunched over. Coming up behind him, he used the wooden club he carried to silence the man. Captain Yun began to speak, launching into a long and, even to Lyons, who couldn't understand a word, tiresome speech. It went on for at least twenty minutes. Lyons was curious as to what the man was ranting about. He didn't ask Rinaldi. There were too many guards around, just waiting for someone to dare to speak during Yun's speech. When the Korean had finished, he turned and looked directly in Lyons's direction, jabbing a finger at the American.

"For your benefit," he said in perfect English, "I have given these miserable traitors some uplifting reports about the glorious achievements of the Democratic People's Republic of Korea. None of them will understand because they are stupid. It is why they are here. To be reeducated so they can be sent home."

In a box, Lyons thought.

"Do *you* understand what I am saying?"

Lyons kept silent. He was studying Yun carefully, not sure what the man expected him to say. Yun stepped down off his stand and crossed to the silent crowd. As he approached, the prisoners stepped aside, allowing him to confront Lyons.

"You may speak," Yun said. "Or are you a unique American who has nothing to say?"

Lyons checked behind him.

"What are you doing?" Yun asked.

"Just making sure there isn't a guard with a club just waiting for me to open my mouth."

Yun smiled. "They do nothing unless I tell them. Then they obey me without question. Now tell me what you think of our establishment."

"I wouldn't house my dog in it."

"And the food?"

"Hard to describe."

"Your treatment?"

"You haven't killed me yet."

Yun nodded. "Exactly. You have described the regime here perfectly. I would have been disappointed if you had said anything to our credit. This is how I wish you to view the camp. It is where the prisoners are treated with contempt. Made to feel less than human. All dignity stripped from them and placed in constant fear for their lives. A death here means less than nothing. Yours included. The fact you have been sent here because it is believed you may have important information will not protect you. Break any of the rules and you will suffer. The guards themselves are only a step above the prisoners. They often need something to distract them from the boredom. Violence against the prisoners becomes a pastime. I do not like being here, so I may fall victim to the same feelings.''

"So we understand each other," Lyons said. "What next?"

Yun clasped his hands behind his back, gazing around the crowd of prisoners. They all stood with heads bowed, refusing to make eye contact with the man who held their lives in his hands.

"You join our community and try to survive. A word of warning. These men are North Koreans. All their lives they have been told about the evil Yankees who wish nothing more than the destruction of their country. I doubt you will find many friends here. It will be interesting to see how you deal with that."

Lyons got the message. If trouble started, he could expect little or no help from the guards. He accepted the condition and made a mental one of his own. Whatever the outcome, he was not going to stand by and allow himself to be used. If he had to kill to survive he would.

"One more thing," Yun said. "As far as you are

concerned, the gate you came in by is one-way only. The only time you step outside is when you are sent to work." He smiled again. "You do not go home. Ever!"

Yun turned away and left Lyons alone with his thoughts.

The guards began yelling, dispersing the prisoners. Rinaldi moved to Lyons's side.

"Jesus, Lyons, he talked to you more just now than he ever has to me in three years."

Lyons glanced at him. "That's just my personality, Chuck. People can't help liking me."

They moved across the compound, shivering as a cold wind brought icy rain with it.

"Chuck, tell me all about this place. Everything you can."

"What for?"

"So I can figure the best way to get the hell out...."

# CHAPTER ONE

*Stony Man Farm Firing Range*

Rosario "the Politician" Blancanales adjusted the earmuffs, picked up the M-16 and began firing at the distant target. There was a defiant set to his shoulders and a more than offensive attitude in the way he was standing. He emptied the magazine, ejected it and snapped in a fresh one. His finger stroked the trigger as he aimed and fired repeatedly. At the far end of the range the cardboard figure target was reduced to shreds. Blancanales rested the M-16 as the second magazine was drained. He jabbed a finger at the button and stood watching as the flapping target was winched toward him. As it came to a stop, Blancanales gazed at it with little interest.

"Anyone we know?" a voice asked.

Blancanales turned and saw his partner, Hermann "Gadgets" Schwarz, leaning against the wall behind him.

"I only asked in case it was me."

"Why would I be mad at you?" Blancanales asked.

Schwarz shrugged. ''You've been through everyone else, so I figured my turn had to come up sooner or later.''

Blancanales slammed down the M-16, his face taut with barely concealed anger.

''Almost ten days,'' he snapped, ''and tell me what's being done to find Carl? Don't bother 'cause I'll tell you. Not a damn thing. They sit and talk. Go away. Come back and talk some more. Jesus, they're worried about upsetting the Koreans. But Carl? He's expendable. Just one of the grunts. An acceptable loss.''

Blancanales began to strip the M-16, his fingers locating and removing parts even as he was staring hard at the target he had reduced to slivers of cardboard and plywood.

''They're doing what they can, Pol. Carl's position is a difficult one to pin down. We know the Koreans have him. They know we are aware, but there isn't a damn thing we can do because they just deny any knowledge. Okay, so there might not be much going on surface-wise, but that doesn't go for the undercover people. We have agents in North Korea, ones who have been there for years. They live there. Work there. And they have their ear to the ground all the time. Those people are sweating their balls off trying to get a murmur about Carl. But we're talking about North Korea here, which isn't exactly a model of openness. Pol, that country is one of the most repressive around. It makes China look like Disneyland. Communication is basic. The government runs a hell of a tight ship. You don't sneeze in North Korea without half the country getting to know.''

"Never stopped us before," Blancanales muttered. "We've been into places the Marines wouldn't even look at. All I know is we have one of buddies on his own, with no way out. Maybe wounded. I can't stand around and listen to nothing but cheesy talk. Gadgets, we have to go in there and pull him out.''

"Look, I know how you feel. He's my partner, too. Or had you forgotten that?''

"So how do you handle it?''

"I'm lucky. I have a buddy who is the best listener in the world. All I do is tell him how I feel and he puts me right.''

"Oh?'' Blancanales looked up in surprise. "Do I know him?''

There was a drawn silence. It extended until Blancanales glanced around and saw that Schwarz was standing, arms folded, staring at him with a ghost of a smile on his face.

"Funny guy,'' Blancanales said. "One day you'll do that and I'll ice you.''

"Hey, clean your damn gun and I'll buy you a coffee.''

"Buy? It's all free here.''

Schwarz shook his head. "Work with me here, buddy. Let's pretend I'm buying. You know, imagination time.''

"Can I imagine you still owe me twenty bucks?''

"My imagination doesn't stretch that far.''

"I knew there'd be a catch.'' Blancanales gathered his gear and trailed the way to the workbench at the far side of the firing range. "Did you actually come all the way down here just to make small talk? Or were you sent?"

"They need us in the War Room," Schwarz said. "I get the feeling it's decision time."

*War Room*

"THEY'RE ON THEIR WAY," Barbara Price said, replacing the phone.

"Anything we need to discuss before the main agenda?" Hal Brognola asked. Out the corner of his eye he saw McCarter's hand go up, and he groaned inwardly. Despite his promotion to leader of Phoenix Force, the Briton still couldn't resist the occasional bit of mischief. "David?"

"Any thought been given to us carrying luncheon vouchers when we go on a mission?"

His request was delivered with a straight face and a reverential tone that caught Brognola off guard.

"The way I see it, if we had them there wouldn't be a need to carry cash. When we go jumping from country to country it gets awkward. I'm sure the others will see the advantage."

"Why not go further and open credit accounts?" Katz said. "Just bill everything to Stony Man, then all Hal has to do is write the checks every month."

McCarter leaned forward. "That's even better. Bloody great idea, Katz. Hal?"

The penny had dropped and Brognola knew he was being set up. The big Fed leaned back in his seat, fumbling in his pocket to see if he had any antacid tablets. He had a feeling he might need them any minute. When he looked up again, McCarter was sitting back, the merest hint of a grin on his face. Across from him Katz was pretending to examine the tip of his prosthesis.

Any thought of admonishing the pair slipped away as swiftly as it rose. Brognola knew the strain they were all under. Carl Lyons's disappearance, the possibility of his death, weighed heavily on them all. McCarter's humorous moment was simply a way of easing the tension, even if it was only for a few seconds. It took them away from the somber mood they were all in, gave them a chance to redefine their thinking. The moment would be over soon enough, and the business at hand would reassert itself.

Aaron Kurtzman spun his wheelchair in through the door and rolled it up to the table. He dumped the stack of files he was carrying on his lap onto the table. Fishing a single sheet from the top of the pile, he slid it across to Brognola, who read it, then addressed the people seated at the table.

"Update on T.J.'s condition. The final fragments of the bullet have been removed from his shoulder. Apparently he came out of surgery last night. Prognosis says all the fragments have been removed and there shouldn't be a need for any more surgery. No damage to muscles or tissue, but due to the fragmentation it's going to take time for him to get back to operational fitness. So you're going to be one man down this time around, David."

"If I know T.J., he isn't going to like that," Calvin

James said. "That boy just doesn't like sitting still doing nothing."

"Reminds me of someone not far from where I'm sitting," Brognola said quietly, his gaze fixed on McCarter.

"You can add me to that list," Rosario Blancanales said as he and Schwarz entered the War Room.

"Point taken," Brognola said. "Take a seat, guys. I think I can give you some good news this time."

Blancanales and Schwarz joined Phoenix Force, Katz and Kurtzman at the big conference table, facing Brognola and Price.

"Give," Blancanales demanded. "And it better be good."

"Given the fact you people are not entirely happy over the way things have been progressing," Brognola said, "I've been liaising with the President. He's just as concerned over Carl being missing as we are."

"Really?" Blancanales said.

"Pol, give Hal a chance," Schwarz said.

Brognola didn't react to Blancanales's comment. He was aware of the closeness of Able Team. The loss of a team member hit hard, especially in their case, as there were only three of them in total. Despite the constant banter and seemingly endless bickering, the trio was closer than most. Since its inception, through the countless missions that had plunged its members into constant danger and both physical and mental aggravation, Able Team had become a loyal and competent group. That closeness, created by the stresses and pressures placed on them, had developed over time until it had become unshakable.

Losing Carl Lyons was like losing an arm or a leg. He was part of them, and they needed him so they could function again as the best there was.

"The U.S. intelligence agencies have their own people in North Korea. No names. No ID. We don't get to meet them unless it's decided the need justifies the risk."

"And is our need justified?" Blancanales asked.

Brognola only smiled. He pushed a sheet of paper across the table for Blancanales's attention.

"That was taken three days ago," the big Fed said, "by one of our people in North Korea. The operative had been doing some checking based on the satellite image we got of Carl arriving at the Korean base. We needed something more convincing, so our guy got it for us. Long-range shot of a light-haired foreigner being put in a truck. Tell me who that is in the shot."

Blancanales grabbed the photo. It was black-and-white, blown up to an eight-by-ten. The image was sharp and clear. No mistaking who it was.

"Carl," Blancanales said. *"It's Carl."*

Schwarz slid the photo closer and took a look himself. He shook his head in disbelief, passing the photo around the table so everyone could take a look.

"Well, I'd recognize that face anywhere," McCarter said. "You don't think he's pissed them off so much they're sending him back?"

"We won't get it that easy," Gary Manning said. "Hal, any intel on where they might be taking him?"

Brognola shook his head. "Our guy was lucky to get what he did. No chance of anything else at the point of contact. Once he took his shots he got out fast. He's been trying all his sources but hasn't come up with anything yet. He won't give up. If there's something out there, he'll come up with it."

"In the meantime all we can do is wait, guys," Price said. "It's not what you want to hear even from me, but I can't see we have any other choice right now."

"For now," Blancanales agreed. He glanced across at Brognola. "At least we have something. Now what else have you got for us, Hal? Has to be more than the info about Carl."

"Paul Curtis did us no favors when he died," Brognola said. "The guy knew a lot more than we first realized. Whatever his motives, he was a smart operator. We now know that he got into the computer mainframe, accessed restricted areas and took out information on Slingshot that goes one step on from the Militia Men's target. Curtis turns out to have been a greedy man and looked at the bigger picture. He got his hands on vital information and did a deal with the North Koreans because they were the ones who would benefit from it more than anyone. Cash transactions have been traced coming from a source we know belongs to the North Koreans. It's an obscure account they use to pay for information. And the recipient was Paul Curtis. We're talking big money here. Not that it's going to do him any good now."

"What is it Curtis sold?" Calvin James asked.

"Okay, recap time. I told you that Slingshot was an ongoing project. Each system will operate on its own initially. The long-term plan will incorporate each of the earlier concepts, making Slingshot increasingly sophisticated. The design allows for improvements to be brought on-line as and when the technology and hardware meets the requirements.''

Brognola paused and nodded to Kurtzman.

One of the TV monitors brightened as Kurtzman activated it. A computerized image filled the large screen.

''Slingshot phase one. A system capable of detecting and tracking incoming missiles and taking them out with interceptor missiles. Stage two was the addition of even better radar and tracking. The Alaska project. You prevented the sabotage of the main sites. When the Militia Men sank those barges, they delayed the construction. But that's all. The project will still go ahead.''

He used his remote to alter the image.

''Phase three. A ring of satellites scanning the globe. They're connected to the Slingshot system. They see a missile launch, track it and work out its target trajectory. Once the missile has been designated as hostile, the satellites send instructions to the interceptor system and give it the command to destroy the incoming missile. The timing is so precise that the hostile can be detected and taken out even before it reaches optimum height. This can work with single and multiple launches.''

The images on-screen showed a simulated launch, intercept and takedown.

Gary Manning broke the silence when he asked, ''Is this the data Curtis passed to the Koreans?''

Brognola nodded.

''So they know what we're planning to do? That

when this is up and running we'll be able to detect missile launches from anywhere in the world, point the finger and stop them?''

"That's about the size of it.''

"Not going to make their customers feel very secure," McCarter said.

"The North Koreans have been throwing massive investment into the development of their missiles," Katz said. "Bigger, better, longer range. Intelligence reports have shown continued developments of improved facilities at the Musudan-ri launch facility. We know the Koreans have an advance on the No-dong missile now with the Taep'o-dong. Our intelligence believes this missile has a range of somewhere in the region of four thousand kilometers. Possibly more. That would make it a big threat if the Koreans brought it to production and sold it on the open market. What holds them back is the fact they don't have the most advanced technical development base, which is why they depend on outside help. Beg, borrow or steal, they need it to move on. It's no good having a big missile if you don't have the power to fly it, or a guidance system to get it where it's supposed to go.''

"Hence the Paul Curtises?" Price said.

Katz nodded. "There will always be people like him around. They see their contribution as nothing more than industrial espionage. They steal a concept and sell it, pocket the cash and plan for an early retirement.''

"Sounds good in theory," Rafael Encizo said. "But don't these people see the harm they do? If the

Koreans buy the information, neutralize Slingshot, build their rockets and sell them to some unstable regime, Curtis would be as vulnerable as the rest of us if there was a major incident.''

"I agree. That never seems to cross their minds. All they look at is the rising bank balance. The consequences of their actions don't come into the equation.''

"Not that it matters now as far as Curtis is concerned," James said. "But what bothers me is the all the shit being thrown around by these people. The Koreans, the Chinese, even the Russians. They all keep bitching about how sneaky we are just because we want to defend ourselves. Now it's a crime to want to stand up against the bullies? That's crazy.''

"Funny you should bring that up, Cal," Brognola said. "It's exactly what the President said when I spoke to him earlier. He's getting angered by the rest of the world telling the U.S. it shouldn't look after its own. One way or another other regimes are going to make preparations to have their own defense systems. The President doesn't see why we shouldn't do the same. All the fuss the Chinese and the Russians are making is intended to throw us off the idea. No way we're about to do that.''

"Tell me I'm being old-fashioned," Katz broke in.

"You are," James said. "Have you taken a look at your wardrobe lately?''

Katz ignored him. "All this is leading the world back to the cold war mentality. Didn't we leave that behind?''

Brognola sighed. "It looks that way, Katz. Tell me

what else can we do? We get all the media hype about peace and love. The Koreans in talks with the U.S. China opening up tourist facilities. Suddenly it's sunshine time. Sit back and look beyond that. China still has a repressive regime. We have Islamic hard liners urging hell on earth for the nonbelievers. Dissident groups, dispossessed people. Wars still going on in Africa. This might be the new millennium, but it sure isn't the return of flower power.''

"I wasn't being naive, Hal," Katz said. "No one is suggesting the world has turned. Every time I hear Palestine and Israel mentioned on the television, my stomach shrinks. We all know the way things are going out there. And we still have Hussein peddling his threats all over the Gulf. I just get a feeling we're about to jump back on that runaway carousel again. Back to the bad old days.''

"Let's hope you're wrong," Brognola said. "Believe me when I say I'd be the first to quit if I was told Stony Man had outlived its usefulness. In the meantime we carry on as long as something like this Slingshot problem exists.''

Blancanales leaned forward, staring across the table at Brognola.

"Curtis sells the Slingshot data to the Koreans. Gives them the advantage. They can take it out before it gets fully on-line?''

Brognola nodded. "The simulation I told you about last time insured Slingshot's survival. But the system isn't fully operational yet. Now would be the best time for the Koreans to take out the satellites.''

"And if they do, the U.S. will retaliate?'' Manning

said. "If the Koreans try to shoot the satellites down, it won't be a slap on the wrist and a few diplomatic discussions. This could escalate out of control."

"The President wants it dealt with before any of that can happen. He's committed to Slingshot, and he's dug in his heels. No way the system is going to be sabotaged. He's given it to us because we're already up to speed with the players. And he wants the Koreans made to see they can't screw around like this and get away with it."

"Sounds good to me," Blancanales said.

"There are twenty orbiting satellites in place," Brognola said, "all ready to be activated and linked to the Slingshot system. There will be more added at later stages."

"How soon before the initial satellites are brought on-line?" Manning asked. "In a week? A month? Next year?"

"Within six to eight months if the rest of the project falls into place."

"Talk about sneaky," McCarter said. "I'm impressed. How did it happen without details getting out?"

Brognola shrugged. "The President just gave the order. There were no discussions. He pulled in all his military advisers, issued the order and told them to get on with it. The military couldn't believe their luck. Here was the chance they'd been asking for being handed to them on a plate. Took just over five months to get all the satellites in place. The logistics were formidable, but our people did it."

"You realize what's going to happen when the

news does break?'' Katz said. ''The U.S. is going to be on the receiving end of a lot of criticism.''

''It'll be a bit late, Katz,'' McCarter said. ''The job's done. The satellites are in place. The world might kick and scream. Too late and not enough, though. And before you say it, I'm not being cynical. Just stating facts.''

''I'm aware of all that, David. My worry is that once the news does get out, as it will, the U.S. is going to be extremely unpopular.''

''Hell, Katz, what's new about that?'' James asked. ''We get the blame for most everything that happens. If we send in the troops, we're interfering. If we don't, they blame us for standing by and letting something happen. This time we're doing something for ourselves. For the safety of America. If the rest of the world doesn't like it, what do we do? Shut down Slingshot?''

''These are all the arguments the President has had to deal with,'' Brognola said. ''He's had to make a decision that's going to make him unpopular with a percentage of the nation. There'll be those in the military who won't like it. And the administration. Especially when they find out he went over their heads.''

''Hal,'' Encizo asked, ''how do you feel?''

Brognola leaned back in his seat.

''The idea of creating the old cold-war mood doesn't thrill me. On the other hand I can't say I feel too comfortable having the rest of the world tell me I can't defend myself because it makes *them* feel insecure. That puts me in a tricky position. Makes me feel I've got my back against the wall, a guy coming at me, and I don't have a thing in my hand to protect myself. By my calculation there's something wrong with that setup. If it gets to that situation, it's too late. If we let ourselves be talked into throwing down our weapons, we deserve what we get.''

The big Fed glanced around the table. No one spoke for the moment.

"Look, maybe I made it too simplistic. Nothing is as black-and-white as that. Hell, I understand politics and diplomacy. We live in a—''

"Hal, you explained it just fine,'' Barbara Price said. "The truth is we get too tangled up in the fancy discussions. Maybe that's what it needed. Someone saying it as it is.''

"Our main concern is the fact that the Koreans have got hold of Slingshot data,'' Schwarz said. "I take it this information could help them get at the satellites?''

Brognola nodded. "What Curtis gave them was the satellite ring orbiting positions. These satellites are a new design. Smaller than your average orbiter and fitted with advanced technology inside. The electronics and guidance are based on new microcircuitry. They also have low-emission exterior coatings to reduce the ability of being pinpointed.''

"What? Stealth in space?'' Manning asked.

"Guys,'' Kurtzman said, "look at this as next generation. Every time something new is designed it incorporates the latest advances. Compare it to television. The first sets were huge with little screens and poor sound. A few years later the sets were smaller and the screens had got bigger. Next time we had better sound. Then color. And each time the overall performance got better. Now we have wide screens. Dolby sound. The sets have slimmed down. Still TVs but everything has moved on."

McCarter shook his head. "You watched some of the shows lately?"

Kurtzman grinned at that. "Got to be a downside to everything."

"Okay," Manning said, "So Slingshot is the framework for future defense systems. Designed to be added to on an expanding basis?"

"More or less."

"So what comes next? A manned platform in space that can monitor any hostile move on Earth?"

Brognola shifted in his seat, glancing at Kurtzman.

"Ouch," McCarter said. "I think you scored pretty high there, Gary."

Holding up his hands, Brognola said, "We're getting ahead of ourselves here, guys. The future can take care of itself. Our priority is to take care of the immediate problem. If we don't, Slingshot may not have a future."

"The data the Koreans have is on compact disks. Two of them," Kurtzman explained. "They're both encrypted. And if the encryption can't be broken, then the information stays exactly where it is."

"I feel a 'but' coming on," James said.

"If the Koreans break the encryption, they're in business," Kurtzman said. "The information on the disks relates to every control command and protocol. If they get into the disks, they can identify and lock on to the satellites. Feeding that data into their own missile-control data banks would give them clear targets, and they would be able to take out the satellite ring.''

''I said there was a 'but','' James repeated. ''I guess what you're saying is we have to go and find these disks and bring them home.''

''Simpler than that,'' Brognola said. ''Just destroy them.''

''Wait a minute,'' Encizo said. ''Assuming we locate the disks, how do we know the Koreans won't have made copies?''

''The guy who wrote the programs set a copy restriction. If anyone tries to duplicate the disks, they simply corrupt. Wipe themselves and send a virus into the operating system. The only way in is by the front door, but to unlock it the encryption has to be broken first.''

''Curtis would have known about this,'' Kurtzman said, ''So he would most likely have told his buyer.''

''What you're saying is the Koreans have got hold of the means to shoot Slingshot out of the sky,'' Manning summarized. ''If they can break the encryption, they're in.''

''Can't the codes be changed?'' Blancanales asked. ''Set up a new sequence?''

Kurtzman shook his head.

''The codes are an integral part of the operating system. It was done that way so that if anyone tries to tamper with the main program, they'll cause the same corruption they would if they try to copy the disks. These are fail-safe protocols placed there by the guy who wrote the program."

"I hope he's still on our side," McCarter said.

"Dr. Raymond Gilman is definitely one of the good guys," Katz said. "The man is a computer genius. Born to live in the cyber world."

"Katz is right," Kurtzman said. "Ray Gilman leaves me at the starting gate."

"Why do you never have a tape recorder running at moments like these?" McCarter asked. "Aaron admitting he isn't the best."

Kurtzman grunted.

"And that means you've been lying to me all these years," McCarter went on.

"What it means is we have two different lines to go for," Price cut in. "Depending on what Curtis told his buyers, we might find Dr. Gilman becoming the center of attention."

"So why not have him put under observation, or placed in a secure unit until we know any danger has passed."

Encizo gazed around the table, waiting for an answer.

Brognola cleared his throat.

"What?" Encizo asked.

"No one knows where he is," the big Fed admitted.

"You're joking," James said. "He's gone missing?"

"Ray Gilman has always been a loner," Kurtzman said. "I've known him for around six years. He likes his own company. Same goes for his work. He's never been a team player. When he went into government work he laid down ground rules. No interference. No colleagues breathing over his shoulder. The government didn't like it, but they had no choice. They couldn't do without his input, especially when he saw the potential of the Slingshot system. He drew up the program all by himself. Only passed it to a small group when it became even too much for him. But once it came down to the final program to be written, Gilman took over."

"And?" Manning asked.

"They put up the satellites, Gilman initiated his program for a simulation and the thing worked." Kurtzman shrugged. "But there's more work to be done before the system goes fully operational."

"So they have the program installed in the defense system computers?" Schwarz asked. "Who has the disks?"

Brognola consulted one of his sheets. "A couple of sets at the Cheyenne Mountain missile-control facility. Then a couple more at the department where Curtis worked."

"And Curtis had access?" McCarter asked.

"As he did to other classified material."

"Taking your work home is one thing," McCarter said. "This was something else."

"All this started when the Chinese walked off with Slingshot data," Manning said. "Didn't anyone learn from that?"

"Yeah, and that was where we came in," Encizo pointed out.

"The whole damn thing has been a cock-up from

the word go,'' McCarter snapped. ''Bloody good people have been hurt and killed because of it.''

Brognola held up a hand. ''No one is denying the mess we got ourselves into. Sitting here pointing the finger won't change a damn thing. Somehow we have to shut this down for good. Too much has gone into Slingshot to just write it off.'' The big Fed glanced at McCarter. ''David, I haven't forgotten what this has cost in terms of people.''

''I wasn't having a go at you, Hal. Let's get this into perspective. Curtis sold out to the Koreans. He handed over the disks, but at the moment they can't use them because of the encryption. The only sensible way around that would be for the Koreans to get their hands on this Gilman bloke. But knowing the Koreans, they'll also be doing their best to try to break the encryption themselves.''

''That sums it up pretty well,'' Brognola said. ''It presents us with two priorities. Find Gilman before the Koreans and destroy the disks already in Korean hands.''

Manning smiled. ''Sounds so easy when you say it like that.''

''Hey, let's back up a tad,'' James said. ''We were talking about Gilman going missing.''

''Maybe the Koreans already have him.'' Blancanales said.

''Put me right, Hal,'' McCarter said. ''If Gilman is so bloody high profile, how come he wasn't under the eye of the security people?''

''Gilman has always resisted being monitored. He fought it from the word go, made it into a game. He's given security the slip so many times now it's beyond a joke. On the other hand he always delivers the goods, meets his deadlines. He works around the clock and more when he's on a project, and never does anything to put his work in jeopardy. The problem is he doesn't like people hanging on his coattails. He needs his time alone.''

"Great," McCarter said. "That's all we need. We have a major security problem in the offing, and the bloke who could hand it to the opposition has done a runner.''

"Don't the security agencies have any ideas?" Schwarz asked.

"Apart from his work and his home, Gilman has no external life to speak of," Price said, checking her notes. "Unmarried. No women—or men—friends. His parents are dead, and he was an only child."

"The guy is one step away from being a recluse," Manning said.

"His choice, Gary," Encizo said. "Nothing's written that says you have to be a party animal.''

"I guess not," the Canadian said. "He probably figures he's normal.''

"Take a look around this table, then tell me *he's* not normal," McCarter said.

"Aaron, you've met him?" James said.

"Couple of times at computer seminars. Last one was six months back when he was presenting a paper.''

"He say anything that might help?"

"Nothing comes to mind. The man was no conversationalist. When he did talk, it was always about his work. He doesn't seem to have anything else on his mind. He told me he even takes his laptop with him when he goes to Albuquerque." Kurtzman paused, glancing around the silent table as he realized what he had just said. "Damn! I never gave it any thought at the time. Why should I? It came out one evening. The only time the man ever mentioned his private life. He never brought it up again, and I didn't make a connection with anything at the time."

"Well, we've made one now," McCarter said. "Aaron, if this works out, I'll buy you a new coffeepot."

"Oh?" Kurtzman said. "There something wrong with the one I got?"

McCarter made a face. "Pass," he said.

"Gilman lived outside a town called West Barnstable, near Cape Cod Bay. According to his file, he doesn't own a car. He likes to take the train to wherever he goes. All he had to do was travel up to Boston, buy a ticket and head for New Mexico."

"That's assuming he's gone to New Mexico," James said. "The guy could be anywhere. He might have gone abroad."

"Gilman doesn't own a passport," Price said. "Aaron ran a check. He's never even applied for one."

"Does he own a cell phone?" Katz asked. "If he does, he could have used it to make reservations."

Kurtzman nodded. "We'll run a check."

"Better do it now," Brognola said. "If we've thought about it, so could the opposition."

"Here we go," McCarter said. "The ball is starting to roll."

# CHAPTER TWO

*Albuquerque, New Mexico*

The moment Raymond Gilman stepped down from the train he felt the New Mexico heat envelop him. He had spent the majority of the train journey in his private compartment, only stepping out a few times to stretch his legs when the Amtrak liner had stopped. His meals had been served in the compartment, which suited Gilman fine. As the train had rolled deeper into the Southwest, the temperature rose. Gilman had turned on the air-conditioning, relaxing in the comfort of his cocoon.

The long hours of the train ride were relaxing. He was on his own, away from the demands of his work. He had admitted to himself that he needed a break. That in itself was unusual. Gilman was dedicated to the point where it isolated him from the world and people in general. That suited him. He just didn't get along with people. He felt safer on his own. Luckily, the kind of work he had chosen allowed him that privilege. Programming the highly technical material he worked with demanded total concentration. There were no margins for error. For example the Slingshot system he had developed was his greatest achievement to date. He had spent long, intense, lonely months writing and refining the program that would command the Slingshot satellite system. Even he had felt the strain toward the end, and being aware of his own feelings he had taken one of his rare vacations.

As usual he had just packed a bag, left his house on Cape Cod Bay and climbed into his ordered cab. It took him to Boston's South Station, where he picked up the ticket he'd ordered the day before and boarded the train. He settled in his compartment, content to sit back and watch the landscape slip by.

Despite his preoccupation with work, Gilman was able to push it aside once he had made the decision to take a break. He felt no anxiety, no guilt. He had completed his Slingshot contract. Before he moved on to a new project, he needed a break. And New Mexico was the only place he could find contentment.

Gilman spent the trip reading magazines he brought with him, sleeping and simply enjoying the scenery as it changed.

The liner pulled in at Albuquerque just after 9:00 a.m. Gilman had been ready for the past half hour. He stepped down the moment the train came to a stop and made his way out of the station.

Gilman glanced around as he emerged, obviously looking for someone. His face brightened when he recognized the person he was seeking.

She was standing beside a dusty, bright red Cherokee 4×4. She had the raven-black hair and profile of a Navajo, but stood slightly taller than the norm. Young, around nineteen, she wore faded blue jeans and a bright cotton shirt. On her feet were ankle-high, soft moccasins. The moment she saw Gilman, she raised a hand, waving wildly, then ran toward him. Reaching him, she threw her arms around his neck, hugging him. Gilman let his bag drop to the ground as he returned her embrace, gripping her tightly. The girl finally let go, stepping back to smile at him.

"Hi, Dad," she said.

"You're looking well," Gilman said. "How are things?"

"No change since you spoke to me last time," the girl said. "Mom's been better this week. You'll see for yourself when we get home."

She picked up Gilman's bag, slipping her free hand under his arm as they headed for the Cherokee.

"Rachel, I wish there was more we could do for her."

"I know you do. But no one can do anything. We've all known that for the past few years. It isn't anyone's fault."

Gilman turned to stare at her. "Isn't it?"

"Your being here all the time, or away because of your work, didn't contribute to Mom's illness. Dad, we've been through this a thousand times. It is not your fault."

"Do I deserve you?"

Rachel grinned. "No. But we all have crosses to bear. You're mine, and I wouldn't have it any other way."

They reached the Cherokee. Rachel placed Gilman's bag in the rear, then climbed behind the wheel. Gilman was already in the passenger seat. She fired up the engine.

"Hey, fasten your belt," she said.

"Bumpy road?"

"No, just a very fast driver."

Gilman sat back and watched his daughter out of the corner of his eye. She drove well, with the confidence of youth, sure of herself and the world she inhabited. He wished his own existence had such a firm base. He could feel the warm sun on his face. It felt good. Very good, and suddenly he was glad to be here.

He had a feeling things were going to go well.

RAYMOND GILMAN'S arrival in Albuquerque hadn't gone unnoticed. A cream-colored Ford was parked at the curb across from the station exit. Two men sat in the front, watching the arrivals. Casually dressed and seemingly relaxed, neither man missed a thing. The one behind the wheel sat drinking from a paper cup of coffee. His partner, who seemed to be suffering from the heat, had his window open, despite the car's air conditioner being on.

The coffee drinker leaned across and nudged his partner.

"I think we've got him," he said.

The other man glanced in the direction being indicated. He studied the tall man in crumpled clothing who walked out into the sunlight, gazing around until he recognized the attractive, dark-haired young woman standing beside a Cherokee 4×4. He watched the meeting between the two people.

"There you go," he said. "How come I never have something like that waiting for me at the end of a long train ride?"

Coffee drinker emptied his cup, crushed it in a powerful hand and tossed it into the rear of the car.

"For one thing, Jesse, I don't ever recall you taking a train ride."

"I guess you got me there, Wes," Jesse said. "Time to go."

Wes started the car and eased into the lane well behind the Cherokee. It picked up the on-ramp for Interstate 40, heading west. Traffic was thin and it was possible to keep the Cherokee in sight even way back.

"Where do you think they're heading?" Wes asked.

Jesse took a long look around. The highway ran ahead of them, vanishing in the soft heat haze. Around them the land lay open and empty now they had left Albuquerque behind. A soft wind blew in off the flatlands, bringing pale wreaths of dust with it.

"Maybe they're just going for a ride."

Wes shook his head. "I don't think so."

"Hey, we got any of those bottles of water left?" Jesse asked.

"Some in the cooler in the trunk."

Jesse muttered under his breath. "Ain't much good to me back there."

"What can I say?"

"You could say, 'I'll stop the car, Jesse, so you can get some.' That's what you could say."

"Can't you wait?"

"No, I can't wait, Wes. If I could wait, I wouldn't be fuckin' well askin', would I?"

Wes eased the car to a stop. He sat with his gaze fixed on the distant Cherokee while his partner made his way to the trunk and hauled out the cooler. He brought it back and placed it on the floor between his feet.

"Can we go now?" Wes asked.

Jesse nodded as he concentrated on opening the lid of the cooler. He plunged his hands into the ice cubes filling the box and pulled out a plastic bottle of water. He held it up and studied the frosted surface of the bottle, watching the beads of moisture run down the side.

"That looks real nice," he said.

Wes only grunted. He was pushing the Ford hard now, wanting to close the distance between them and the Cherokee. He had to pass three vehicles before he had the red 4×4 in clear sight again.

Removing the cap from the bottle, Jesse took a long swallow of the cold water. He slumped back in the seat, rolling the water around inside his mouth.

"Christ, Jesse, I never heard anyone make such a noise over a drink of water."

"I don't like these hot places," Jesse said. "Never have."

"Yeah, well, that's fine. But you don't have to make like you're having a sexual experience just 'cause you're thirsty."

Jesse swallowed the water, making sure he didn't make any more noise than he had to.

"Days are when you can be a pain in the ass."

Wes smiled. "Can't I just."

They stayed behind the Cherokee for the next twenty miles. Then it slowed and pulled off the road, drawing up outside a long, low adobe-and-timber building that advertised itself as Rachel's Diner. Set away from the diner was a gas station with pumps and a repair shop. The area was clean and well tended. There were a number of big rigs and semi-trailers parked, as well as cars.

The Cherokee pulled to a stop outside a section of the diner marked Office. The girl and Raymond Gilman climbed out of the Cherokee and went in through the office door.

Wes hauled the car to a stop in the parking area. He killed the engine and sat studying the place.

"At least we can get a cup of coffee while we figure this out," he said.

Wes picked up a cell phone from the seat beside him and punched in a number. He waited until his call was answered.

"We got him spotted. Some girl met him at the station. They drove west out of Albuquerque on Interstate 40. About twenty miles west there's a place called Rachel's Diner. That's where they stopped. We're going to check the place out. We won't do anything until the rest of you arrive... Yeah, okay."

He cut the connection and placed the phone back on the seat.

"What they say?" Jesse asked.

"They'll be with us in a hour."

"Some time to kill sitting here."

"We'll just have to have a slow breakfast," Wes said.

They climbed out of the car and made their way to the diner. The interior was cool. About half the booths were in use, and three customers sat at the counter, perched on high stools. Wes chose a booth where they could see the kitchen area of the diner, as well as the entrance door.

They had only been seated for a couple of minutes when a red-haired young woman came to take their order.

"Couple of your breakfast specials and coffee," Wes said, smiling easily at the girl.

"Okay."

Wes watched her go, admiring her supple figure in the blue jeans and yellow T-shirt. The back of the T-shirt bore the legend Rachel's Diner in red letters.

"Nice place," Wes said. "Reckon it makes good money?"

Jesse looked at him and shook his head. "How the hell am I supposed to know that?"

"Jesse, you're a slight touchy this morning. Have a bad night? Figured you'd be fine with that blonde. Hey, buddy, couldn't she shake the knots out of your tail?"

"I don't know where you got her, *buddy*, but she had a hard time shaking her fuckin' butt. Times are I think you do it on purpose."

Wes held his hands up in mock surrender. "Man,

don't blame me. All I did was hire 'em. I don't road test 'em first.''

''Maybe next time you should.''

Their food arrived shortly after, and the pair busied themselves with eating. The food was good and plentiful, and the redhead kept their coffee mugs well filled.

A DUSTY PANEL TRUCK pulled off the highway and parked beside the cream Ford. Five men were inside. The one in the middle took out a cell phone and tapped a speed-dial number. He was looking across the parking lot to where he could see Wes and Jesse sitting inside the diner. When the phone rang, Wes took his phone out of his pocket and answered.

''We're in the lot. Parked next to your car.''

''Okay, I'll join you.''

Wes said something to Jesse, got up and made his way outside.

The three men climbed out of the panel truck.

The one with the cell phone leaned against the side of the truck and took out a pack of thin cigars. He lit one with a slim gold lighter.

''Wes,'' he acknowledged.

''Gilman is still in the back with the girl.''

''Any idea who she is?''

Wes shook his head. ''The way they acted when they said hello, I figure they're pretty close. Nobody mention her, Hutch?''

The man called Hutch shook his head. ''Doesn't matter. All we're contracted for is to snatch Gilman and deliver. If the girl gets in the way, we deal with her.''

"How do we play this?''

"Quiet as possible.'' Hutch took a look around the area. "This place is too damn busy. We wait until we can get Gilman alone. No point havin' a bunch of truckers gawkin' when we take him. No point makin' a fuss and getting the local law on our tails.''

"I'll go back inside. Me an' Jesse can keep an eye on things from there for a while longer.''

"Don't make it too long. Somebody might wonder why you're hanging around.''

*Stony Man Farm, Virginia*

"ANYTHING YET?'' Price asked.

Huntington Wethers swung his chair around, shaking his head.

"No. I'm just waiting for the next bird to come on-line. Be about forty minutes. We've had clearance to use the Canadian SAR satellite again. It gave us some good scans last time around so all we can do is give it a try.''

"Give me a yell if anything shows,'' Price said. "I'll be with Hal.''

BROGNOLA SAT hunched over the papers strewed across his desk. This was one of the parts of the job he hated with a vengeance. Paperwork was a necessary evil, though. It didn't matter how sophisticated the electronic function became, there were always pieces of paper coming in at an alarming rate. Surveillance reports. Statistical readouts. Current and future overviews. He picked up a twenty-page security assessment that had been prepared by Buck Greene, the Farm's security chief. Brognola accepted them as part of the furniture, but he certainly didn't have to like the chore.

When Barbara Price tapped on his office door, he welcomed the break.

"Come on in, Barb," he said.

She sat, placing her clipboard on the edge of Brognola's cluttered desk.

"Looks like my desk's twin," she said.

"Tell me about it," the big Fed said, leaning back in his seat. "This business or pleasure?"

"Hal, you should know even when it is business, it's always a pleasure to see you."

"I can see why you got the job."

"Hal, tell me if I'm pushing too far. I'm just curious about Slingshot. You didn't say anything when you were asked about the possibility of there being more to the project, but I picked up the vibes."

Brognola couldn't hold back a grin. There was little Barbara Price missed. She had her own built-in radar that could reach out and pick up the slightest hint of something unsaid, an inflection in a voice that was trying to hide something. He had given up trying to fool her.

"Long term, Slingshot is seen as our main defense project," he said. "New stages will be added. It maintains continuity. Keeps the logistical problems down because we're not starting from scratch each time."

"So that remark about a platform in space wasn't so far off the mark?"

"It all depends how the satellite system performs. There's a way to go yet. A lot of development still to be done."

"Sounds impressive, Hal."

"If it works it will be impressive. But this is way ahead of anything that's been tried before, Barb. Which is why it's being done in stages. And why the President is determined to keep it up and running."

Brognola waved a hand at the paperwork on his desk.

"Every day I get another threat analysis from somewhere. Hostile governments, unstable regimes, terrorist organizations, the possibility of conflict between A and B, and whether that conflict will drag us in. Religious groups, militia groups, the disenchanted, the poor. Christ, Barb, we still live in a mixed-up world. There are a hell of a lot of people and groups who all want their own particular grievance or injustice put to the top of the list. If they don't get what they want, they might decide to go out and blow up something. We don't live in a peaceful world, and it'll be a long time before it ever is. In the meantime we have to survive."

Brognola pushed away from his desk. He reached for his jacket, draped across the back of his chair, and pulled it on.

"Let's go get a sandwich," he said. "Then you can update me on how the guys are doing."

# CHAPTER THREE

*North Korea*

As soon as breakfast was over, the prisoners were herded into a line of trucks and driven north. The journey took two hours. The trucks were packed tight, so there was little room to move around. Not everyone was able to sit. That and the fact that the trucks were open to the weather made for an uncomfortable ride. The prisoners were issued with quilted coats and rough leather boots. They were even issued crude, stiff gloves. Lyons had a hard time getting his on over his large, long-fingered hands. He managed it, taking some comfort from the protection they offered.

It seemed to rain most of the time, a cold and constant downpour that swept in from the north, bringing with it a penetrating wind. Sometimes snow was mixed with the rain. The terrain they passed over was bleak and empty A dark, lowering sky hung over it all. As far as Lyons was concerned, it was one of the most depressing places he had ever seen. The trucks brought them to a large site housing low concrete structures and large bunkers. The whole place was surrounded by concrete walls topped with razor wire. And once again Lyons saw guard towers manned by machine-gun emplacements, tall pylons supported powerful searchlights.

Lyons assessed the place as the trucks drove in through the heavy wooden gate. There was still a great deal of construction taking place, but what he saw was enough to tell him he was inside some kind of missile launch facility. It wasn't the first time he had seen this kind of layout, with its blast pits and cradles. What interested him was the realization that much of the construction seemed to have been underground. There was a wide concrete entrance ramp leading below the surface. Soldiers were carrying equipment down this ramp and into the underground complex.

The trucks lurched over the muddy ground, passing long, open trailers loaded with the covered shapes of missiles. He saw, too, a communications center, with radio masts and aerials. There was also a large radar dish on top of the com center building. All the buildings and equipment were low to the ground. Someone was going to a great deal of trouble keeping the place deliberately low profile.

As soon as the trucks stopped, the prisoners were unloaded, given their tasks and quickly put to work. Lyons and Rinaldi were together in a party of about twenty men. They were given shovels and picks and directed to an area. Orders were given and the men set to work immediately. They were leveling an area of ground, Lyons saw. The extracted dirt was shoveled into barrows and taken away to another part of the site.

The work carried throughout the morning, with no letup. Lyons, who was probably fitter than most, felt the strain on his back and arm muscles. The ground was hard and took some breaking up before they were able to start taking it away. The continuous rain soaked into everything. The sodden lumps of earth were heavy, dripping with freezing water.

"When do we stop for lunch?" Lyons asked his American companion. "Or are you going to tell me we work right through?"

Rinaldi, shoveling the sodden earth into a barrow, said, "Some days we get fed. Others we don't. Depends how busy we are."

"Where's the union when you need them," Lyons muttered.

That day they did get fed. It was somewhere around early afternoon. Section by section the prisoners were taken to a makeshift kitchen, where large metal containers held the familiar cabbage soup and boiled rice. Lyons and Rinaldi took their bowls and found some scant shelter beside one of the trucks. The hot food went a little way to ease their discomfort. It was only for a brief time. The cold rain still fell, soaking their clothing and chilling their bodies.

"Chuck, you still haven't told me why that guy went for you my first day in camp," Lyons asked.

Rinaldi frowned. "Oh, yeah. The guards stir them up. Keep telling them how bad Americans are. How we deny the people food and medical help. All kinds of crap to get the prisoners worked up. It's one of their little games. Great sense of humor, these North Koreans.''

Gets better all the time, Lyons thought.

"How long you been working on this place?" he asked.

"Three, four months I figure."

"Know much about it? What it's for?"

Rinaldi shrugged.

They were unable to carry on their discussion as a shout went up. The prisoners moved to return their bowls to the food point, then got back to work. Rinaldi and Lyons were a little slow. Two of the guards headed for them brandishing their clubs. Rinaldi speeded up, lost his footing in the mud and went down on his knees. One of the guards loomed over him, lashing out with the club. It cracked down across Rinaldi's shoulders, drawing a cry of pain from the man. The guard raised his club again. Lyons slammed into the man and sent him sprawling. The second guard came at the American, swinging his club in a wide arc. Lyons ducked under the badly timed blow, then drove a clenched fist into the guard's stomach. The man grunted, sagging forward. Lyons sledged his fist into the side of the guard's face, splitting his cheek open to the bone.

More shouts went up. More guards appeared, some of them carrying rifles with fitted bayonets. They formed a circle around Lyons and Rinaldi, closing in until there was nowhere for the two Americans to go.

Lyons stood his ground. He had no intention of backing down. If they had the idea Americans were weak cowards, they didn't know Carl Lyons.

Someone shouted an order and the guards backed off. A moment later Captain Yun stepped into view. He was warmly clad in thick, weatherproof clothing, even down to leather gloves.

"So! Already you are in trouble. If you were any of these other prisoners, you would be dead."

"Comes to us all," Lyons said. "What should I do? Let your guards beat someone just because he fell down? Or don't they have the sense to realize an injured prisoner can't work as efficiently as a healthy one?"

"American sentimentality?" Yun said.

"American common sense. You beat a man until he's crippled, what good is he for your workforce?"

"There are plenty of replacements."

"Sure. Plenty of your own people, Captain Yun. How long before you realize what you're doing to your own country?"

Yun smiled. "Now a lesson on the American way."

"We made our mistakes. Still are. But we don't imprison our people just for the way they think."

"We had a war over this very thing," Yun said.

"That was great success. Since then you've had a divided country and North Korean poverty. Don't bullshit me, Yun. I don't swallow it. If you used half your damn brain, you'd know all that propaganda your government pumps out is just a crock of shit.

Now let me get back to work or shoot me, because I'm cold and wet, and right now I don't give a fuck."

Yun held Lyons's angry stare. His face was immobile, but his eyes bored deep into the American's, and Lyons knew the man was debating which way to go. The only thing Lyons had going for him was his halfway sure knowledge that Yat Sen Took wanted him kept alive despite sending him to the camp. If Yun was under orders, there was no way he would dare defy Took. It was Lyons's only lifeline. If he had read it wrong, he had certainly placed himself in the firing line. Having a stand-up argument with the camp commandant, in front of guards and prisoners, was not a wise move.

A smile etched Yun's mouth. He stepped back and began to speak in his own language, making himself heard by all those within earshot. Whatever he said brought a burst of laughter from the guards. It was obvious that Yun was belittling Lyons before the assembly. If that was the case, Lyons didn't give a damn. Being made to look stupid was easier to take than a bullet in the head.

"Shit, pal, you must be important if Yun's taken what you threw at him," Rinaldi muttered.

Lyons shrugged. "Long as he isn't saying I'm gay, I don't care what he says.

"Not exactly gay," Rinaldi said. "Only don't go bending down in the showers."

"We don't have any showers."

"You're safe, then."

Yun turned back to Lyons when he had finished speaking.

"Get back to your work. Consider yourself lucky. My only consolation is that I know you will try to escape soon. You are not the kind of man to live in a place like this. If you do get beyond the camp perimeter, I will follow you. I do not think you will stay alive very long in my country. But if you do and I recapture you, then you *will* die. Even Yat Sen Took will not be able to save you then."

The Korean turned away.

"Captain Yun," Lyons said.

"Yes?"

"Same goes for me. Come after me, I promise I *will* kill you."

Yun smiled, almost pleased. He nodded very briefly.

"I look forward to that day."

THE WORK CARRIED ON until it became too dark and cold for even the guards to maintain control. Tools were handed in and the trucks were started. As soon as the prisoners had been loaded, the trucks began the return journey toward the distant camp.

Huddled in among the other prisoners, Carl Lyons studied the terrain. There was only a pale moon, laying a misty light over the land. He wasn't viewing the landscape for any purpose other than assessing it for a possible break. The more he considered the trip back and forth between the camp and the missile site, the truck journey seemed to offer the best chance.

The camp was far too well guarded and closed in for him to effect a successful escape. The effort would require a great deal of planning. There were also the logistics of breaking out from an enclosure. He would need information, which was near impossible given his situation and the animosity of the Korean prisoners. There wasn't one of them he could use in any way. He didn't understand the language, and that alone rendered any kind of contact nil. Rinaldi understood some Korean. The problem again was who could be trusted. The other difficulty would be equipment needed to get out. From what Lyons had seen, the camp had little in the way of useful tools. The prisoners were denied even the most basic items. Nothing was allowed that might be turned into a weapon. The only utensils they were allowed were the wooden spoons handed out at meal times. They were clumsy, basic items, made from soft wood, and wouldn't make any kind of deadly weapon. Added to that was the fact that every prisoner had to hand in his spoon after each meal.

The truck swayed as it hit a depression in the ground. The bulk of standing prisoners were pushed off balance. Lyons felt himself pressed against the side of the low-sided truck. In the momentary confusion he might have been able to roll over the side and lie flat to the ground as the truck moved on. It was a tempting moment, but Lyons resisted. He wasn't ready to make his break yet. Basic as it might be, he needed to gather some kind of survival kit together. He was going to need to do some thinking on the matter.

"Hey, buddy, you okay?" Rinaldi asked.

Lyons glanced at him, nodding. He didn't want to say anything to Rinaldi yet. He needed to make certain the man was to be trusted. Lyons made no excuses for his thoughts. Rinaldi was an American, sure, but how far had he been pushed in the years he had been in the camp? The man had lost his sense of time. What else had he given up? Maybe the will to escape. Strange as it might seem, it had been known for long-term captives to accept their fate and see their place of confinement as home. Loss of contact with their homeland and isolation in a new country left them in a vacuum, seeing the close perimeters of their jail as the world and the universe. The very thought of leaving could cause them to panic. They would refuse to run away, happy to remain where they were, and at least, understand what was happening around them day to day.

Carl Lyons had no intention of remaining a prisoner of the Koreans. Captain Yun's threats didn't worry him. He faced threats every day of his life when he was on a Stony Man mission. Yun was no different than any uniformed thug. Surrounded by his armed guards, with their weapons and ravenous dogs, the man could afford to throw his weight around. His whole existence at the camp was to cow the prisoners. To tear away every scrap of dignity they had. As far as Yun and his masters were concerned, the mass of the people were there to be controlled and dominated. Told what to say and what to think, to passively absorb the endless streams of puerile political cant that was fed to them. Day after day, extolling the wonders of the North Korean leaders. How lucky they were to live in the earthly paradise of the Democratic People's Republic of Korea. No mention was ever made of the poverty, the deprivation, the lack of food and decent clothing, the backward culture forced on them by a repressive regime more concerned with building vast stocks of destructive missiles.

Captain Yun was as browbeaten as the prisoners he controlled. In truth he was a prisoner himself, trapped within the web of deceit and falsity foisted upon his charges. Lyons knew that if he did escape, Yun would follow him until one of them was dead. The man was so steeped in the doctrine of his masters he would be unable to do anything else.

Lyons felt the rain increase. It fell from a dark, swollen sky, lashing the prisoners in the back of the truck, soaking through their already wet clothes until they were sodden. The cold leeched through to their very bones. There would be little respite when they reached the camp. They would be herded into their huts, the doors closed, trapping them in the damp environment where they would attempt to sleep until the dawn and the start of another day.

"Bastards!" Rinaldi muttered, wrapping his arms around his lean body in an attempt to gain a little warmth. "They could at least give us trucks with some covers. At least that..."

He trailed off, sinking into his black depression. His head fell forward, chin resting against his chest. Watching him, Lyons knew how he felt. He could see how easy it would be to give in, to let the time and the place overwhelm him. Giving up took away responsibility, and when that was gone the mind and body shut down, moving into a semihibernation state. It was an option Lyons would never accept. His stubborn nature would never allow him to go down that path.

From that moment Carl Lyons moved on. He saw his internment as a temporary setback. Something he would change as soon as he saw the opportunity.

# CHAPTER FOUR

*Stony Man Farm, Virginia*

While Raymond Gilman was still en route to New Mexico, Aaron Kurtzman's cyber team was running checks into his recent movements, using every data file they could access. Using the same logic that Gilman himself seemed to favor—the direct and simple approach—they checked cab companies in his locality and ran checks on his most recent calls from his home telephone. Akira Tokaido, the youngest member of Kurtzman's staff, ran a program of his own and came up with an account for a mobile phone in Gilman's name. When he accessed the call list he found only a few calls had ever been made. All of them were to a number near Albuquerque, New Mexico. The most recent had been two days ago. The next call had been to Boston's South Station. Moving on, Tokaido found a call to a local cab company in West Barnstable.

"Check this out," he said, as he sent the data to Kurtzman's monitor.

"Okay, Akira, what do we do next?"

"Hack into South Station's system and see where Gilman booked his ticket to."

Kurtzman spun his wheelchair and rolled it to his bubbling coffeepot. "Get her done, then."

Tokaido, grinning, turned back to his keyboard. It took him less than five minutes to access the information he wanted.

"His train arrives in Albuquerque in approximately four hours. That makes it 9:00 a.m."

Kurtzman picked up a phone and dialed the number that would connect him to Able Team. They were on standby at Andrews Air Force Base, where an Air Force jet had been made available. There had been a direct request via the Oval Office for full cooperation, which made Hal Brognola's task a lot easier. The aircraft would take Blancanales and Schwarz and land them at Kirtland Air Force Base just outside Albuquerque, where they would transfer to an unmarked car.

FORTY MINUTES LATER Able Team was airborne.

"This is the way to travel," Blancanales said, using the aircraft's telephone system.

"Don't get used to it," Barbara Price told him. "Listen up, now. We have more detail on the location Gilman has called. It turns out to be a diner on Interstate 40, heading west out of Albuquerque. The place is called Rachel's Diner. The owner is Rachel Noon. Aaron got hooked and dug a little deeper. This Rachel Noon is only nineteen but she owns this diner."

"And Gilman is involved somewhere in the equation?"

"That's right. It seems it was his money that helped to set the place up. All legal but done very low-key via his bank."

"Tut-tut, have we been prying into Gilman's bank account?"

"You see how low we have to stoop in the cause of national security," Price said.

"I wonder what his relationship is with this girl?" Blancanales asked.

"That's something you'll have to ask Dr. Gilman, Pol."

There was a pause as Price was interrupted. She came back on the line a few moments later with a description of Rachel Noon's vehicle, a red Cherokee 4×4 and the license number.

"I'll fax the information through to you," she said. "We have your on-board number."

"We should be able to locate Gilman from all that," Blancanales said. "Thanks, Barb."

Blancanales told Schwarz what he had just learned from Stony Man.

"Hell of a way to go for a romantic break," Schwarz said. "If that's what it is."

Blancanales shrugged, settling back and closing his eyes.

"And they say the art of conversation has died," Schwarz muttered.

THE C-12 TOUCHED DOWN at Kirtland just after 9:30 a.m. Able team was met by an Air Force major who escorted them to the car that had been made available. It was a dark, late-model Chevrolet. The major was a lean, tanned, noncommittal individual who was working to orders, but obviously resented the intrusion by these civilians.

"Never knew it could get so frosty in New Mexico," Schwarz said as they left the base and headed for Interstate 40 West.

"Some you win, some you lose," Blancanales said.

Schwarz glanced at his partner, figuring that the four hours of sleep on the plane had left Blancanales in a philosophical mood. He decided to leave it alone and concentrated on his driving.

THEY HAD NO PROBLEM locating the diner. As Schwarz pulled off the highway and drove across the dusty parking area, he spotted the red Cherokee parked outside the main building close to a sign that said Office.

"I guess we made it," he said, parking and shutting off the engine.

Before they had a chance to climb out of their car, the office door opened and two people stepped out. One was a young woman with dark hair, wearing jeans and a bright shirt. She was followed by a tall, lean man recognizable—from the ID photograph Able Team had been given—as Raymond Gilman. They crossed to the red Cherokee and climbed in. The girl took the driver's seat. She reversed away from the diner, swung the 4×4 around and rolled on to the highway, turning west.

Schwarz fired up the engine of their car and prepared to follow. As he turned the car around, a cream Ford and a dirty panel truck headed off in pursuit. The two vehicles picked up speed as they fell in behind the fast-moving Cherokee.

"Hmm. Company," Blancanales said.

Schwarz hit the pedal and sent the Chevrolet after the three vehicles ahead of them.

"Any bright ideas?"

Blancanales reached inside his jacket and pulled out the fax sheet that had been sent through to them during the flight. He scanned the printed information, then took out his cell phone.

"What are you doing?" Schwarz asked.

"Playing a long shot," Blancanales said. "Hoping Doc Gilman has his cell phone in his pocket and it's switched on."

He heard the phone ringing. It rang for a while.

"Come on, Doc," Blancanales begged. "Pick up. Pick up."

A voice came on the line. "Hello? Who is this?"

"Dr. Gilman, please do not hang up. Just listen to what I have to say. You and the young lady could be in danger. There are two vehicles behind you. A cream Ford and a panel truck. They appear to be following you."

"I don't understand. Who are—?"

"Right now all I can say is that me and my partner are with the Justice Department, assigned to protect you from just exactly what seems to be happening. We're in a dark Chevy directly behind the two vehicles following you."

"If this is true, what are we supposed to do?"

"I'm working on that, Doc. Problem is we don't come equipped with a manual of instant solutions."

Gilman went off the line and Blancanales could hear him conversing with his companion. Her voice rose, defiantly angry. Blancanales had a sudden feeling she might do something reckless.

"Doc, come back. Doc."

"The Cherokee is speeding up," Schwarz said. "And I mean speeding."

Blancanales couldn't get Gilman back. The cell phone line was still open, but no one was listening. He could hear the howl of the 4×4's powerful engine and the subdued voices of Gilman and the woman.

"Damn! He isn't listening."

"They probably figure they can outrun the tail cars."

"The girl must do it every day," Blancanales said. "No problem."

Schwarz glanced at the speedometer. He was doing almost eighty.

"Warp factor five coming up," he said dryly.

"And not a patrol car in sight."

Schwarz saw the panel truck sway, smoke coming from the rear tires as brakes were applied. The truck veered from left to right.

"What the hell are they doing?" Blancanales yelled, hunching back in his seat as Schwarz hit his own brakes, swinging away from the rear of the panel truck.

He overshot the truck and the Ford, and as they cleared the two vehicles the Able Team pair saw that the Cherokee had made a sudden left turn onto a dusty side road. The tail cars followed, leaving dark burn marks on the road surface as they dropped speed to negotiate the upcoming turn. The panel truck was moving fast, and it came close to rolling as it lurched into the turn.

Schwarz stood on the brake pedal, swinging the wheel to bring the Chevrolet around. He fought the heavy car's slide and brought it to a near stop, then pushed down on the gas and turned off the highway. The side road was rutted and had a loose, gritty surface. Thick dust spewed up behind them as Schwarz pushed to pick up speed. The three vehicles ahead of them were obscured by their own dust clouds and the undulating surface of the side road.

Blancanales took out his Beretta and checked it.

"Think we're going to need them?" Schwarz asked.

"I don't think we're on our way to a local barbecue," his partner said.

Schwarz handed over his own weapon, and Blancanales checked it, then laid it on the seat next to him. He tried the cell phone once more, but Gilman appeared to have broken the connection.

GILMAN GLANCED over his shoulder. He saw the hazy outline of the Ford still following and presumed that the panel truck was also still in pursuit. Beside him Rachel fought the wheel as the Cherokee bounced and jarred its way along the rutted road.

"Where is this taking us?" he asked.

"Cross-country eventually," she said. "I didn't

think they'd be able to follow this far in those road vehicles. I guess I was wrong, Dad. Sorry.''

"Don't be.''

"Shouldn't you talk to that man who called?''

"Is he genuine? Maybe he's one of those men behind us.''

As they slid around a bend in the road, a faded signboard showed up.

Interstate 40 Salvage.

Just beyond, a wind-eroded tin fence extended alongside the road. It seemed to go on for some distance. There was an opening where gates had once been. They were long gone, adding to the deserted air of the place.

As the opening approached, the Ford made an attempt to pass the Cherokee, swinging out to run alongside, then pull ahead. Rachel's response was to yank down on the steering wheel and send the Cherokee slamming into the Ford, crushing the front door and knocking the Ford aside. As she made to right the Cherokee, the right front wheel hit a deep rut. The steering wheel was torn from Rachel's hands, and the big vehicle lurched to the right, heading directly for the tin fence. Grabbing the wheel again, Rachel hauled the Cherokee back under her control. Her speed was still too high to effectively correct her course. The right fender clipped the steel gate post, bouncing the vehicle in a quarter turn that left it straddling the entrance to the scrap yard.

Behind them the Ford and the panel truck were hauling to a dusty stop, blocking Rachel from returning to the road. In the rearview mirror Gilman saw someone lean out from the Ford, a stubby SMG in his hands.

"They have guns," he yelled.

Rachel stepped on the gas and took the 4×4 in through the gate. The scrap yard spread out before them, a mass of abandoned vehicles and metal. There were buildings ahead, long and dark, but at that moment they seemed the only place that might offer them some kind of sanctuary from their pursuers. Rachel held the pedal down as the 4×4 sped along the rows of rusted scrap.

"DAMN, THEY GOT themselves boxed in," Blancanales said.

Schwarz took the Chevrolet in through the gates, following the other vehicles.

The panel truck's rear door flew open, and they saw a figure hanging on to the interior with one hand and brandishing a weapon at them. The weapon opened up, sending a stream of slugs that pounded the ground only feet in front of the Chevrolet. Schwarz swerved from side to side, presenting a harder target. The gunner in the truck had problems, too. His vehicle was bouncing and jerking as it careered along the rutted track. It meant he was having a rough ride, and there was no way he could settle his aim. He fired once more and his shots were feet above the Chevrolet's roof.

The Cherokee made a sudden stop just short of one of the abandoned buildings. Gilman and the woman scrambled out and made a run for the closest entrance. The Ford pulled up just behind the 4×4 and the panel truck did likewise.

Schwarz spun the Chevrolet around a pile of steel girders and snatched up his Beretta as he followed Blancanales out of the car.

THE FIVE OCCUPANTS of the panel truck joined Jesse and Wes. Hutch, the man Wes had talked to over the cell phone, glanced around.

"We know why we're here. Gilman is our target. He has to be unharmed. That's the contract. If he dies, that's an end to it. I don't give a fuck about the girl or those two in the Chevy. Easiest thing to do is get rid of them. Once they're dead, we can forget them. Alive, they're just going to get in our way. Let's do it."

"THEY'RE SPLITTING UP," Schwarz said.

"Time to earn our pay," Blancanales replied. "I'll go around the side of the building. You take the other end. Okay?"

"No problem, pal. Just watch yourself."

They separated, moving quickly to close in on Gilman and his unwelcome visitors.

An access door allowed Blancanales entry into the building. It was gloomy inside, the air hot from heat radiating through the metal structure. Shafts of sunlight came in through holes. Scrap metal was strewed around the floor.

Blancanales could hear voices somewhere toward the far end of the long building. Someone was yelling orders. He made for the sound of the voices.

GILMAN AND RACHEL found themselves suddenly confronted by one of the gunmen. He held a large automatic pistol and he gestured with it.

"Let's go, Gilman. Fun's over."

Gilman hesitated. The gunman stepped forward, anger showing in his eyes.

"Don't fuck with me, Doc," he snapped, raising the pistol.

Rachel pushed her father aside.

"Leave him alone," she yelled.

"Out of my way, bitch."

Rachel ignored him. She swung a balled fist that caught him across the cheek, stinging him.

"You…" he said, and lashed out with the hand gripping the pistol. It caught Rachel alongside her right cheek, knocking her to the ground.

*"No!"* Gilman shouted, and went for the gunman.

The muzzle of the weapon was jammed into Gilman's stomach. It brought him up short, his anger diminished by the immediate threat of the gun.

"Now move it," the gunman said. "Outside."

He pushed Gilman ahead of him. They reached an access door and went through, stepping into the bright daylight. As they emerged, a shadow caught the gunman's eye and he turned, expecting to see one of his partners.

Hermann Schwarz slammed the barrel of his Beretta across the gunman's skull, dropping him in the dust. Reaching out, he grabbed Gilman's arm and moved him away from the building.

"Wait…we can't…" Gilman protested.

Schwarz ignored him. He had seen armed figures

emerging from around the end of the building. Someone opened fire with a badly timed burst that did at least make Gilman aware of their situation.

"That way, Doc, and don't stop to think about it," Schwarz yelled.

He pushed Gilman in the direction of a rusty forty-foot steel tank lying amid other scrap. Formerly some kind of storage tank, it would at least offer them a degree of protection. Bullets clanged against the steel tank as Schwarz and Gilman rounded the barrel end of the large structure. A mass of metal girders and pipes was stacked on the far side. Schwarz pushed the muttering Gilman through the tangle of metal.

BLANCANALES HAD SEEN the gunman with Gilman and Rachel, but he was too far away to do anything. There was no chance of taking a shot at the gunman while Gilman and the girl were so close to him. As he made his way toward them, Blancanales saw the gunman strike Rachel and then hustle Gilman out of the building.

As he reached the prone figure, Blancanales heard shooting from outside the building. Rachel groaned and sat up.

"Are you okay?" Blancanales asked as he helped her to her feet.

She stared at him with a blank expression. Shock. Blancanales could understand why. Neither she nor her father had been ready for anything like this. They had resisted, and the result was the attack on Rachel. Now she found herself confronted by another stranger, wielding a gun. Blancanales lowered the weapon, keeping it down by his side.

He could hear a commotion toward the front of the building. Schwarz confronting the others?

The crackle of gunfire sounded again.

The moment she heard the shots, Rachel snapped out of her daze. She raised a hand to explore the ragged gash on her cheek, exploring the inside of her mouth with her tongue and tasting blood.

"Where's my father?" she demanded. "What are you doing to him?"

At least, Blancanales thought, we have the connection now.

To Rachel's second question he simply said, "Trying to keep him from getting hurt."

"I don't understand what's happening. Who are those men? Why are they—?"

"Later. Right now we need to get you both out of here."

Blancanales showed her the Justice Department badge he carried. She studied it, then looked at Blancanales as if he had the imprint etched across his face.

"You were the one who called on the cell phone?"

He nodded.

"Has Dad done something wrong?"

"No."

Putting the badge away, Blancanales retraced his steps through the building. At the side door he peered through the gap where it hadn't closed securely. He could see the Cherokee, with the Ford and the panel truck behind it. The Chevrolet was farther back.

Movement to his right caught his eye. The gunman who had taken Gilman out of the building was standing close by. He looked dazed, holding a hand to his head. Gilman was nowhere in sight.

Schwarz.

Gunfire was being directed at a large steel tank some twenty feet from the building. The fire was coming from beyond the building.

"Go and get the girl," someone yelled. "We can use her."

The gunman responded slowly. He turned and headed back for the access door. He put away his pistol and pulled a 9 mm Uzi from under his coat. It was suspended by a strap from his shoulder. He snapped back the bolt to cock the weapon.

"Stay away from the door, Rachel," Blancanales said.

"Is there someone out there?"

"Yes. And it's not your dad."

The gunman reached out to push open the door.

"Bad choice, pal," Blancanales muttered.

He reached behind him to push Rachel away from the door, then stepped to the right of the opening.

The gunman strode to the door and kicked it open. It swung away from Blancanales, and he watched as the Uzi muzzle poked inside. He held back, waiting until the gun's owner showed in the door frame. Head and shoulders leaned inside as the gunman scanned the interior.

Blancanales reached out with his left hand, catching hold of the gunman's wrist and yanking him off balance. As the gunman stumbled, trying to regain control, Blancanales backhanded him with the Beretta. The slide casing struck across the bridge of the man's nose, caving it in. Blood gushed from his nostrils as the man roared in pain. Blancanales didn't allow him any time to recover. He hit the guy twice more, this time in the side of the head, where the skull was thin. All the man's resistance ceased abruptly and he slumped against the opposite side of the door frame, knees sagging. As the man went down, Blancanales unclipped the shoulder strap and snatched the Uzi from his passive hands. The downed man was sprawled at his feet, body in spasm as he reacted to the fatal blows Blancanales had delivered.

Turning to Rachel, the Able Team commando caught hold of her wrist, pulling her close.

"Don't look at him," he snapped. "All we have to worry about is getting out of here. Okay?"

She nodded, still trying to come to terms with the dramatic turn of events. The sudden explosion of violence had changed her perceptions of life. It didn't seem real, but it was certainly different from the sanitized violence that was shown on TV, where people died neatly and cleanly. This was nothing like that.

SCHWARZ WASN'T exactly pinned down. He just had poor choices of which way to go. Added to that, he still had the responsibility of Raymond Gilman. To his credit the man was doing exactly what Schwarz telling him, despite being terrified. He might have created a missile system capable of killing, but he had never been involved in any kind of violence in his life. He seemed to be handling it calmly, but it was hard to tell if that would last. The last thing Schwarz needed was Gilman going to pieces.

"I don't like the idea of sitting here all day," Gilman said.

"Those guys aren't about to let that happen," Schwarz told him. "This was supposed to be a quick, clean snatch. Pick you up and leave. Last thing they need is a standoff and maybe the local law showing up."

Gilman, sitting with his back to the steel tank, cleared his throat.

"Can I ask you something?"

"Sure, Dr. Gilman," Schwarz said.

"Did we establish why these men want to *snatch* me?"

"Something to do with the Slingshot project. About you being the only man capable of breaking the encryption code on the disks the North Koreans have."

Gilman stared at Schwarz as if he had sprouted a second head.

"Do you want to say that again?"

"Maybe later," Schwarz said. "This isn't the time to go into it."

He had spotted movement.

"Looks like our boys are going for it," he said.

One of the gunmen had broken from cover and was coming across the open at an angle that would bring him to the far end of the steel tank. If he achieved his goal, Schwarz and Gilman would find they were being covered on two fronts.

An autoweapon opened up, laying down fire that

pushed Schwarz back behind the tank, covering the gunman making the run.

"He's making for the far end of the tank," Schwarz said.

He looked around, saw what he wanted and grabbed Gilman's arm, moving him to an opening in the tank.

"What are you doing?" Gilman protested.

"Doc, just get inside and stay there until I come for you."

Schwarz turned and sprinted the length of the tank, jumping over any of the scrap metal that lay in his path. His burst of speed took him to the far end of the tank in time to meet the gunman who had been congratulating himself on a smart move.

The gunman flattened himself against the end of the tank, raising his Uzi as a signal to his partners, then turned to round the end of the tank so he could confront the opposition.

He walked into a confrontation with Schwarz, waiting with his raised Beretta.

"Not today, pal," the Stony Man commando said.

Anger etched itself across the gunman's face. He made a vain attempt at lining up his Uzi, pulling back on the trigger. His burst was way off. Schwarz's wasn't. His 9 mm round punched in through the gunman's chest, knocking him back a couple of steps. Schwarz's second shot put him down for good.

HUTCH SAW the gunman tumble into view.

"This was supposed to go easy," he said. "It's getting to be like a fucking turkey shoot."

"I figure we got two options, Hutch," Wes said. "Play this out, or back off."

"I don't like quitting."

"You wouldn't like dead, either," Wes pointed out.

"You forgetting we took the man's money?"

"No. And I know he doesn't like jobs going sour. Only he ain't the one getting shot at."

Jesse pushed himself between them.

"Guys, let's do the it. We can take this pair. Quit pissin' in the sand, okay?"

He yanked back the Uzi's cocking bolt. "We know where they are, boys. Let's smoke them out so we can go home. Al, go get the truck and bring it around."

Al broke away from the group and ran to where the truck was parked. He slid in behind the wheel and started the vehicle. Turning it, he drove back toward the group, hitting the horn to let them know he was coming.

Jesse broke from cover and zigzagged his way across to the tank, laying down covering fire. He crouched against the front face of the tank, waving the others to join him. They converged on the tank, flanking Jesse.

The panel truck came alongside Wes and Hutch. They slid open the side door and climbed in, bracing themselves as the truck moved off, lurching across the rough ground.

"Let's do it," Hutch yelled.

The truck swung around the end of the tank, Hutch and Wes leaning out, Uzis cocked and ready.

At the same time Jesse and his partner moved around the far end of the tank, stepping across the body of the gunman Schwarz had shot.

The area behind the tank was empty. Scuff marks in the dust showed where the two men had been standing.

"Where the...?"

"Over here," Jesse's partner yelled.

His warning came a fraction late.

Schwarz had rolled out from beneath a stacked section of metalwork. He carried the Uzi he had picked up from the man he had shot. Now he opened up on the two gunmen, dropping both of them with his first burst.

HUTCH WATCHED with a mix of anger and surprise. He saw his team going down under the withering fire coming from the man wielding the Uzi, and he could hardly believe what he was seeing. It was as if they were unable to retaliate, taken so much by surprise that their responses had withered away as fast as they took the hits.

He raised his Uzi, leaning out the truck door to locate his target, and felt Wes grab his arm.

"Don't forget the other one."

The warning came too late. Something flickered in the corner of Hutch's eye. He responded, bringing up his Uzi.

Hutch yanked the Uzi around to track in on the guy.

Blancanales had his Uzi set on single-shot mode and he fired twice, his shots merging. He saw Hutch's chest recoil under the impact. The man slumped to his knees, head dropping, so that Blancanales's next round drilled into his skull, tearing away a chunk of bloody bone as it angled to one side, coring into hutch's brain.

The panel truck jumped as the driver tried to reverse away from the firing line. Blancanales hit him high in the left shoulder, shattering bone. The man cried out, clamping his right hand over the shredded flesh, feeling splintered bone under his fingers. The truck swung around, out of control, and slammed into a stack of scrap metal. It came to a jolting stop.

The Able Team commando stepped away from the tank, moving toward the truck as he saw a dark shape pushing past Hutch's still form.

WES HAD DECIDED it was time to move out. The hell with completing the contract. That was out of his hands now. The only thing that mattered was staying alive.

His free hand was absently brushing at the sticky debris that had spattered his clothing when Hutch's head had burst open. Wes hit the ground, sensing someone close. He looked up and saw Blancanales closing in.

"Fuck this," Wes said.

He curled his finger around the trigger of the Uzi.

Blancanales saw the gesture and shook his head. He triggered a shot that punched into Wes's left leg, just above the knee. Wes felt his leg go from under him and he went down, the Uzi spilling from his fingers. He made a grab for it. Blancanales swung his right foot, the toe of his shoe catching Wes under the chin. The force of the kick slammed the man against the side of the truck. He stayed there, clutching his leg and feeling blood fill his mouth from a tear in his cheek.

Blancanales nudged the Uzi to one side.

"You had enough?" he asked.

Wes wanted to say something, but the pain in his leg was too severe.

The gunfire had stopped as quickly as it had started. Schwarz covered the survivors with the Uzi as he removed weapons and made sure none of them were hiding any backups.

"You okay?" Blancanales asked.

Schwarz raised a hand. With the two survivors disarmed he crossed to the steel tank and brought out Gilman.

Gilman surveyed the scene, his face paling.

"All this because of me?" he asked.

"Somebody must have wanted you real bad, Doc," Blancanales said.

Gilman leaned back against the tank.

"I suppose so." A look of alarm crossed his face. "Rachel! Is she all right?"

"She's fine, Doc. She'll have a nasty bruise and a headache, but I think she'll live," Blancanales said. "I'll go and get her."

"Give me your cell phone," Schwarz said to his partner. "I'd better call the local cops. Ask them to send an ambulance, as well."

Blancanales nodded. He wondered what the law was going to say when they arrived on the scene.

AN HOUR LATER the area was sealed off, with police vehicles of every shape and size blocking entry and exit. There was even a state police presence. Lights were still flashing, radios chattering and uniformed figures were milling around. Ambulances had been and gone, taking away the wounded, under escort. They would have their injuries tended to and while in hospital would stay under police guard.

The man in charge of the police was a lean, tanned man with black hair and a worried expression. His name was Ned Turner. He seemed more concerned with Rachel's welfare than anyone else. The fact that Raymond Gilman was her father had thrown him more than the gun battle within his jurisdiction. It was obvious he and Rachel were an item.

"You sure he's her father?" he asked Blancanales.

Blancanales nodded. "It's the truth."

"Hell of a way to find out," Turner said.

He crossed over to where Schwarz was checking out the panel truck.

"Find anything?" he asked.

Schwarz shook his head. "Looks pretty clean."

"Rental?" Turner queried.

"Looks that way," Schwarz said. "They could have picked it up anywhere. Probably paid cash to avoid any problems."

"We can trace the registration. Find out where it came from," Turner volunteered. "Then, I suppose your people could do that a lot faster?"

Blancanales, approaching, held up his cell phone. "They're already on it. Thanks for the offer."

Turner rolled the brim of his hat between his fingers.

"Government man, huh?" he asked, nodding in Gilman's direction.

"That's right," Schwarz said.

"Hey, go talk to him," Blancanales said. "The guy won't bite."

Turner made his way across to where Gilman was standing with Rachel.

"Ain't love grand," Blancanales said.

His cell phone rang and he answered it.

"Your panel truck was rented by a guy named Clyde Hutchinson," Huntington Wethers said over the phone. "I ran a check and the guy looks genuine. He paid in cash for the truck. His home address is in Cabot Crossing, New Mexico. It turns out to be a gun store. The man has no police record, and has a military background in the Army. Special ops. He and a couple of buddies set up the store a number of years back. Wes Loomis and Jesse Lyman. I can't find anything on them."

"We've got something now," Blancanales said. "They just tried to kidnap a government computer specialist. Not exactly the normal way gun-store owners act."

"I'll run checks on all the other names you passed along," Wethers stated. "Nice of them all to be carrying wallets with ID."

"Way we see it," Blancanales said, "they expected this to be an easy deal. Just grab Gilman and drive away with him."

"Not their day, huh?"

"You pay your money and take your chances," Blancanales said. "Thanks for the intel. Talk to you later."

Blancanales put away his cell phone and made his way to where Turner was standing by his patrol car, talking on the radio. The cop finished his call as Blancanales approached.

"The guy who seemed to be running this bunch was Clyde Hutchinson. He ran a gun store in a place called Cabot Crossing."

"I know it," Turner said. "It's a small town about forty miles away from here. I could call the local law and let them know you're on your way. That's if you're planning on calling."

"We are," Blancanales said. "I'd appreciate it if you kept our visit private for the time being. Until we have a chance to look the place over on our own."

"Sure. Give me a call if you want me to contact the locals."

Blancanales made his way to Schwarz, Rachel and Dr. Gilman. The medics had seen to Rachel's injury. She was sitting just inside the Cherokee, talking to her father.

"Are we going to be watched now?" Rachel asked. She was staring at Blancanales, eyes sharply focused on him. "Trailed day and night like criminals?"

"Rachel, we can't take it out on these people," Gilman said. "If they hadn't turned up when they did, we might not be sitting here discussing the matter. You saw what those men were like."

The girl's face softened. "Yes, I suppose you're right. I'm sorry. It's been a bad day."

Schwarz smiled at her. "Tell me about it."

"Can we discuss this matter of the Slingshot disk going missing?" Gilman said. "You realize what this could mean to the whole program if the Koreans do manage to break the encryption?"

"We understand the implications," Schwarz said. "So do the Koreans, which is why they wanted you."

"My God, this is unbelievable. If the Koreans get into the program, they would be able to pinpoint every satellite we've launched. If they do that, they—"

"Bring them down with a missile attack," Blancanales said. "And there wouldn't be any means of stopping them because Slingshot isn't on-line yet."

Gilman ran a hand through his hair, staring around as if he expected an answer to leap at him from the sky.

"We create a defensive system to protect us and it could be destroyed even before we get it operational." Gilman rounded on Blancanales and Schwarz. "How the hell did this happen? How *could* it happen? I was told the security of the project was the best there was."

"Look, Doc, we only came into this after the event," Blancanales said. "All we know is someone within the project sold out. It's complicated. Too complicated to explain here and now."

"The main thing is to make sure you're safe,"

Schwarz said. "Until this matter is settled, you'll need protection."

"Do you think they'll try again?" Rachel asked.

"Whoever arranged the attempted kidnapping is going to know it failed when your father isn't delivered. They'll do some thinking about it. They're going to know the doc will be under guard from now, so they might decide to call it quits."

"But no guarantees?" Rachel added. "Oh, great. I suppose we'll have round-the-clock Secret Service agents standing over our shoulders. Dad, this is not good. We have think about Mom."

"Rachel's mother is terminally ill," Gilman explained. "It's cancer. She's been on treatment for a couple of years now, but nothing seems to be working. We do what we can for her. I visit when I can. Not as often as I like."

"Dad feels guilty about everything," Rachel said. "He didn't want to create any problems when Mom became pregnant with me because she's Navajo. He arranged things so we had a place to live. He set me up in the diner a few years back and helped Mom so she could paint. He added a studio to the back of the diner. And he comes to see us when he can."

"Not enough," Gilman said.

"Oh, come on, Dad. If you didn't do all that work for the government, how would you have been able to help set up the diner and everything?"

Gilman put his arm around Rachel's shoulders. "I'm sorry this happened. This wasn't the way it was meant to be." He looked at the Able Team duo. "I've tried to keep Rachel and her mother out of my work. It's why I left her out here where she belongs. There are going to be those who'll say I brought all this on because of my behavior. What the hell, maybe they're right. I thought I was doing the right thing. Maybe I should spend more time out here.''

"From what I've heard, Doc, you've done a pretty good job. Nothing wrong trying to keep family safe,'' Blancanales said. "Let's look on the bright side. If the Koreans can't get their hands on you, it could give us more time to track them down. If your encryption code is as hard to get into as you say, they're going to be busy people.''

"Maybe not,'' Gilman said in a low voice.

"Is there something we need to know?'' Schwarz asked, not expecting to like the answer.

Gilman sighed. "If these Koreans are as smart as they do seem to be, they'll know about Berkoff. If they can't get to me, they'll go for Berkoff.''

"Doc, let's have it all,'' Blancanales said urgently. "Who is Berkoff?''

"Jerome Berkoff. He's the one man who *could* break my code. We worked together some years ago. The man is brilliant. We used to create encryption codes for each other to break as part of our research. He understands my way of thinking, the way I construct codes. If the Koreans get hold of him, he would probably be able to break into the Slingshot program in a short time.''

"Oh, great,'' Schwarz said. "Doc, we're going to need information about this guy. Description. Where he lives. Everything and anything you can tell us.''

"No problem there,'' Gilman said. "I haven't

heard from him for a long time. Can't tell you where he is these days. He used to live in New York, but I believe he moved to France somewhere. We lost touch after he quit the program in the early days. Jerome just couldn't take to the restrictions. He hated taking orders and working to a plan. Government research wasn't for Jerome.''

''Just one question, Doc. This Berkoff guy. Would he take on this job if the North Koreans asked him?''

Gilman nodded. ''Yes, he would. Jerome had no qualms about betraying loyalty. He once told me that offered the right amount of money, he'd take on any challenge. That's his weakness. He has to prove he can outsmart anyone. Take his genius and use it for his own ends.''

Blancanales glanced at his partner.

''That wasn't the answer we wanted, Doc,'' he said.

''So what does happen to us now?'' Gilman asked.

''The way I see it, Doc, you need to be under protection until this is all over,'' Schwarz said. ''Same goes for Rachel and her mother. We'll get it arranged.''

''You'll probably have to put up with a degree of isolation for a while,'' Schwarz said.

''But I have a business to run,'' Rachel said.

''To put it bluntly,'' Schwarz said, ''you were very nearly the late Rachel Noon today. Understand that these people would use anything and anyone to get to your father. None of us want any harm to come to any of you. So we have to face facts. Rachel, you and your mother would be a hell of a bargaining tool if these people got their hands on you. And they would do it. Which is why you all have to be protected. We will do our best to make sure they don't come after you again.''

She sighed. ''I know you're right. It's just so...so...''

''Unfair?'' Blancanales suggested from the sidelines.

''Damn right it is,'' the girl said.

Schwarz grinned. ''She always had this stubborn streak?''

''It's from her mother's side,'' he said.

Rachel left them to join Ned Turner.

''That is one lovely girl, Doc,'' Blancanales said.

Gilman smiled. ''She's the image of her mother when I met her. She was the same age. I was on vacation. We met one day and that was it. I'd never met anyone quite like Beth. You know the rest.''

''Doc, I hope when this is all over you work things out.''

''Thanks to you, I might get that chance.''

Blancanales watched Turner and Rachel together.

''Was I ever that young?'' he asked. He knew the answer was yes, but readily admitted it had been a hell of a long time ago.

# CHAPTER FIVE

*North Korea*

Yat Sen Took felt a tinge of apprehension on hearing of the arrival of Duong Chin. The man's reputation was something to be feared. His control of the Chinese covert unit was absolute, and it was a known fact that he had personally executed two of his own men for failure on assignments. Chin maintained an unwavering loyalty to the Party and considered all defections from the line as being weak and doomed to failure. He wouldn't tolerate any lessening of state control over the population, and his allegiance to the hard-line Party members went a long way to keeping a tight rein on anyone trying to influence them.

Took was only given a few hours' notice of Chin's visit. It gave him little time to make any preparations, which he decided against. Chin hated any kind of formalized welcomes. He liked to make his entrance and get down to work immediately. Took wasn't sure why Chin had decided to make his visit. He could only assume it was to do with the Slingshot affair. China still showed great interest in the Koreans' attempts at neutralizing the project. It was as much in their interest as anyone else's. China had as much to lose as the Koreans, security wise, if the Americans brought their missile-shield technology on-line. With all that had happened concerning Slingshot, the Chinese had probably decided to become actively involved in the current crisis.

China still wielded influence in North Korea. The country was one of the few that still adhered to the Marxist doctrine and wasn't going to lose its position of favor with its great neighbor. It was a meeting of like minds. Each making outward gestures to the rest of the world while maintaining national integrity within its own borders. There had been some disagreements between the two, with China stepping back as she tried to improve her lot with the rest of the world, but behind the scenes the two countries still had much in common.

As he finished dressing, an achievement he was proud of, due to his crippled hand, Took couldn't help wondering what Chin might say or do. The man was known for coming to his decisions quickly and acting on them just as speedily. He would expect total obedience from anyone in his presence, and the fact he would be on Korean soil would mean nothing to Chin. He would still expect people to jump when he gave an order. A thin smile edged Took's lips. How would Gagarin react to Chin? The Russian may have looked harmless enough on the outside, but Took knew there was a steel core that would make Gagarin hard to push around. It would be interesting to watch what happened when the two met.

Tugging his tunic jacket into place, Took left his room and made his way down to his office. Gagarin was already there, standing at the window, overlooking the compound where uniformed soldiers were rushing about trying to avoid the constant rain. Gagarin turned as Took entered. The Russian was holding a mug of steaming tea in his hand.

"Does the sun ever shine in this place?" he asked.

Took helped himself to a cup of the tea.

"You are visiting us at the worst time of the year. It can be very pleasant in the summer."

"No offense, my friend, but I hope I don't have to stay that long."

"You have heard about our visitor?"

"I heard."

Took sipped his tea. "Have you met Duong Chin?"

"On a number of occasions. Some of them I try to forget about."

"Oh?"

"We've had our differences."

"Ideological or personal?"

Gagarin laughed. "Something of both."

"It should be an interesting meeting," Took said.

Gagarin had turned back to look out the window.

"If the weather is like this farther north, our American friend will be very uncomfortable."

Took smiled to himself. "I certainly hope he is."

"He won't break, Took. You'll never find out whether he knows anything or not, because you will never break him."

Took joined the Russian at the window.

"Why are you so certain?"

"I know his kind. His ability to resist is part of his makeup. He would die rather than submit to your threats. The more you push him, the harder he will fight back. He is one of those genuine Americans who took a continent and made it into the most powerful nation on Earth. Deny the Americans all you want, Took, but they are who they are because of what they did. A people of dreams made good. Success out of nothing. Built by their own hands and the blood they shed. You cannot create a nation such as America without an inner strength. And that strength comes down through the generations. This man you have working in your labor camp is one of those Americans. I truly believe he will survive, my friend, and if you achieve nothing else with him you will at least understand who he is."

Took sat down, facing the Russian.

"Is that admiration in your words?"

"A man can be admired in spite of being your enemy, Took. It's easy to kill a man. That doesn't take much effort, or skill, if you have him in your power."

"I have no time for your emotional baggage, Nikolai. This American is our enemy. The enemy is to be defeated. Through victory comes strength. The Americans are intent on destroying us. If we allow it, they will make us weak."

"Have it your way," Gagarin said. He was growing weary of Took's party-line arguments. He wanted a conversation that didn't include the latest predtions direct from the great leader. He also knew he would not get it talking with Took. The man lived and breathed his nation's doctrine. The only way for Took was in a straight line down the Party road. No deviation of any kind. Nothing that would detract from his purpose. Took's destiny was that of North Korea. He would live and die by that principle. Gagarin had no argument with any man who stayed the course. He just wished it didn't make such total bores out of them.

Duong Chin arrived midmorning. His helicopter touched down in the center of the compound where a rain-soaked guard of honor had been standing at attention for more than an hour.

Took went down to greet the Chinese, while Gagarin stayed in the warm office, watching the proceedings through the window. He recognized Chin the moment he stepped from the helicopter. He had a dark coat thrown over his shoulders. He was a big man, very broad, the thick fingers of his square hands gripping the lapels of the coat to prevent it slipping. He spoke briefly with Took, threw a cursory glance at the line of soldiers, then followed Took into the building. Gagarin crossed the room to stand by the blazing fire.

The door opened and Took entered, followed by Chin and the pair of bodyguards who followed him everywhere. The Chinese slid the wet coat from his shoulders and threw it to one of his men to shake and fold. Chin's keen eyes settled on Gagarin. He looked the Russian over, noting the well-cut suit Gagarin was wearing. Chin wore the plain dark tunic and pants that were the universal garment of China.

"Making another attempt?" Chin asked. "I hear your people experienced problems in Alaska."

Gagarin raised his hands. "What can I say, Chin? I suppose our embarrassment must have been similar to yours when the Americans leveled Colonel Li Cheng's island facility and wiped out his security force."

Chin's expression didn't change. Then his eyes settled on Gagarin and gave the merest hint of acknowledgment.

"The Americans have shown great resourcefulness over these incidents," he said. "It is time we put an end to it once and for all."

Chin sat down, staring into the fire as he gathered his thoughts.

"The failure to kidnap Dr. Gilman means the breaking of the encryption has not been resolved. Am I correct, Took?"

"Yes. But our people are working on the disks at this very moment. I am sure they will break the code in time."

"Time is not on our side," Chin said. "The longer we take over this matter, the more opportunity it gives the Americans to consolidate the system. While it is in its embryonic state, it is vulnerable. The moment it comes on-line it will have the capability of detecting any missiles we send at it. Which is the very purpose it was built for."

"The code is an extremely complex one," Took said. "Without Gilman the task *is* difficult."

"Then we overcome it."

"With respect, Comrade Chin, the thought is far from the deed."

"Have you heard of Jerome Berkoff?" Chin asked.

"German. Works independently for whoever pays his way. Very clever man," Gagarin said. "An expert at breaking encryption codes."

Chin nodded. "He is on a retainer with my department. We can call on him at any time. As we speak, I have people going to meet him and start him on his journey here. My assessment of the problem suggests we have little time to spare. The Americans are going to put their people on the Slingshot project to working full-time. It is coming down to a simple race. Whoever completes first will determine the future of Slingshot. I would prefer that we were the first past the post, Comrade Took."

Took inclined his head. "I agree."

"Good. How is the construction of the missile complex progressing?"

"Ahead of schedule. We expect to be commissioning the unit within the week. All the major construction on the subterranean level is being finalized as we speak. Electronic equipment, including the computers and tracking systems, passed their checks. They are virtually on-line."

"Good," Chin said.

He turned to Gagarin. "These Americans, the ones who destroyed Colonel Li's facility? They are also responsible for the Alaska attack?"

"I believe it was the work of a single group,"

Gagarin said. "It is not the first time we have encountered them."

"Who do they work for?"

"That is the problem," Gagarin said. "They are not responsible to any of the known American agencies as far as we can tell. They are well equipped, have excellent communication expertise and are superb combat fighters."

"A covert organization?"

"So we believe," Gagarin said.

"When they attacked Li's complex, there was talk of a highly sophisticated helicopter coming to their aid," Chin said.

"We made an attempt to get our hands on it in Siberia. Unfortunately we failed."

"My informants tell me this helicopter was instrumental in destroying one of your MIG fighters."

"Don't remind me," Gagarin said. "I requested it be launched against the Americans."

Chin almost smiled. He leaned forward. "I sympathize. There is nothing worse than trying to resolve a problem and having it escalate into something far larger."

"I just hope they don't extract the cost of that damn MIG from my pension."

"If they do, I will personally contribute to a collection to help you."

"This is all very amusing," Took said. "However, it does not solve any of our problems."

"True," Chin said. "As I see it, we have two distinct matters to deal with. The breaking of the encryption code. If we can get Berkoff to your facility, he can concentrate on the disks. Our second task is the elimination of this American group. As long as they are allowed to remain operational, there is a threat. We must stay alert to the possibility that they will know about Berkoff. I recall that he and Gilman know each other. Undoubtedly Gilman will warn the Americans there is another individual capable of breaking his code. When Gilman tells this to the American authorities, they will do their best to prevent him from offering his services to us.''

"If they send this American team to detain him," Gagarin said, "we may have an opportunity to put them out of action."

"Where is Berkoff?" Took asked.

"At this present moment he is in France," Chin said. "Took, is there a secure telephone I can use? I need to talk to my people. Warn them that the Americans may try to interfere with their transportation of Berkoff."

Took arranged for the call to be made, then returned to where Gagarin was sitting.

"You seem to find all this somewhat amusing," the Korean said.

"We become so involved with all these matters of state. Secrets, projects and such," the Russian said. "When is there time for living?"

"Is this not living?" Took asked. "What we are doing is vital to the future of my country. If we succeed, we prevent the Americans from destroying us."

"Took, do you really believe there is a fat, bloated capitalist sitting in some underground bunker, just waiting for the moment he can launch hundreds of missiles in your direction?''

''Didn't you before the Soviet Union fell apart? Wasn't that why your country built all those missile sites and sent submarines all around the world?''

''I never succumbed to the total paranoia,'' Gagarin said. ''We were all a little crazy in those days. And frightened. Fear was the key, Took. Fear of what might happen if some idiot pressed the wrong button or misread a blip on a radar screen.''

''But you fought the Americans, sent your agents to deal with them.''

''True. It was a children's game being played by adults. Running around stealing from each other. Lurking in the shadows. Passing secrets back and forth. Spreading the word about communism to the oppressed in Central America. In Africa. And what did it get us, Took? Are we all better off for it? Living in a shiny utopia? Look around, my friend. We are not better off. Any of us.''

''But you are here,'' Took said. ''If you don't believe, why are you working beside me?''

''One thing I learned a long time ago was how to survive. That's what I'm doing now, Took. Surviving. For a simple reason. Sooner or later Russia is going to stand back and make its mark on the world again. I want to be around when that happens. To be able to do that, Russia has to be able to hold the Americans down. put it on a leash while she gathers herself. Allowing the Americans to hold the whip hand with this Slingshot system would be like surrendering. Like it or not we're in this together. For different reasons.''

Took leaned forward. "You also have a personal stake in this, too.''

"The American commando team?'' Gagarin laughed. "The frosting on the cake. My little whim. I'll admit to that. It's an indulgence that will make my day, as our American cousins would say.''

Chin came back into the room. He seemed extremely pleased with himself.

"My people inform me that the task of bringing Jerome Berkoff here is under way. In order to put our American off the scent, they are employing a degree of subterfuge.''

"Excellent,'' Took said.

"In the meantime,'' Chin said, "why don't we go and take a look at your missile site, Took?''

"Of course Comrade Chin.''

Chin looked across at Gagarin. "Are you going to join us?''

"Oh, yes,'' Gagarin said. "I couldn't turn down such an opportunity. Could I, Took?''

The Korean maintained an icy indifference. Chin didn't fail to observe the slight derision in Gagarin's tone when he spoke to Took. He caught Gagarin's steady gaze and smiled very briefly and knowingly. He found Took's unremitting steadfastness to the cause a little wearying himself. It was quite possible to be a true believer without becoming a mechanical, clucking puppet. It was something Took seemed unable to grasp, and Gagarin pounced on it at every opportunity.

# CHAPTER SIX

*New Mexico*

Cabot Crossing straddled the rail tracks and the highway. It had a history that went back to the days of cattle and range wars. Now it was a backwater community that offered some degree of comfort to workers from outlying ranches and anyone else who decided to stop off. On the outskirts were houses that had seen better days, a few service businesses and a quietness that was almost eerie.

As Schwarz coasted along the dusty main street, looking for somewhere to park the Chevrolet, he began to experience a feeling of unease.

"You okay?" Blancanales asked. He had become aware of Schwarz's mood. "No one knows we're coming."

"That's what's worrying me," Schwarz said.

"What? You figure the local sheriff might be in with Hutchinson's bunch?"

"Him or one of his staff. Did anybody check on them?"

Blancanales took out his cell phone and dialed the

Stony Man secure number. He got through to Barbara Price and explained what they wanted. She took the details and told him they would call back with whatever they found.

Schwarz turned in at a parking slot outside a local café. The Able Team duo went inside and located an empty booth. The waitress sauntered over and took their order for coffee. Their window seat allowed them a view up and down the main drag.

"Looks peaceful enough to me," Blancanales said.

"Let's hope it stays that way."

"What do you expect? Truck loads of seed pods and people walking around with glassy stares?"

Schwarz smiled. "Pol, that was only a movie. It wasn't real."

"Scared the hell out of me. Black-and-white movies always seemed more realistic."

The waitress arrived with their coffee. Just as she moved away, Blancanales's cell phone rang softly. He answered.

"We ran a check on all the employees on the Cabot Crossing sheriff's department," Price said. "They all came up clean except one. Name of Walter Neuman. He runs the department's motor pool. He was also in the military along with Hutchinson and company. Cozy arrangement."

"We'll keep our eyes open," Blancanales said. "Anything else we need to know about?"

"Phoenix is on the way to France. We picked up information that Jerome Berkoff has been seen there recently."

"Thanks, Barb."

Blancanales ended the call and put his phone away. He drank some coffee.

"One of Hutchinson's old Army buddies is working in the motor pool over at the sheriff's department. Name of Walter Neuman. And Phoenix is on the way to France. Looking to find Berkoff."

"If this guy Neuman has heard about his buddies getting retired, he might decide to move on himself," Schwarz said. "Maybe we need to pay our visit to the gun store sooner rather than later."

"Look at how many people turned up at the scene," Blancanales said. "If news didn't get out one way or another, I'd be surprised. Let's go."

They paid for the coffee and left the café after getting directions for the gun store from the waitress. It was located at the far end of Cabot Crossing, a stand-alone building with parking at the side and access to the delivery ramp at the rear. A sign on the front door stated that the store was closed. Schwarz took the Chevrolet around the side. There were no cars in view there, but as he nosed the Chevrolet around the rear of the building he and Blancanales were able to see a couple of vehicles parked up against the ramp. There was a gleaming Buick limousine and a dusty Ford Mustang.

"Cleaning house?" Blancanales suggested.

"Could be."

They climbed out of the Chevrolet, making sure their weapons were accessible. Schwarz led the way up the steps to the loading ramp. Just as they reached the ramp a man stepped out of the door marked Deliveries. He was carrying a carton and he wore a pair of coveralls that had Cabot Crossing Sheriff—Motor Pool over the right pocket. The left pocket identified him as Neuman.

"Moonlighting, Wally?" Blancanales asked. "Times must be hard."

"Who the fuck are you?" Neuman asked.

He was a big man, paunchy but still a formidable figure. His sandy hair was cut in a military style close to his skull.

"Interested party," Schwarz said. "Concerned about the late Clyde Hutchinson's affairs. And especially his property. You got permission to remove it, Wally?"

"He was a friend of mine," Neuman snapped.

"I didn't ask whether you slept with him," Blancanales said. "I just want to know why you're stealing his stuff the minute he's dead."

"Weird thing for a friend to do."

Neuman shot a glance at Schwarz. He was working on an answer, but his mind couldn't get around it fast enough. Sweat popped out across his forehead.

"He's helping me," someone said.

The man behind the voice stepped into view. He was dressed in a suit that had to have cost as much as the Buick. Everything about him screamed money. This man had it and wasn't afraid to display the fact. Lean, with a tan that had to have come out of a bottle, the man was perfectly groomed and his smooth manner blended with his appearance.

"You are…?" Schwarz asked.

"Leopold Spenser. I represent the late Mr. Hutchinson."

"News does travel fast in this burgh," Blancanales said. "Well now, I work for the Justice Department and I shot the late Mr. Hutchinson while he was in the act of trying to kidnap someone. So now that we understand each other, I suggest you replace everything you've moved and get the hell out of here."

Spenser considered Blancanales's statement.

"I have no proof you are who you claim to be."

"As far as we're concerned, you haven't proved anything," Schwarz said. "For all we know you're an opportunistic thief."

Blancanales was watching Neuman out the corner of his eye. The man was staring at him, his face working as he absorbed the facts about Hutchinson's death.

"I resent that," Spenser said. "I'm going to reach inside my jacket and take out a card."

He did so slowly, holding out the card for Schwarz to take. It stated that he was indeed an attorney with offices in a number of locations around the country.

"Very impressive," Schwarz said. "You print them yourself?"

Neuman was building up a head of steam. Blancanales could see it in the man's expression.

Schwarz took out his badge holder and showed it to Spenser.

"Mr. Spenser, I don't have time for games," Schwarz said. "We have a job to do, and we can't allow you to remove anything pertaining to the affairs of Clyde Hutchinson."

Neuman made a sound that might have been a spoken word, or just as easily an angry growl. His fingers closed tightly against the carton he was holding, digging in through the cardboard.

"We need to discuss this, gentlemen," Spenser said. He was starting, ever so slightly, to become aware of his predicament, and he was going to try to talk his way out.

"No. We need to put all of Hutchinson's property back where it belongs because this building is now in our jurisdiction."

"I must pro—"

"Do all the protesting you want, Mr. Spenser, but do it from your own office, without the aid of Mr. Hutchinson's property."

Neuman erupted with a yell of pure frustration. He hurled the carton at the Able Team duo, lunging at Blancanales with his large hands spread wide. For a big man he moved quickly, closing the gap in seconds. Blancanales stood his ground initially, reaching for his Beretta. He pulled the gun free as Neuman loomed large in his eyes, then executed a sidestep that moved him away from the grasping hands. In the same move Blancanales swept his pistol up and around, catching Neuman behind the left ear. The blow stunned the man. He overshot Blancanales and went over the edge of the loading ramp, falling with a heavy thump across the hood of Spenser's Buick. His head smacked against the windshield, and a jagged crack appeared in the glass. Neuman made no attempt to remove himself from the hood of the car.

"Discussion over," Schwarz snapped. "We need to go back inside, Spenser."

He pushed the now silent attorney back inside the gun store, leaving his partner to deal with Neuman. When Blancanales did show up, hauling the groggy Neuman with him, Schwarz and Spenser were in the store office. Blancanales shoved Neuman into a chair. Neuman's face was bloody, and he had a nasty gash down the left side. Blancanales closed the door.

"I need a doctor," Neuman moaned.

"You have to earn that right," Blancanales said.

"You can't get away with this," Spenser said, still trying to talk his way out of trouble.

"I believe we are," Schwarz said.

He spotted a computer on a separate desk and went across to it. He turned it on, watching the monitor light up.

"I wonder if we'll find anything interesting in here."

Out the corner of his eye Schwarz saw Spenser's left hand start a move to his jacket pocket. It was purely a reflex move, done out of anxiety over his present position. The attorney let his hand resume its former position almost immediately as he realized what he was doing.

Schwarz eased his Beretta from its shoulder rig and moved over to stand behind Spenser.

"If he moves, shoot him," Schwarz said to his partner.

"Really?"

"Yeah. He is pissing me off big time."

With the muzzle of his pistol pressed against Spenser's skull, Schwarz went through the man's coat pockets. He tossed his findings on the desk. What interested him most was the computer disk he found. Schwarz returned to the desk, picked up the disk, pushed it into the disk drive slot on the computer and clicked it open. A number of files were listed. Schwarz opened them one by one, and what he found brought a smile to his face. He checked the computer and found it was capable of connecting to the Internet. He opened it and tapped in Kurtzman's E-mail address. As soon as he was on-line, he mailed the contents of the disk through to Kurtzman, with a brief message: "Read these and weep. From Uncle Able."

As soon as the e-mail had been delivered, Schwarz ended the connection. He ejected the disk and put it in his pocket.

Spenser looked devastated. He obviously knew what the disk had contained. Its discovery by Schwarz and the transfer of the information caused him a great deal of agitation. He stared around the office, eyes flicking back and forth like a cornered animal trying to find a way out.

"There's nowhere to go," Blancanales said.

"You guys are dead," Neuman blurted out. "Stupid bastards don't know what you've got yourselves into."

"Coming from a guy who just tried to head butt a car windshield, calling us stupid is a bit lame," Blancanales said.

"Yeah? Well, I still need a fuckin' doctor."

"We're still thinking about it," Schwarz said. He glanced at the ashen-faced Spenser. "What is it *you* want, Spenser, apart from a hole to swallow you up?''

The lawyer opened his mouth, then thought better of it. He slumped back in his seat, all the earlier brashness lost as he tried to figure how to get out of his current position and stay alive.

Blancanales picked up the telephone on the desk and dialed Ned Turner's number.

''I believe the term is we hit pay dirt. Or more like the mother lode. Listen, Ned, you still got the state police around? Good. We need them here at Cabot Crossing. Let them deal with the local law. We haven't been in contact yet because we don't know if there's any connection. Better if the state cops handle that side. If there's no connection, fine. Okay, I'll leave that with you.''

Blancanales hung up. He took out his cell phone and showed it to Schwarz as he crossed the office and stepped outside. He dialed Stony Man and eventually got Brognola on the line.

''Can you get a team in here fast? Let them take our prisoners off our hands. I only got a quick look at the contents of that disk. It looked pretty interesting.''

''Yeah?'' Brognola said. ''You want to be back here. You guys must lead a charmed life to have picked this up. And you're right. I do want you back here. The FBI can take over down there. I'll contact the local field office and have them send in a full team. I can liaise with them later. Soon as they arrive, you hand over and then head back to Kirtland and the Air Force will bring you home.''

"This lawyer we picked up. He's starting to act like the world's come to an end. He knows what's on that disk."

"If he does, I'm not surprised he's in a panic. Keep him away from any telephones. He doesn't get to call anyone. We need to keep this nailed down."

"You got it," Blancanales said.

He returned to the office. Schwarz was standing quietly by while Spenser deluged him with demands about his rights, his need to call his associates and what would happen if his requests weren't met.

"You can tell he's a lawyer," Blancanales said, ignoring Spenser's ranting.

He beckoned Schwarz to him and repeated what Brognola had said.

"I demand to know what you are saying," Spenser said.

"I don't think so," Schwarz told him. "It's personal."

"Never mind that. What about my telephone call?"

"You don't get one."

"You have to give me that call. It's a legal requirement. Every person who has been arrested is allowed a telephone call."

Blancanales nodded. "Exactly right, Mr. Spenser, with one small flaw in your argument."

"What?"

"Did you forget? We haven't technically arrested you. Now shut up and sit quietly unless you want me to commit another illegal act."

Spenser didn't say another word.

# CHAPTER SEVEN

*France*

Jerome Berkoff was renting a house south of Évreux in Normandy. According to information supplied, he lived alone, frequently making business trips that took him away from the place for weeks at a time. The information supplied via Kurtzman's team was no more than a few days old. Phoenix Force was flown to England and from there the team took a commercial flight from London's Gatwick airport to Rouen, France. They hired a car for the trip to Évreux.

Due to high security at airports, they were forced to make the flights unarmed. However while they were in the air from the U.S. Katz made arrangements via his contacts within Mossad, and one of their agents in France met Phoenix Force at a service area a few miles from Rouen and passed over a package. The delivery took less than a minute, Katz having set up the exchange with his usual expertise. Once the team was back in its car and on the move, McCarter opened the package. Inside they found four

9 mm Glock Model 34s, each with two extra loaded magazines.

"I don't know how he did it, but I owe that man a drink," McCarter stated.

"Okay," James said. "While you're buyin' I'll have one, too."

"Don't push it."

They passed through Évreux around 11:00 a.m., continuing their trip through the region. They bordered the River Eure, moving along winding country roads where timber houses gave way to the Dreux Forest.

Encizo, driving, asked, "How we doing, Gary? Are we lost yet?"

"We should see a church on the right," Manning said. "Couple of miles along from here."

The forest faded away, leaving open fields. They spotted the church, perched on a low hill, with its gray stone spire rearing against the cold blue sky. On the far side of the church was the cemetery, and, beyond, the road curved down the other side of the hill. A spread of farm fields stretched for a mile, then a line of trees edged the road. As they drove on, the trees increased and by the time they had gone another couple of miles, they were again passing through the dense forest, thick stands of trees on either side of the road. The tranquil vista continued for as far as the eye could see.

"Berkoff's place should be about a mile from here," Manning said, checking his map again. "There should be a turnoff and a narrow road."

They picked up the turnoff. Encizo slowed the car

and turned off the main road. The new road was wide enough to allow one vehicle at a time. Every so often there were areas where opposing vehicles could pull to one side to allow safe passage for one coming in the opposite direction.

"House up ahead," James said. "Off to the left through the trees."

"Rafe, pull in," McCarter directed him.

Encizo pulled the rental car under the cover of low-hanging foliage and cut the engine.

"We don't know if this bloke is on his own," McCarter said. "We go in carefully. Check the place out. Then we'll decide how to do it."

They moved off the road and into the trees, using the thick foliage as cover to hide their approach to the house. They worked their way to where the forest had been cut back to create room for the house and its grounds. Crouching in the shadows, they were able to study the big old house and its surroundings. The gardens might once have been the pride of who-ever lived in the place. Now they had been allowed to run wild. The carefully planted flower beds and ornamental hedges were thick with wild grass. Their unkempt growth did little to add to the view but did at least provide cover for Phoenix Force. Thin spirals of smoke issued from stone chimneys on the roof of the house.

"Looks like someone's home."

"Probably the Addams Family house-sitting," James muttered.

McCarter took out his Glock, checking the action. "Two teams," he said. "Cal, you're with me. Rafe and Gary, cover the rear. We don't have time for anything fancy on this. Let's check out the opposition if there is any. Our main objective is Berkoff.''

"If he's home," James said.

They had already prepared themselves for that probability. If the Koreans had made contingency plans, Berkoff might already have left France, his destination North Korea.

"Okay," McCarter said. "How long do you need to get established at the rear?"

"Make it five," Manning said, glancing at Encizo and getting a nod of agreement.

They checked and synchronized watches.

"Go," McCarter said.

Manning and Encizo faded into the overgrown foliage, leaving the others to settle down and wait.

THE DENSE FOLIAGE covered Manning and Encizo as they skirted the side of the old house. As the tree line faded, they used the thick grass and heavy bushes to conceal their movements. The only windows in sight on this side wall were on the upper floors.

It took them a full four minutes to reach the rear corner. Easing to the very edge of the wall, they checked the area. Beyond the house were extensive lawns and gardens that at one time had been ordered and neat. Paths were overgrown, flower beds choked with grass. Sagging net fencing showed where tennis courts had stood. The grass courts themselves were barely visible due the untended grass. Tiered sections of the gardens, landscaped in another era, were unkempt and marked the deterioration of the gardens as a whole.

Manning and Encizo scanned the area. Nothing moved except for the tall grass rippling under the effects of the slight breeze.

"If there is anyone around, they must be inside," Manning said.

"Time's up," Encizo said.

They eased around the corner of the house and flattened against the stone wall, weapons held ready. Some yards to their right a large window gave them viewing access to the interior.

Manning peered around the edge of the wooden frame. He looked in on a room filled by dark furniture and ceiling-high shelves holding countless books. On the wall directly opposite the window was a large stone fireplace. Logs burned in the hearth.

Just as Manning was about to pull back from the window, he saw a broad-shouldered figure step inside the room and cross to sit behind a desk. A computer was set up on the desk, and the man began to use the keyboard. The room wasn't brightly lit but from what Manning could see, the man fit the description of Jerome Berkoff they had been issued with. The man had pale hair worn long, exactly as the photo image they carried with them.

"Looks like our man," Manning said.

He moved aside so Encizo could double-check. When he had finished the little Cuban leaned back against the wall, a thoughtful expression in his eyes.

"Not Berkoff?" Manning asked.

Encizo shrugged. "We'll tell better when we get inside."

"Rafe? What is it? I hate that look."

Encizo shrugged. "Maybe me just being suspicious."

They skirted the window and moved across the rear of the house, searching for a way in. They found a door that led into the kitchen. Manning tried it and the door opened without a sound. The kitchen was fitted out with what looked like the original units. The wood was dark and shiny from polishing. A wide cooking stove threw off a degree of heat. Along one of the working surfaces were modern items. A microwave oven and a coffeemaker in stainless steel. The floor underfoot was stone slabs.

Manning and Encizo crossed to the door that led through to the house. It stood open, giving access to a short passage that took them deeper into the house.

While Manning watched the way ahead, Encizo maintained a check on their backs. He still had a feeling things weren't right within the house. Something was out of sync. He couldn't put his finger on it, but Encizo stayed with his gut feeling. It had served him too well in the past to be ignored.

If he hadn't been wary, listening for any sound or movement that might suggest trouble, the Cuban's ears wouldn't have been finely tuned to the slightest disturbance.

The floors in this part of the house were wooden. One of the problems associated with wood floors, and especially old ones, was a tendency to creak. Unless an individual lived in a house full-time and knew all of the peculiarities of that building, it was an easy matter to overlook something.

Like the merest whisper of a creaky board when someone placed his weight on it. When the brief sound did reach Encizo's ears, he didn't register having heard it. He simply maintained his alert presence behind Manning. But in his mind he placed the source of the sound as having come from a door they had passed moments before. He had noticed the door, on their left, and had briefly wondered where it led.

Manning paused, raising his free hand to indicate they had reached the door to the library they had seen from the window. Encizo moved up close behind the big Canadian and said quietly, "Somebody's behind the door we passed on the left."

It was enough. Manning concentrated on the task ahead of him, trusting Encizo to deal with whatever might come from his warning.

Leaving Manning to deal with the man in the library, Encizo dropped back a step, bringing his Glock across his body, so that as he turned, the weapon moved before him, and as the door was thrust open Encizo was already facing it.

He saw a bulky figure framed in the doorway, the muzzle of an SMG catching soft light. He saw the man's trigger finger pulling back, a deliberate movement that broadcast the man's intentions.

Encizo was already committed. His finger completed its pull on the Glock's trigger, and he felt the weapon punch back against his hand as it fired. The bullet caught the gunman in the chest, just above the heart. It shoved him back against the door frame, jerking his SMG off target. It fired, sending a stream of 9 mm slugs into the wood wall paneling above Encizo's head. The Cuban ducked, hunching his shoulders as he pushed the Glock forward and triggered twice more, sending a pair of 9 mm rounds into the gunman's chest. This time they were on target, coring through the chest cavity and puncturing the man's heart. He flung himself back, arms windmilling as he went down, the SMG bouncing from slack fingers. Thin veils of bloody spray misted the air over the turning body.

Manning raised a foot and kicked open the door to the library. He ducked, broke to one side and went in low, his Glock tracking the air ahead of him. He saw the man at the computer turn, shoving back his chair and reaching for an automatic pistol lying beside the keyboard.

The door swung wide as Manning went through. He continued his forward motion, pushing hard, and executed a final half leap that took him crashing into the man behind the desk. They collided with stunning force. The big Canadian had already braced himself for impact, so he was ready. The other man hadn't, and the breath was driven from his lungs as Manning struck. They went over the top of the desk, sending the computer monitor crashing to the floor, then followed it down as they slithered across the desk. Manning kept the other man under him, and he took the full impact of the fall. The autopistol he had snatched up from the desk was jarred from his fingers. It slithered across the polished wood and vanished under a chair.

MCCARTER AND JAMES had reached the front of the house when they heard the rattle of gunfire.

"Bloody hell," McCarter said. "I think sneaky time is over, Cal."

He bolted for the main door, James close behind. The Briton slammed his shoulder against the door, which yielded, flying open to reveal the entrance hall. Ahead of them a wide staircase led to the upper sections of the house. To the left stood an open door, and farther back Encizo loomed over a downed figure.

"David!" James yelled, reaching out to push McCarter aside as an armed man showed from an alcove to their right.

The ripple of autofire was followed by the whine of bullets scoring the marble floor. James, dropping to a half crouch, tracked in on the man who had fired and punched two bullets through the attacker's chest. He had taken a fraction of time to aim, and his shots were hard on target. The gunner slumped back, dropping his weapon and curling up at the base of the wall.

McCarter crossed the hall, homing in on Encizo.

"In there," the Cuban said, gesturing toward the door to the library.

McCarter stepped into the room and saw Manning dragging a panting figure to his feet.

"Berkoff?" he asked.

Manning pushed the figure toward McCarter.

"What do you think?"

McCarter stared at the man. He reached out and took hold of the man's hair, pulling his head up so he could look in his face. At first glance he could have passed for Jerome Berkoff, but something wasn't quite right in the set of his features.

"Different-color eyes," Encizo said from behind McCarter.

Stepping around the man Encizo held up the photo of Berkoff they had been supplied with. There was a similarity that would have convinced at a distance. Up close the differences were evident.

This man wasn't Jerome Berkoff.

Phoenix Force had been drawn into a deception. While they had been busy here in France, the real Jerome Berkoff had been spirited away and was most probably heading for North Korea.

"Sit him down where I can see him," McCarter ordered. He reached for an inside pocket and took out his cell phone.

The stand-in Berkoff crossed to a chair and sat. He obviously understood English.

"Go check out the rest of the house in case there are any more of his chums around," McCarter said.

The seated man raised a hand. "I'll save you the bother. There were only the three of us. We were told to wait around until you showed up and make sure you didn't leave."

"Just two guns and you?" Manning said. "Your people must have some confidence if all they sent were two guns to back you up."

The man shrugged. "I knew my job. If those two weren't able to cut it, that's their funeral."

McCarter crossed to the far side of the room and dialed Stony Man. He waited while the signal was sent to the satellite link, then bounced back to the electronic system that diverted it through to Stony Man. He asked for and got Brognola.

"How's France?" the big Fed asked.

"Not my idea of a fun day out," the Briton snapped. "We've been neatly shafted here. The guy we collared isn't Berkoff. He's just a look-alike, and not a very good one up close. While we've been putting our arses on the line, the real Berkoff has been laughing up his all the way to North Korea."

Brognola sighed. "You'd better finish up there and come on home."

"We could stay on here and have a break," McCarter said dryly.

"I don't think so," Brognola told him. "Arrangements are being made to send you somewhere else."

"I don't like the sound of that."

"Wait until you find out where it is."

*Stony Man Farm, Virginia*

THEY WERE GATHERED in the Computer Room. Barbara Price, Katz and the cyber team.

"David is not a happy man," Brognola said as he replaced the phone. "Not that I can blame any of them. All that way for nothing."

He explained what had happened. "Good thing we have all the details fixed, then," Price said. "It looks as if everything is focusing in on North Korea."

Kurtzman tapped in commands, and one of the large wall monitors came on-line.

"This is the playback of the imagery we picked

up via the SAR satellite. This is the base where we saw Carl, and this is a recent scan of the same base. We've been keeping an eye on the place. Picked this up day before yesterday. A chopper is delivering a visitor. We managed to record a pretty clear shot of the guy while he was on view. I ran it through all the databases and we finally came up with an ID.''

Kurtzman punched in another command, and a full face image came on-screen, with accompanying data.

''Duong Chin, a hard-liner from mainland China. Information has him down as the control of a unit of enforcers who work all kinds of operations for the government. Chin is a tough cookie. He doesn't put up with anything less than the best from his people. He has the blessing of the top Chinese men. According to the background, his influence is pretty widespread. Hong Kong. Taiwan. Most of Asia where the Chinese have interests. He also has contacts in the West, Europe, Russia. He pays well but expects results.''

''I know the name,'' Katz said. ''I never came across the man myself, but from what I've picked up he's no beginner. He understands his business.''

''And he's paying a visit to North Korea at a busy time,'' Price said. ''You think maybe he's got a hand in the Berkoff business?''

''We know the Chinese had a hand in the previous Slingshot deals,'' Brognola replied. ''Could be they're keeping their options open and playing house with the Koreans.''

Kurtzman put up another image.

''This is from further sweeps, using the information the deep-cover operative sent in. This shows the labor camp we've been looking for.''

''Where Carl might be?'' Price asked.

''Yeah.''

Kurtzman let them watch the image. It wasn't the best he had been able to obtain previously due to the severe weather. He had sharpened the image as much as possible, so they were able to pick out the formation of the camp, with its perimeter fence and watchtowers. Within the confines of the camp they could see the shuffling figures of the inmates as they moved around. There was a hopelessness in the way they moved, an aimless lethargy that was made all the more distressing by the silent, impersonal view afforded by the cold eye of the satellite camera.

''It's hard to believe these places still exist,'' Price said. She didn't like what she saw but forced herself to keep watching. That way the image would burn itself into her mind, and it would help when she had to make decisions about why they were doing what they did at Stony Man.

''This is how they make their people toe the line,'' Huntington Wethers said. ''Criticize the government over there, and they send you to one of these places to reeducate you. It's how the top people stay in power. Through intimidation and the threat of arrest.''

''And this might be where Carl is?'' Carmen Delahunt said. ''Pray God he's okay.''

''Aaron,'' Brognola said, ''you got anything else?''

Kurtzman nodded and flashed up another image.

"We did scan this. They got a lot of people working on it. It's hard to figure out exactly what it is. Some new base. It could be a missile-launch facility, or some kind of military establishment. Whatever, there isn't much aboveground, so we're second-guessing at the moment. I'm going to try again when the satellite is available."

"Calculated guess would suggest if the Koreans are going to be launching missiles at the Slingshot satellites, they'll need something other than a standard system," Katz said. "The technology required to knock satellites out of the sky will need to be pretty sophisticated. It would have to handle the kind of data on those disks the Koreans have. It might be worthwhile checking on any movements of high-tech computer systems. See if we can link the purchase of the required hardware to the North Koreans. If you want, I'll look into that, Hal."

Brognola nodded. "Good idea, Katz. Give it a shot."

Katz crossed to have a word with Tokaido.

"Okay, people, thanks for your efforts. I know this has all been a rush, but that's the way this thing is running. All we can do is stay with it so we can give the guys all the backup they can use."

"Any feedback from the information you passed to the FBI?" Price asked.

Brognola managed a smile. "They think it's Christmas come early. Some arrests have already been made. They're keeping the lid on this so no one else can be alerted. When they do go, it'll be a nationwide operation. If it goes as planned, they should be able to grab most of the names from that database.''

''Some find,'' Price said. ''An organization coordinating infiltration of government organizations. Run like a business, and tied in with groups like the Militia Men. Able to supply hit teams, arrange kidnappings, and all on a national footing with international connections. Even in Russia. Hal, what the hell is happening to the world? The way that was set up, it had the structure of a corporation. Even down to lawyers like Spenser.''

''No different than the Mafia in the old days. That had its hierarchy. From the capos right down to the street men. Chains of command. Legal people to make sure they always had someone on hand to bail out the ones who got themselves busted. These days it's antigovernment cells. Trading in secrets between countries. Somebody had to see the advantage of putting it on a business footing.''

''Hal, there were people in there from security agencies. If they can get them on their payroll, what hope is there for the rest of us?''

''Not the first time that's happened,'' Brognola said. ''Won't be the last, either. But at least we can take a few of them down thanks to Able Team. By the way, where are Pol and Gadgets?''

''Down at the firing range. Now that Gilman's safe, they're feeling a little out of the action.''

''How are we on the Phoenix operation?''

''Jack is already on his way to South Korea. As soon as Dragon Slayer is off-loaded, he'll fly her out to rendezvous with the carrier. They'll look after him and make sure the chopper is all fueled up and armed.

Then he goes on standby until Phoenix signals for pickup.''

"The sub?"

"The Navy will pick up Phoenix from South Korea. When they leave, they'll head out to sea, then basically double back once they're submerged and head for the drop-off point along the North Korean coast. Phoenix will swim in using scuba gear to the prearranged point. From there they'll go on foot until they meet up with the undercover operative, Quo Lam Sun. He can lead them in and get them to the locations we've discussed. It's the only way we can do it. The way the Koreans have stepped up security, Phoenix needs someone with-on-the-spot knowledge of the country.''

Brognola shoved his hands deep in his pockets as he stared at the monitor screens.

"Let's hope they can find something. As we all assume Jerome Berkoff is being taken to North Korea, wherever he ends up might at least point to where those damn disks are.''

"Hey, we'll get there, Hal," Price said.

Brognola stared at the wall for a moment, then squared his shoulders as he reached a decision.

"Get Pol and Gadgets up here. I want them geared up and ready to go soon as. Then get me our Air Force contact. I want the guys on a fast jet.''

"Where to?"

"They can join Jack on standby. When he goes in to lift Phoenix out, they might need some help. Better Pol and Gadgets are out there than sitting around here stewing about having nothing to do.''

"Consider it done," Price said.

# CHAPTER EIGHT

*Sea of Japan*

Joseph DeVere eased down beside McCarter. He had a mug of coffee in his hand. He looked far too young to be commanding a nuclear submarine, let alone making an illegal run under North Korean waters.

"Our luck seems to be holding," he said. "Another twenty minutes and we can off-load you bums. Then my boys and I can go home and put our feet up."

"Typical Navy," McCarter commented. "Make a quick voyage, drop off the real fighting men, then duck for cover."

Calvin James tapped DeVere on the knee. "Ignore him. He's jealous. Can't understand why we're special."

"You Navy?"

James nodded. "Did time with the SEALs before I fell on hard times and had to join up with this crew."

"There you go." The sub commander grinned at

McCarter. "Two against one, pal. Must be extrahard for you being a Brit. Royal Navy and all."

"Cross I have to bear," McCarter said.

DeVere drank his coffee, screwing up his face. "All this high-tech gear we have on board and the coffee is still crap."

A crew member leaned around the bulkhead. "Message just come through for you, sir," he said to McCarter.

The Briton took the paper and scanned it.

"We're still on schedule," he said. "Our contact maintains he can still meet us at the rendezvous point."

DeVere flicked a switch on one of the intercom boxes. "Cannelli, this is the captain."

"Sir?"

"Weather situation topside?"

"Still rough, sir. Rain coming in from the north. Wind speed is still strong, too."

"What's your forecast for the next twelve to twenty-four hours?"

"You want actual, or one of my guesses, sir?"

"Give me your best shot, Cannelli."

"I'd say she isn't going to get much better. This time of year the weather's unpredictable. We could be looking at a drop in temperature. More rain and even some snow in with it."

"That the best you can do for us, Cannelli?" McCarter asked.

"I could lie, sir, but it wouldn't do me any good. You know the name of the sub, so you could find me. Sorry I can't give you anything better."

"Not your fault, mate," McCarter said. "Thanks anyway."

"You're welcome, sir. And, sir, good luck to you and your guys."

DeVere flicked off the switch.

"Cannelli is good. If he says snow, you'll most likely get it."

"We'd better wrap up warm, then," James stated.

"Time we geared up," McCarter said. "Let the others know."

James nodded and left to find his teammates.

"I'll check if everything is ready," DeVere said.

McCarter sat for a moment, staring at the bulkhead. He was thinking ahead, assessing the mission and their chances of pulling it off. Though the Stony Man teams always hit their missions head on, going all-out for success, there were always those quiet and private moments each of them experienced. In the lull before the storm they each took time to consider the possibility, however remote, that one or more of them might not come back. That they might die in the hectic and often confused combat situations they were likely to become involved in. It didn't matter how good any of them were. It took no more than a fraction of a second for someone to make a false step, hesitate just long enough to catch a stray bullet. It could happen so quickly. None of them had any say in the matter.

The sub rolled gently under McCarter, the movement jolting him out of his reverie. He pushed off the bench and went to join the rest of his team.

James had his medical kit open, checking if he had

everything he needed. His weapons were stacked against the bulkhead beside him, ready to be stowed away in the waterproof bags they would take with them. Manning and Encizo were checking their own gear.

"Someone packed my gear for me?" McCarter asked casually.

He received three identical blank stares.

"Fine, I'll do it myself. Just wait until one of you wants a favor."

"You've been giving out favors?" Manning asked.

"No, but someday one of you is going to want one."

"I wouldn't say no to a transfer right now," Encizo said.

For the swim to the shore they donned wet suits over their thermal body underwear and buckled on scuba apparatus. As the distance was comparatively short, they were able to limit themselves to a single tank. Each man would have his land gear in sealed waterproof bags provided by the Navy. The Marine sergeant they had met when they boarded the sub came and checked them over once they were kitted up. He went over every item with cool efficiency, his unwavering gaze not missing a thing.

"How are we doing, Sarge?" McCarter asked.

"Almost there, sir," the Marine said, maintaining his appraisal.

DeVere joined them.

"Soon as you've been checked out, you can move to the aft escape hatch. We're on stop about forty feet below the surface. Cannelli got it right. Rain, some wind. Plenty of cloud cover so you're not going to get much moonlight. Water shallows out around ninety feet from the shore. Keep in mind the current is unpredictable close in. It's why we chose this spot. Less likely to be under close watch. Don't let it make you lazy. The Koreans might have the area well spotted just because it is a hard landing.''

"We'll keep that in mind," McCarter said.

They all moved to the chart table, establishing their position so they knew the course to take when they exited the sub. Each man wore a wrist compass, encased in thick rubber. There was a snap top on the compasses, enabling them to uncover them for reading by the built-in light even in the darkest underwater conditions.

"Okay?" McCarter asked. He received positive nods. "Let's do it, then."

They shouldered their waterproof bags and followed DeVere and the Marine sergeant through to the aft escape hatch. Two crewmen were on standby to open the access hatch, allowing Phoenix Force to step inside the cylindrical chamber.

"She'll take about two minutes to fill," DeVere said. He indicated a small panel showing a red light. "Once the water fills the chamber, the light next to it will show green. When the pressure has equalized, the outer hatch will open automatically. After that, gentlemen, you're on your own."

"Thanks for the ride, Captain," McCarter said.

"My pleasure. Good luck, guys."

The hatch swung shut and locked tight as the crewmen sealed it. Water began to flood the chamber, foaming as it rose swiftly. It rose up the bodies of Phoenix Force, chilling them through the wet suits. Glancing upward, McCarter could see the circular hatch at the top of the escape chamber from which they would exit the submarine. Before they knew it, the water was over their heads, rising to fill the chamber. The Phoenix Force warriors were breathing through their air supply now. Turning his head, McCarter watched the indicator lights. The red light went out, and after a couple of seconds the green one lit up. After a short delay the upper hatch opened, releasing the last few bubbles of air trapped beneath it.

Using their flippered feet, Phoenix Force rose up out of the escape hatch and emerged into the near darkness of the Sea of Japan. It was colder out here. The four gathered together, checking their compasses, then followed McCarter's pointing finger. They powered away from the gray bulk of the submarine, making for the shore.

Behind them the sub began to move slowly, coming about and sinking deeper, then picked up speed as it headed out to sea.

PHOENIX FORCE MADE steady progress. They checked their course often, making sure they all stayed within sight of one another. The weight of the equipment bags they were hauling weight impeded progress to a degree. They adjusted their speed to compensate, not trying to force the pace. It would only have tired them. They conserved their strength for the final stretch, where they would be nearing the surface. There they would have to deal with the prevailing weather conditions and also the possible drag of the undercurrents.

As they closed on the shore, those currents came into play. Gentle at first, then increasing until they could feel them pulling at their bodies, swelling over their efforts and moving them off course. At McCarter's signal they closed up, narrowing the gaps between them. The currents, invisible but definitely present, seemed to reach out and grip them. One moment they were lifting them toward the surface; the next the eddies were attempting to pull them deeper. Luckily they had reached the section where the seabed began to rise as it neared the shore. More often than not they were swimming only inches above the loose seabed, stirring up the silt and gravel, disturbing clinging seaweed that wrapped around their limbs.

As the water became shallower, it began to show the effects of the weather. The wind and falling rain added to their struggles. The churned water brought up more sand from the seabed, creating a swirling fog that impaired their vision. The final push for the shore was where they needed their strength. They were combating the currents, the surging tidal movement and the strong wind that was whipping the surface water into a boiling mass. Even when they were able to get their feet under them, it was a struggle to stay upright as the water lashed at them, tugging them back and forth. Waves came in at regular intervals, threatening to knock them off their feet.

David McCarter swung his waterproof bag over his shoulder, out of the water that was trying to tear it from his grasp. If he hadn't had the safety cord looped around his wrist, he would have lost the bag more than once. He leaned into the rain and wind, muttering to himself as he pushed his aching leg muscles forward. Stumbling and slipping, he worked his way out of the water and up onto the stony beach. Clear now, he pulled off his breathing mouthpiece and sucked in some of the cold, fresh air. The Briton pushed his mask up out of the way and turned to check out the rest of the team as they followed him out of the water.

"Bloody hell," he said, "that should keep us fit for the rest of the day. Nothing like a bracing swim first thing."

Calvin James took off his mask and mouthpiece.

"You think so? Then you're crazy."

McCarter just grinned at him. He watched Encizo and Manning move up to join them.

"Looks like the stand of trees we were told about," he said, indicating the small stand to their right, a couple of hundred yards up from the beach. "Sooner we get there the sooner we can get out of these wet suits and into dry clothing."

They reached the cover of the trees, opening the bags and pulling out their combat clothing. They had weatherproof gear, the jackets having hoods they could use to keep out extremes of weather and thermal gloves. Each man had a medium-sized backpack holding additional clothing and equipment. They dressed quickly, adding their combat harness, complete with fragmentation and stun grenades. Next up was a full weapons check, followed by making certain their communications were working. As well as team communications, there were signal devices to be used when they were ready to call in Jack Grimaldi for their extraction. They all knew that the Stony Man pilot would be monitoring their wavelength while he sat out the mission period on the aircraft carrier out in the bay. McCarter also had a Tri-Band cell phone in his backpack.

Gary Manning opened his explosives pack and examined his preset devices. Each of the compact, solid packs was ready for use. They only needed their timers activated when Manning decided where and when to plant them.

McCarter and Encizo opened the entrenching tools they had brought along and quickly dug a pit in the soft earth around the base of one of the trees. First they skinned off the top layer, removing a carpet of grass that they rolled into a bundle and put aside. Then they dug down so they were able to bury the bags and all their scuba gear. They replaced the earth, leveling it out before replacing the grass layer. Surplus earth was scattered around in the undergrowth. The continuing rain would help to cover the area after they had bedded it down.

"Not too bad, lads," McCarter said as he surveyed the scene. "Might not fool a determined hunt, but we don't have time for a full landscaping job."

He glanced at his watch, then reached down and swung his backpack into position, adjusting the strapping until it felt comfort able. He looped the strap of his MP-5 around his neck, cradled the M-16 under his arm and stood waiting until the others had completed their final preparations.

"Time for a walk," he said. He eased the compact GPS unit out of its pouch at his side and keyed in the activating code. He studied the screen, establishing their current position. "Encizo, take the point. Who wants to be tail-end Charlie?"

Manning accepted the position by giving a low grunt.

"I love enthusiasm," McCarter said. "Let's go, girls. I don't want to be here all week."

"I hate it when he gets to be so cheerful," Manning said from the rear.

"Hearing you," McCarter said.

"You were supposed to, *mate.*"

They set off at a steady pace, fully aware of their situation. They were in unknown territory. Their insertion onto North Korean soil was intentional and illegal. If they were discovered, they were on their own and would be up against military forces of staggering numbers. The North Koreans might not have had the most up-to-date, sophisticated weapons available, but what they did have was men by the million. The Phoenix Force commandos, as good as they were, couldn't hope to outfight such a force. They were going to have to ensure that whatever they did was carried out quickly and with the maximum amount of force.

They had at least four hours of darkness ahead of them. It would give them a good start. Once the daylight came, matters would change and they were going to have to alter their tactics.

The poor weather conditions persisted. Rain and wind continued to hamper their progress. The ground was soft and muddy in many places, dragging at their boots as they progressed. The stretch of coastline they were traveling was dotted with straggly lines of thin trees that offered a minimum of cover. It helped to conceal them to a degree.

McCarter called a number of halts to verify their position and allow them to check the way ahead and behind. Crouching on the wet ground, they checked every point of the compass, watching for sign of any movement and listening for sound that might indicate they weren't alone.

"Nothing," James said, joining McCarter. "If there is anyone out there, I can't see or hear them."

"This bloody weather doesn't make it easier."

"Only consolation is it's the same for anyone else," James said.

"Maybe, but this is their home ground. Gives them some knowledge."

James wiped a hand across his wet face. "Man, this rain is cold. David, this is one damn miserable place."

"Tell me about it."

They moved on at McCarter's signal. At this point they were starting to move inland, leaving the coastline behind them. The terrain was still as barren and inhospitable. Away from the trees the full force of the weather hit them, wind tugging at their clothing and the cold rain seeping into their clothing. On a number of occasions they found themselves having to ford swollen streams of rushing water. Snow began to appear in the rain, adding to their discomfort.

They had been traveling for just over two hours when McCarter raised a hand and pulled them together. In the lee of a low hill they sheltered as best they could from the weather.

"Meeting point shouldn't be far off," he said. "We have to be close now."

"That's the best news I've heard for a while," Manning said.

"Probably be the only good news you'll get while we're here," Encizo replied.

"Keep it down," McCarter snapped. "I heard something."

They stayed low, hugging the ground, weapons cocked and ready. McCarter strained his ears, attempting to pick up any other sounds. He was convinced he had picked up a soft rustle of someone passing through the undergrowth off to their left. He concentrated on the area, peering through the poor light, his vision hampered by the rain. The Briton knew the problems associated with this kind of weather. The falling rain and the drifting wind made their own distractions, sometimes creating what looked like movement and sound. It was easy for someone to be fooled, especially if the individual was listening out for a contact.

McCarter had a feeling there *was* something else. Something not quite right. Instinct, intuition, he didn't give a damn what it was called. He was convinced he had heard something.

"Heads up," he said. "I don't like this."

Bright lights pierced the gloom, striking at Phoenix Force. The slanting rain showed silver in the powerful shafts of light. The lights came from a number of sources, all converging on the crouching Stony Man warriors. The lights stung their eyes, preventing them from seeing what lay behind them.

An amplified voice boomed out of the darkness beyond the lights.

"Put down your weapons now! Your choice. Surrender or die!"

McCarter held back his anger. That would come later. The choice was simple. As much as he hated the fact, Phoenix Force was compromised. He had no doubt over the threat. The choice was simple. Death or captivity. Not much of a choice, he decided.

"Do it," he said. "They've got the advantage for now."

Phoenix Force lowered its weapons and stood. Uniformed figures rushed from behind the curtain of light and surrounded them. The armed soldiers wore the uniforms of the North Korean army. While the main group held their weapons on Phoenix Force, others moved in to strip away the team's arms and equipment.

A lean figure stepped forward. He wore a long leather coat that glistened with rain. His left hand was bandaged and held in a sling against his body. For some reason he was bare headed, ignoring the rain that plastered his black hair to his skull. He stepped up to McCarter. In his right hand was the GPS unit.

"Very efficient," he said in English. "I am impressed you made it this far. However, your journey is over now. From here you will be the guests of the Democratic People's Republic of Korea. Let me add that it will not be a pleasant experience. In the end you will be glad to die.''

"Bloody hell," McCarter said, "I hope they all don't jabber on like this one.''

Yat Sen Took turned to one of his soldiers and snapped a command. The Korean moved quickly, swinging the butt of his rifle in a short arc that connected with the Briton's body. McCarter grunted and doubled over. The Korean swung again, this time clouting McCarter behind the ear. He slumped to his knees, supporting himself with his hands.

"Any more clever remarks?" Took asked, scanning the impassive faces of the others. "Good. You will pick him up and go where my people direct you.''

James and Encizo hauled McCarter to his feet. There was a wash of blood streaking the side of his head. His weight dragged as they moved him. The Koreans herded them in the direction of a canvas topped military truck. The tailgate was dropped, and Phoenix Force was forced to climb inside. They were made to sit on one of the wooden benches fixed to the floor of the truck. A half-dozen soldiers joined them, sitting across from the Stony Man commandos, weapons aimed at them. Two more Koreans dumped the team's weapons and equipment in a deep steel box at the top end of the truck. The box was bolted to the floor and butted up against the back of the cab, reaching to just below the cab's rear window.

Calvin James glanced over the now closed tailgate. He saw two more trucks falling in behind. They had searchlights fixed at the rear of the cabs. The rest of the troops climbed into those trucks. A third vehicle, some kind of all-terrain military truck, pulled ahead of the small convoy and moments later they were all moving, bumping and rocking across the uneven ground.

The Koreans were talking among themselves. Every so often one of them would point toward the floor of the truck. The man farthest along kicked out at a shape on the floor. A man groaned. Adjusting his eyes to the gloom, James began to make out the huddled form of a body on the floor. He saw wet clothing, then the pale oval of a face. He also saw a great deal of blood and raw gashes and bruises. One of the man's arms lay across his body, bent at an unnatural angle.

James had the sudden bad feeling that he was looking at their contact man, the Korean undercover operative who was supposed to be guiding them to their target.

# CHAPTER NINE

*North Korea*

When McCarter stole a careful glance at his watch, he saw they had been traveling for almost an hour. The truck was having a hard time. The weather hadn't eased, and the ground conditions were poor. They were traveling cross-country, where there didn't even seem to be anything as basic as a track. The muddy, soaked ground held the truck to a slow crawl, and on more than one occasion it was almost forced to a stop, wheels slipping.

From the angle of the truck, it was negotiating a long slope. The rear wheels had lost their grip a couple of times. McCarter noticed that the Korean guards were getting a little uneasy as they hung on to whatever they could as the truck swayed dangerously. They shouted at the driver, banging on the rear of the cab. He ignored them, concentrating on his driving.

McCarter caught Manning's eye. The big Canadian was sitting on the opposite side of the truck, with Encizo next to him. James was beside the Briton. The moment Manning looked at him directly, McCarter mouthed a silent command.

"Get ready."

Manning gave a slight nod. Next to him Encizo had deciphered McCarter's instruction. He signaled his awareness by a brief movement of his right hand.

They had to wait a couple more minutes before their chance came.

Soft mud under the wheels slowed the truck almost to a standstill. The rear wheels began to spin and the driver, instead of easing his foot off the gas pedal, jammed it down hard, struggling to maintain forward motion. The truck's rear began to slide, geysers of wet mud spurting from beneath the tires. The Koreans in the back of the truck renewed their yelling at the driver. Their yells only angered him. He couldn't figure out a way of getting out of the mud, so he simply stood on the pedal, hoping that full power would break the truck free. All it achieved was to send the vehicle into a long, rocking slide until the right side wheels went over the edge of the slope. The truck began to tilt, toppling slowly until it was hanging at an awkward angle to the slope.

In the back of the truck Phoenix Force and the guards were thrown together in a messy tangle. They all slid to right side of the tilted truck.

"Let's do it," McCarter yelled.

The moment was the best they were going to get. It was a difficult situation, with captives and prisoners thrown together due to the position of the truck.

McCarter hit out at the guard closest to him, his fist slamming the Korean full in the face, connecting with a solid thump. The Korean's head snapped around, blood bubbling from torn lips. Before he could even begin to wonder where the blow had come from, McCarter hit him again, this time driving the point of his elbow into the man's throat. The Korean was unable to make a sound, his shattered throat devoid of sound. All he could do was start to choke on his own blood. McCarter followed the man to the floor of the truck, snatching the Kalashnikov from his grasp. As McCarter straightened, his finger was already on the trigger. He saw two of the guards, still clear of the mass, struggling to stay on their feet and bring their weapons on target at the same time.

The Phoenix Force leader didn't hesitate. He snapped the Kalashnikov into target acquisition, finger stroking the trigger. The sustained burst from the AK sent a red-hot stream of slugs into the bodies of the two North Koreans. The pair was knocked back by the burst, bodies bubbling red from the ragged wounds.

Calvin James had hurled himself bodily into two of the Koreans, toppling them. He followed them down, his booted foot connecting with one man's skull, the kick uncompromising in its ferocity. Falling across the downed man's body, James crashed against the second soldier, his hands reaching to clamp around the Korean's throat, his fingers squeezing against the arteries, cutting off the blood flow. James hung on, maintaining his grip despite the frantic squirming of the gasping man. The Korean struggled to the last, desperate to hold on to life even as it faded away.

There was a moment when Gary Manning thought he had missed his chance as he slammed against a Korean, almost missing the AK the man was trying raise. Manning's big hand batted the muzzle to the side in the instant the Korean pulled the trigger. The bullet burned its way through the canvas that covered the roof of the truck. Keeping a grip on the AK, Manning wedged his free hand under the Korean's jaw. He shoved hard, forcing the Korean's head back, exposing the taut throat. Manning released his grip on the AK, bunched his hand into a fist and punched down hard on the Korean's throat. He repeated the blow, rolling off the man as the Korean started to flail, attempting to draw air in through his crushed throat. The Canadian snatched up the forgotten AK, lining it up on one of the remaining guards. He triggered fast bursts that punched in through the Korean's padded tunic and cored into his body.

Rafael Encizo, seeing that his partners were handling the situation, ducked low and scrambled along the tilted floor of the truck until he reached the large box container where their gear had been dumped. He snapped back the catch and flung the lid open, reaching inside to grab one of the M-16s. Raising the weapon, Encizo triggered shots into the rear of the cab, spacing them back and forth. Above the crackle of gunfire he heard a muffled cry of pain from someone, then heard the shattering of glass as the windshield vanished.

He turned, hauling up one of the combat harnesses, and struggled through the truck to the tailgate. He could see the two other trucks, already halted. Encizo pulled a fragmentation grenade from the harness, eased out the pin, leaned over the tailgate and lobbed the grenade at the closer truck. It landed a couple of feet from the side of the vehicle. The blast lit up the darkness for a brief moment, then the detonation threw its charge against the side of the truck, catching the vehicle and men riding on it. Smoke billowed for a few seconds. Pained screams filled the air. Torn bodies rolled from the back of the truck. Others struggled to keep upright despite their wounds. A hard silence fell in the wake of the detonation. It lasted for only a heartbeat. Encizo freed a second grenade and repeated his maneuver. It struck the hood of the second truck, bouncing and rolling across until it reached the windshield. The blast took out most of the cab, along with the crew inside.

Slinging the harness from one shoulder, Encizo vaulted over the tailgate. He landed in a half crouch, feeling the soft mud grab at his boots. He stayed low, using the M-16 to clear the area in front of him. His sharp, controlled bursts effected losses on the Koreans as they struggled to shake off the effects of the first grenade. Encizo didn't give them any quarter. He hit hard and fast, using their hesitation to his advantage.

Behind him Calvin James leaned over the tailgate, a borrowed AK chattering in his hands. He was concentrating on the second truck, sending the 7.62 mm slugs into the dark shapes emerging from the rear.

"Heads down," McCarter yelled.

He dropped down beside Encizo, a grenade in each hand. He threw them both, one in the direction of each truck. His first hit the rear wheel of the closer vehicle and bounced off, exploding with little effect.

"Dammit!" the Brit muttered.

His second throw landed the grenade in the mud only inches from its target. When it blew, it took the fuel tank with it. Shards of metal and wood, and fiery coils of fire erupted. Smoke billowed into the stormy sky.

"Hey, don't forget the lead car," Manning called.

McCarter turned and moved the length of their mired-down truck. He was in time to see the 4×4 cresting the slope ahead of them. He pulled the M-16 to his shoulder and fired off the contents of the magazine. He couldn't be sure whether he had scored a hit or not. The 4×4 vanished from sight over the crest.

"Bloody great," McCarter said out loud. "Sooner we move out the better. Before the Korean cavalry comes charging over that hill."

He made his way back to the truck.

James had climbed back inside to check over the injured man they had discovered. Between them they brought him to the open tailgate. Someone brought James his medical kit, and he did what he could for the man.

In the meantime Phoenix Force recovered its equipment and weapons from the box. They all felt secure once they had their gear back in place.

McCarter put Encizo and Manning on watch. He went to see how James was faring with his patient.

"He's had a hard time," James said. "Badly beaten around the face and body. Teeth broken. Right arm shattered. Fingers of his left hand all broken. Nails pulled out. Could be internal damage, too. He's bleeding from the mouth.''

"They didn't cut out my tongue, so I can still talk," the man said. "Sorry I couldn't let you know. I am Quo Lam Sun."

McCarter leaned over him. "What happened?"

"They were waiting for me when I reached the rendezvous point. Someone must have picked up one of my transmissions. They got quite upset when I wouldn't tell them how many you were or where you were coming ashore. I got the feeling they wanted to be there when you landed."

Sun began to breathe unevenly. His gaze wandered. He made small gestures with one of his hands, fluttering aimlessly.

James caught McCarter's eye and shook his head slowly, indicating there was little else he could for the man.

Sun reached out to grasp McCarter's wrist.

"Do you have a map of the area?"

McCarter nodded. He opened a pocket in his combat jacket and pulled out the map Stony Man had provided. He held it so Sun could see. The Korean studied it for a time, then reached a bloodied finger to indicate points.

"We are here. The man named Took. The one with the damaged hand. He is in charge of the missile complex here. Some thirty miles to the north is the labor camp where he uses the prisoners to work on the new site being developed. All very high-tech. This is farther north. Around here. The site has been constructed without outside knowledge. It has been kept under strict security. From what I learned, most of it has been built belowground to avoid detection. The last phase is being worked on at this moment.''

McCarter marked the locations and put the map away.

''Any sightings of the American you saw earlier?''

Sun took a long time answering. He seemed to be losing his grip on reality. His breathing became very shallow, and McCarter looked across at James.

''He could be going into shock. His injuries. The temperature out here. And before you ask there isn't a damn thing I can do to help him.''

''You have done what you can,'' Sun said, regaining lucidity. ''I believe your American may have been sent to the labor camp. If so, his life will have become extremely difficult. I know those places. I was in one myself for a time....''

His voice trailed away. Blood bubbled from his mouth, and he became very still.

''Cal?''

''I don't think he's going to make it.''

McCarter leaned against the truck, scanning their surroundings. He looked skyward. Rain was still falling, cold and holding the soft flakes of approaching snow. He took a deep breath, raising a hand to pull the team together.

''We don't have much in the way of choices. As far as I'm concerned, we still have the mission to complete. Nothing changes there. The difference is we won't have our guide to get us there. We'll have to do that ourselves. The other thing is the Koreans know we're here. They're going to be looking for us, and when we reach the target it's going to be hard to crack.''

"Sounds like a regular mission to me," Manning said. "Nothing ever runs smooth on these things."

"What are we talking on distance?" James asked.

McCarter showed them the map and the points he had marked.

"I'd guess at something like seventy, maybe eighty miles."

"With half the North Korean army looking for us?" Encizo said.

"Who said anything about half?" McCarter asked. "I'm guessing more like three-quarters."

"One day your sense of humor is going to get you into trouble," the Cuban warned.

McCarter put away the map.

"See if we can salvage anything from this mess," he said. "We might need some extra artillery."

While Encizo and manning checked out the trucks, McCarter joined James, who had moved back to check Sun. As McCarter approached, he saw James's shoulders slump, his hand resting gently on the Korean's chest.

"Sorry, David," he said. "I did what I could for him."

"No problem, mate. Under these conditions it would have been a miracle if he'd survived."

"Jesus, they didn't have to do all that to him."

"Time to move on, Cal."

Manning and Encizo came back with an AK for each of them, plus a number of extra magazines.

"Best we could find," Manning said. "These guys were traveling light."

"They'll do," McCarter said. He checked his compass, pointing a finger in the direction they were going to travel. "Move out, mates. We've a way to go. Stay in sight of one another. And keep your eyes open for the local military. They're going to be well pissed off with us by now."

Phoenix Force fell into their marching line, weapons at the ready. The only thing they could be sure of was the lack of hospitality of the Korean military. They were in enemy territory—of that there was no doubt. Their presence on Korean soil was strictly illegal, and it gave their hosts the opportunity to deal with them as they saw fit. Confrontation with the Koreans would be deadly in the extreme. Phoenix Force was out on a limb, and a shaky one at that. They were in the unenviable position of being the hunted. How long that condition remained was in their hands.

GRAY LIGHT SHOWED in the distance. McCarter checked his watch. Dawn was nearly on them. In another hour it would be full light. The continuing rainfall and the heavy cloud formations would keep it dull and shadowy. But they would be exposed, allowing any spotters to see Phoenix Force.

The Briton called a halt, and the four gathered in the shadows of a stand of trees.

"Daylight traveling is going to be tricky," he said. "This isn't the way it was supposed to happen. Sun would have guided us through without having to walk into any of the locals. We can't take that chance. We can't work this if we're having to dodge the natives or chance running into an army patrol.''

"You suggesting we stay out of sight until dark?" Manning said.

McCarter nodded. "I don't see any other way. We have to avoid any confrontation if we can."

"I agree," Encizo said. "Moving at night at least gives us some cover. We could walk around the next corner and find we're on the main street of some village. This place isn't big on roadside signs."

Manning nodded, "I guess you're right. In that case we need to find somewhere to bed down."

"We should have at least an hour before full light," McCarter said. "We'll use it to scout some place to stop."

"I'll go ahead," Encizo offered, "and see if the way's clear. I'll keep you in sight. Give you the signal to close up."

"You okay doing this?" McCarter asked.

The Cuban nodded. "I'll be fine."

"Take it easy," James said.

"Caution is my middle name," Encizo said.

They watched him move out.

"No, it isn't," James said after a while.

"What?"

"No way caution is his middle name."

RAFAEL ENCIZO WORKED his way through the rain-drenched landscape, moving with practiced ease. His ability to blend in with his surroundings was something learned the hard way. It sometimes seemed to Encizo that he had been doing it all his life in one form or another. Working his way through minefields of dangerous situations. Times and places when he was constantly evading trouble in a variety of disguises. In a determined effort to survive, no matter where or when, Encizo blended with his environment in the most natural way. To those who might have been observing, he did it without effort. If he had known, Encizo would have taken that as a great compliment. The skill was in doing it as easily as pulling on a sweater.

He had traveled nearly half a mile when he spotted the narrow rock formation just ahead of him. Some straggly foliage bordered the rocks. Encizo made his way across, able to see as he got closer that the formation spread for some distance. Once he reached the first of the rocks, he found himself on the lip of a depression. At the bottom a fast-running stream, swollen by the rain, ran across the edge of the rocks. On the opposite bank Encizo saw the opening to the rocks. It looked a likely spot. He turned and raised an arm, catching the attention of the others. He beckoned them to join him, then went down the bank and waded through the cold water. He moved into the rock formation. As he went deeper in, he found tangled vegetation growing among the eroded boulders. He was able to hide himself in the labyrinth of rock. He saw the mass of rock ahead rising as they became larger. Pushing through some foliage, Encizo found a deep overhang where the ground was reasonably dry. It would have to do, he decided.

He retraced his way out of the rocks and found the rest of the team waiting on the far side of the stream.

"You guys want to check in?"

They followed him back through the rocks until they reached the overhang.

"They got cable?" James asked.

The commandos took off their backpacks, and each man chose his spot.

"Who wants to take first watch?" McCarter asked. "Two-hour rotation."

"I'll go first," Manning said.

"Cal, you next. I'll pick up after you, then Rafe."

Manning checked his weapons. He moved out from under the overhang, scanning the rock formation for a spot to start climbing. Selecting a likely place, he worked his way up the rock, taking his time in the predawn gloom, and emerged on a high point that allowed him unrestricted viewing all around. He worked his way into a slight hollow in the surface of the rock, protecting himself from the worst of the weather against a projection, and settled down. He pulled the AK into position close to his body. A quick glance at his watch established the start of his two-hour shift.

The rain continued to fall. Manning decided this was one of the worst sentry duties he had been subjected to. The rock under him was hard and damp. It was colder up here due to the open aspect of his position. After thirty minutes the rain turned to heavy sleet. Even though Manning had pulled the hood of his combat jacket over his head, the sleet stung his exposed face. He decided that anyone coming out to look for them in such weather had to be crazy. From bitter experience he knew the weather would be the last thing to stop the Koreans searching for them.

MCCARTER AND THE OTHERS settled down as best they could. The relative comfort the overhang offered did little to improve the overall situation. At best this would be the most they could expect. Their incursion into North Korean territory hadn't begun well. The fact that the Koreans knew of their existence and would be actively searching for them only added to the problem. Any insertion into enemy territory had its drawbacks. It was a time of flux, with the boundaries capable of change quickly. Preplanning was fine up to a point, but it could never take into account reversals or situations altering to extremes. The fact that the team's contact man had been taken by the Koreans changed the nature of the operation in an instant. The Koreans knew Phoenix Force was coming. It removed the element of surprise from the team's hands, and placed them in a vulnerable position. Now they were being forced to carry on their mission, aware of the Korean presence, and knowing their every move would need to be protected to the limit. Time was affected, as well. The swift insertion and deployment had been cast aside. Phoenix Force had a long distance to travel, already restricted by only being able to move at night. Daylight hours were being lost now that they had to hide.

As commander of the team, McCarter accepted the facts and planned accordingly. Not for a moment did he allow the situation to cloud his judgment. Whatever the restrictions placed on them, he was determined that the mission be followed through. He didn't have to ask to know that the others would have the same feelings. It wasn't in their nature to quit, or even sit back and bemoan the circumstances affecting their ability to perform well. The only feeling manifesting itself within McCarter was one of frustration, the knowing that whatever had been planned initially had been cast aside by a quirk of fate, pushing Phoenix Force into the spotlight without means of protection. The team had known from the outset that the mission was going to present them with difficulties. Quo Lam Sun, the South Korean agent, had been their man on the spot, able to guide and direct them to the target site with the minimum of interference. Everything he could have offered had been lost with his untimely death. McCarter regretted Sun's death more than the information. He had been a courageous man, undertaking a difficult and life-threatening assignment. Living among the enemy, observing and reporting his findings had left him open to discovery every passing moment. The risks he had taken to help Phoenix Force had resulted in capture, torture and death. His sacrifice would not be forgotten as far as McCarter and Phoenix Force were concerned.

In the meantime the team would have its work cut out making the trek to the target site. No matter how many times he ran the scenario through his mind, McCarter was unable to come up with any other plan than staying out of sight during the day and traveling at night. It would prolong their time on Korean soil, and the simple matter of that extra time would place them in harm's way. Short of a miracle there was no way around the fact.

McCarter sat with his back to the cold rock, staring out at the oncoming daylight. Swirls of snow eddied back and forth, tossed by the chill Korean wind. He pulled his hood closer around his face. He was cold and wet, starting to crave a cigarette. A bottle of Coke Classic. If the truth be known, he admitted, he would have relished the chance to tuck into a real English breakfast of fried bacon, eggs, sausage and fried bread, washed down with a walloping great mug of scalding, sweet tea. The Briton managed a wolfish grin at the thought. It was only at times like these when he missed the simple things in life. He could have asked for dry clothing, a tent to protect him from the weather—but all he could think about was food, Coca-Cola and a bloody fag. Then he rebelled against that and decided what the hell, it was his dream, so he'd ask for what he really wanted.

He shifted position on the hard rock, trying to gain a little comfort. A change in the wind's direction sent flurries of snow into his corner. McCarter felt the chill snow against his exposed face. It was going to be hard catching much sleep under these conditions. And it was going to be a long day, too. The hours would drag. He glanced across at Encizo and James, wondering how they were faring. Encizo was curled up, his head tucked down against his chest and from where McCarter was sitting the Cuban did look as if he were asleep. James was sitting upright, his back to the rock. His head was up, eyes closed, but his body signs suggested he would be alert to anything that might pose a threat to the team.

Manning would be fully awake, watching the surrounding terrain from his position high on the rock formation. He would be suffering more than the rest of them, exposed to the full extent of the weather and forced to stay alert for his two hours.

GARY MANNING WAS HALFWAY through his watch. It was full light now, as bright as it was going to get. The sky to the north was dark and overcast. Clouds in the distance were low against the horizon, so dark they looked black. Snow was drifting down around Manning and had already laid a fine white covering over the surrounding terrain despite the wet ground.

Manning moved as much as he could given his restricted position, flexing his arms and legs to maintain circulation. Although he was wearing gloves, his hands and fingers were cold. At least the temperature hadn't plummeted yet. Manning rotated his neck, rocking his head from side to side. It would have been nice, he thought, to be back home in Canada. If he had been out somewhere in the wilds, at least there would have been the comfort of camping gear or a cabin, shut off from the weather with a roaring log fire and maybe a thick steak cooking on the stove. He could have managed that without too much distress.

His attention was caught by something distant, a couple of hundred feet off the ground. A dark speck. Manning blinked to clear his vision and concentrated on the point in the sky, wondering if he had imagined it. He found the speck again, held it and saw it grow bigger. He maintained his observation, confirming he had not been seeing things. The speck took on definition as it approached.

A helicopter.

No doubt. Too far away yet for him to identify the type. There was no mistaking the shape. Even through the drifting curtain of snow.

Manning backed away from his position and worked his way back down the rock until he hit solid ground. He returned to where the others had settled themselves.

"David, we have visitors."

McCarter opened his eyes, staring at the Canadian.

"Say that again," he asked.

"Chopper coming in from the north, heading in this direction."

"Not Jack, is it?" James asked, pushing to his feet.

"I wish," Manning said.

"More likely a Korean spotter looking for us," Encizo said.

McCarter, fully awake now, checked his AK.

"Maybe we should let him find us," he said.

"Say what?" James asked.

"Sounds like one of your inspirational ideas," Manning said.

McCarter moved to where he could check out Manning's helicopter sighting. He picked it up, watching it come for their rock formation.

"Let's move, guys," he said. "I think this might work."

"What might work?"

McCarter explained his idea very quickly, pulling no punches and promising nothing. His team studied him for a few moments.

"He's been out in the cold too long," James said. "He's lost it."

"Could work, though," Encizo said, his words holding a little doubt. "But I still think it's crazy."

"This is not a good idea," Manning said.

"So who has a better one?" McCarter asked. "Right now we're out on a limb. A long way to go and damn all to help. So we need to improvise." He glanced over his shoulder at the distant helicopter. "And we need to do it bloody fast."

Manning sighed. "If this doesn't pan out, we're all going to look stupid."

McCarter shook his head. "If it doesn't pan out, we'll most probably all be dead."

"Gee, boss, was that the pep talk?" James asked.

"Best you'll get today, chum. Now let's move out and get this show on the bloody road."

# CHAPTER TEN

The drab-colored helicopter was a ten-year-old Mil Mi-2 that did service as a spotter and gunship. It carried a crew of two, plus a gunner who operated the light machine gun mounted in the port hatch. It wasn't a sophisticated aircraft, having standard equipment, much of which was outdated when compared to late-model helicopters. The craft, designated Hoplite, was slow, and struggled in the harsh weather conditions. The crew had been given its orders and had little choice but to carry out their patrol until they were called back to base. They had been out now for almost three hours, and had seen nothing.

That changed as they closed on the rock formation lying directly ahead. It was a good landmark for them to use as a reference point.

The copilot, staring out through the snow-streaked canopy, his eyes straining from scanning the ground below, suddenly leaned forward. He made certain he was sure of his facts before he alerted his superior, the pilot.

"Ahead and to the right, Sergeant," he said. "At least three men. There, you see?"

The pilot followed the soldier's guiding finger.

"I see them. What are they doing?"

"Lying down. Almost covered with snow. Some weapons on the ground near them. Perhaps they have been overcome by the weather."

"We will take a closer look." The pilot called over his shoulder to the gunner. "Arm your weapon in case they offer resistance."

"Do we take them alive?"

"Those were our orders. But it will depend on the men down there. If they fight, I will choose my life over theirs. Both of you remember that."

"Yes, Sergeant."

The gunner checked his machine gun, making certain the ammunition belt was aligned. He snapped back the bolt, swinging the gun on its pivot.

As they hovered, with the rotor wash driving drifting snow around them, they studied the prone figures sprawled on the ground. They wore American combat clothing and carried backpacks. They were armed with M-16 rifles and MP-5 SMGs.

"There are supposed to be four of them," the sergeant said.

"Over there by the rocks," the gunner called. "Curled up."

The sergeant noted the fourth figure. He debated for a moment, then took the helicopter to the ground and dropped the power so that the twin turbines kept the rotors slowly turning. Unclipping his seat harness, the sergeant reached down and lifted his AK from its clip. He checked the action, making sure the weapon was cocked and ready for use. He turned in his seat.

"Keep that gun ready," he ordered.

The gunner nodded, raising a gloved hand.

"Cover me," the sergeant said to the copilot.

They emerged from the helicopter, weapons up and tracking as they moved in the direction of the three bodies lying in the snow. The sergeant motioned for his copilot to cover him as he closed in on the nearest. He stood observing for a while, checking the position of the body. The man lay with his M-16 rifle well clear of his hands. An MP-5 was draped over one shoulder. His head was turned to the right, snow covering his features. Easing his head around, the sergeant glanced at the next man. He was long and lean and black. He carried two weapons slung over his back, an M-16 and a H&K MP-5. The third lay partially on his right side, arms clasped to his body as if he were trying to protect himself.

"What do we do?" the copilot asked.

"First take away their weapons. Just in case."

The copilot, showing his nervousness asked, "In case what?"

The sergeant swung his head around, impatience darkening his features. "Idiot," he snapped. "In case they try any—"

The rest of his sentence was drowned by the sharp, vicious crack of a single shot. Behind the sergeant the machine gunner was knocked back from his weapon as a 5.56 mm bullet cored into his skull, directly between his eyes. He skidded across the cabin and slammed up against the far bulkhead, dead by the time his body stopped moving.

The sergeant's reaction time was fast, and he

brought his head around, seeking a target. The muzzle of his AK was tracking as his vision took in the three figures before him.

Who were no longer motionless.

The black man had pulled an autopistol from under his body. The weapon arced up and fired twice, driving a pair of 9 mm slugs into the sergeant's chest, one catching him in the heart. The sergeant toppled over backward, hitting the hard ground with enough force to jerk his finger against the trigger of his AK. The weapon discharged a burst into the empty sky.

The copilot, unaware of what had exactly happened to his sergeant and the gunner, swung the muzzle of his weapon on the closest of the prone figures. He heard a shot, then felt something thump his chest, high up. The impact knocked him back a step, and he tried to right himself. Then pain flared, spearing into him, and it brought a gasp from his lips. Despite his agony he tried to bring his weapon back on track, only to hear a second shot. He was down on the ground, unaware he'd fallen. Cold snow pushed against his face, filling his open mouth. He slid forward as his knees gave way, pinning his own gun beneath his body.

GARY MANNING PUSHED away from the rocks, uncurling his body, and stamped around to get the circulation going. He kept his M-16 trained on the two Koreans where they lay in the snow, bodies limp in death, blood dappling the white layer covering the ground.

The others were clambering to their feet, shaking

off the snow that had crusted them during the time they had been lying out in the open.

"I'm freezing," McCarter muttered.

"Yeah?" Manning said. "Well, it was your idea, remember."

"Worked, too," the Briton said.

"Still crazy," Encizo said.

McCarter had decided they had talked it over long enough. He strode off in the direction of the idling helicopter. By the time the others were alongside, the Briton was in the pilot's seat, checking and familiarizing himself with the controls. Manning and Encizo slid the gunner's body out of the cabin and laid it on the ground. James went around the three bodies and collected all their weapons and spare ammunition. He placed the arms at the rear of the cabin.

McCarter was winding up the power as Manning dropped into the copilot's seat. He took the map McCarter passed over and they checked their position against the points Quo Lam Sun had given them.

"Okay," Manning said. "Going by the distance we traveled, we should be somewhere here. We need to fly north for the time being, then ease across to the east around here."

From the rear James said, "Way things are going, we're not going to make our extraction window."

"Don't remind me," McCarter said. "Knowing Jack, if we don't send him the signal on time, he'll still come looking for us."

"Well, there goes the North Korean air force," James said.

"This tub got a radio?" Encizo asked. "Any

chance we could hit a frequency he might pick up? At least we could update him.''

"Yes, there's a radio," Manning said. "And it's probably being monitored. We start transmitting, and someone could pick up and track us.''

"So we delay sending until the last possible moment," James said. "Let's not forget, guys, that when this chopper's base starts to figure it's overdue, our time is going to run out fast. So let's make the most of what we got.''

"I take it the night-move-only order has been withdrawn?'' Manning asked.

"If you think I'm flying this thing in the dark, the answer is no," McCarter said.

"I'm with David," James stated. "When we crash, I want to see what we're going to hit.''

"On that jolly note it's time we left," McCarter said.

He increased the power, working the controls gently until he got the feel of the helicopter's responses. The machine lifted, sliding to the right until McCarter corrected. He brought the machine around onto the correct heading and started to gain height.

In the rear Encizo and James swung the LMG inside on its pivot and closed the hatch, shutting out the wind and snow. They dragged out the acquired weapons and went through them, making sure each was fully loaded. They repeated the procedure with their own weaponry. In addition to the box of ammunition for the machine gun, they located two more strapped to the bulkhead.

"We're pretty high on weapons," James announced. "There isn't anything else back here. These boys were flying light."

"Like the troops back with the trucks," Encizo said. "You get the feeling these boys are having to make it on next to nothing?"

"All the goodies are locked up somewhere in the power palaces," Manning said. "The bosses do okay but run the place on a knife edge."

"Ain't it the truth," James said.

A thought struck Manning. "Talking of light, how is this thing on fuel?"

McCarter studied the array of dials on the control panel.

"Buggered if I know," he announced. "Gary, you keep your eye on the dials. Minute you see one hit zero, let me know."

The Canadian glanced across at McCarter, then caught the merest hint of a smile on the Briton's lips.

"Funny."

"Couldn't resist that," McCarter said. "Thing is we might just have to depend on something like that. I'm not certain all these bloody instruments are registering correctly."

He peered through the canopy. The wipers, which had been switched on before he had climbed inside, were struggling to keep the windscreen clear. They were flying into the snow.

"Crate like this makes you realize how good Dragon Slayer is," Manning said.

"Yeah, Jack runs that thing like a luxury limo," James agreed. "Flasks of coffee. Comfortable seats."

"He's probably giving her a wax job while he's waiting," Encizo said.

*Aboard U.S. Navy Carrier, Sea of Japan*

GRIMALDI WAS on a secure line to Stony Man, courtesy of the Navy.

"Weather outlook isn't too promising," he was saying to Barbara Price.

The satellite link was crystal clear. Price's voice came through as if she were standing next to him.

"I know. We have the current situation on-screen now. Looks like the snow might hold for a couple more hours, then move farther north."

"I'm all set at this end," Grimaldi said. "The Lady is juiced up and set. Extra tanks for the run in. Full weapons load. All I need is the signal, then I'm off and running."

"Able Team settled in?"

"Yeah. Glad to have them along."

"You okay?"

"Sure. The Navy is looking after me like one of their own. If I drink any more coffee and down another bacon sandwich, I won't be able to walk."

"I'll bet they're curious about the Lady, huh?"

"Man, they are like kids on Christmas Eve. You can see them drooling every time they go near her."

"She locked down?"

"Yeah. I feel sneaky doing it, but I think they understand it's an outside look only."

"We're running visuals here, but the satellites are having a hard time due to the weather. If we pick up on the guys, I'll let you know. In the meantime just relax. Make the most of it. Could get hot soon.''

"Talk to you later. Over and out."

Grimaldi shut down the connection and stepped out of the carrier's comm room. He was halfway along the corridor when he was confronted by the captain.

"I was just coming to find you, Mr. Pierce," he said.

"Problem?"

The captain smiled. "Only in the sense we just picked up a North Korean ship."

"Out here? I thought we were in South Korean territorial waters?"

"Oh, we are. Both within our boundaries, so to speak. But this happens from time to time out here. They come to look at us and we do the same. Kind of like a turf war. Daring each other to step over the line."

"This might get difficult if I suddenly get my call," Grimaldi suggested. "If they see me take off and head north and all."

"Usually doesn't last too long. If they're still around at the wrong time, we'll have to figure something out to distract them."

"Not going to sink them, are you?"

The captain grinned. "Hell, no. I figure we'll manage something a little less drastic. We'll save that for the last resort."

They wandered off toward the upper level.

"Hey, how about a cup of coffee while we wait?" the captain suggested.

SOME TIME LATER Grimaldi stood on one of the observation platforms, zipped up in a thick Navy weatherproof coat, with a peaked cap pulled low over his face. His hands were deep in his pockets as he stared out across the gray, choppy water. The swirling snow and wind cut visibility severely. He couldn't see the North Korean ship, but he knew it was still out there. It still showed up on the radar screens. Like the carrier, it was riding out the storm, just sitting and watching and waiting. Grimaldi knew what he was waiting for. Did the Korean ship have a similar agenda? Or was it, as the captain had said, simply on a routine watch, playing the game that had gone on between the two countries ever since the end of the Korean War?

Grimaldi wished he knew. He didn't want anything to interfere with his mission once he received the pickup call from Phoenix Force. They had enough to handle without anything stopping him from making his dash into North Korean territory to lift them out.

He leaned against the rail, staring out across the misty seascape. Spray wet his face, chilling his flesh. Grimaldi huddled deeper in his coat.

"Stay sharp, guys," he said into the wind. "Stay sharp."

"Talking to yourself again, Jack?"

Grimaldi recognized Blancanales's voice. The Able Team vet was similarly clad, his face peering out from the hood of his weatherproof coat. He joined Grimaldi at the rail.

"We come all the way out here and run into this

freak weather," Blancanales said. "Next time we'll choose summer."

"Doesn't work like that, pal. We get the call, we go. Choice doesn't come into it."

"Phoenix will be fine, Jack. Those guys are survivors."

"Do I look worried?"

Blancanales grinned. "Damn right you do."

"What about you? Knowing Carl is probably out there somewhere."

"One minute I figure what the hell. This is Carl we're talking about. The Ironman. Hard as they come. Then I see him in one of those labor camps and I think maybe it isn't so good."

"If I know Carl, he'll be giving 'em hell every chance he gets," Grimaldi said. "That guy is the most stubborn son of a bitch I ever knew."

# CHAPTER ELEVEN

*North Korea*

Carl Lyons's search for survival material produced nothing of value except for blankets from the hut. He had noticed a number of them lying around, trodden into the dirt and filthy, but that didn't matter. If he was able to smuggle a couple out, concealed under his padded clothing, they would at least provide him with some additional protection against the harsh weather conditions. The rain, often turning to snow, seemed to have become a permanent feature. The only positive thing to come out of it was that it made everyone—including the guards—miserable. The guards themselves had become despondent to the point where they retreated into a reclusive condition of their own. Once they had the prisoners working, they hunched over in their thick uniforms and did the best they could to endure the long hours of routine.

Lyons studied this over a couple of days while he labored along with the others, mired down in the freezing mud and constant rain. The conditions failed to improve. Lyons found he had adjusted to the climate as much as was humanly possible. It would have been easy to simply lie down and give in, letting the cold do its work and end the misery. He had seen two of the prisoners do exactly that. Having collapsed from sheer exhaustion, they refused to get up again. No amount of screaming and yelling from the guards had any effect on them. Club blows achieved nothing. In the end they were dragged away, and that night on the return journey to the camp their bodies had been placed in one of the trucks.

Lyons resolve not to let that happen to him had been fortified. He had sat during the journey, his eyes fixed on the corpses, steeling himself against the deprivation and squalor he was in and promising himself he wouldn't forget what he had seen in this freezing hellhole.

While the prisoners were working on the site they were allowed to keep the extra clothing that had been provided. It did at least give some extra warmth during the long, cold nights. Lyons took the opportunity, once Rinaldi was asleep, to wrap a couple of the spare blankets around his body. He took off the padded jacket and shirt, wrapped the blankets round his torso, then replaced the clothing. The blankets were thin, so they didn't add too much bulk to his body shape. By the time he had the shirt and padded jacket back on, it was hard to tell. He knew he was taking a risk. He decided it had to be. If he was going to make his escape attempt, it would have to be soon. Once they completed work on the site, whenever that was, the prisoners would be confined to the camp again. There was no telling when, or if, another work-force might be needed.

Lyons maintained his observation of the guards. He also made mental notes on any occurrences out-side the norm. One came when a helicopter touched down beyond the site perimeter. Three men climbed out and were met by Captain Yun and some other uniformed men who had come out from one of the units under construction. Lyons recognized Yat Sen Took. He was accompanied by a heavily built Chi-nese and also the Russian Gagarin. They talked for a time, then the party walked to the unit and went inside. Lyons's curiosity was cut short as one of the guards, noticing that his spade had stopped moving for a few seconds, moved up behind him and slammed his club across the back of the American's shoulders. The biting pain focused Lyons's attention back to the realities of his position, enforcing his de-termination to break out of his captivity.

Later that day another helicopter landed and un-loaded a number of sealed containers that were swiftly moved to one of the site buildings.

On the following day Lyons was wolfing down his midday meal of watery soup and rice when Ri-naldi nudged him.

"Hey, look at that."

Lyons glanced up in time to see a helicopter land. It wasn't a military machine. He recognized it as an AS365 Dauphin. The brightly colored aircraft settled, rotors slowing as the single turbine engine was cut.

A number of men climbed out. Lyons spotted the

heavyset Chinese who had visited along with Took and Gagarin. There were four more Chinese. Clad in thick coats, they carried stubby SMGs and appeared to be watching over the tall, broad-shouldered man with long blond hair in their midst. As soon as they were clear of the helicopter, the tight group made its way to one of the access ramps leading to the subterranean structure that seemed to be the main area of the site.

"This place is starting to get popular," Lyons said.

"Not with me it ain't," Rinaldi muttered with a vengeance.

He had noticed one of the Korean prisoners approaching. It was the one who had attacked him before. His face still bore the marks Lyons had left there. The Korean was staring at Lyons.

"Why can't they leave us alone?" Rinaldi said.

He turned to the Korean and said, "Go on! Get lost for Christ's sake!"

The Korean didn't understand the language, but he had to have picked up the inflection in Rinaldi's tone. He made straight for the American, grabbing him by the shoulders and hurling him aside. Rinaldi was smashed bodily against a pile of stone that had been excavated from the site, his skull cracking against the unyielding surface.

The Korean yelled something in his own tongue, spitting in Rinaldi's direction. He turned toward Lyons, jabbing a thick, callused finger at the American, and started to reel off a litany of Korean that could only have been expletives. As he trudged forward through the sticky mud, his left hand went inside his jacket and when it emerged he was holding a primitive knife with a jagged edged.

Lyons didn't waste time trying to talk the man out of whatever he intended. Other prisoners had formed a ragged line between Lyons and the guards, who didn't appear to be in any kind of rush to prevent what was happening.

Lyons watched the advancing Korean. The man was no knife fighter. Not by the way he was carrying the blade. The guy was just hefty and looked as if he meant what he was about to do. That was enough given the condition Lyons was in. Right there and then he wished he had his Colt Python in his hand.

He shook off the dullness that seemed to be clouding his thought process. He remembered the spade he had been working with all morning. He had stuck it into the ground next to where he had squatted to eat his food. It was still there, no more than a foot or so away from his right hand.

The Korean said something, slashing the air with the gleaming blade. Lyons could see it clearly now and realized it was nothing more than a piece of metal from the site. Still sharp and jagged enough to cut him to ribbons if the Korean got closer.

Lyons pushed to his feet, turning slightly, and reached out to grab the wooden handle of the spade. He yanked it from the soft mud, left hand gripping the crosspiece, his right hand halfway down the shaft. He swung it at the Korean and landed a hard blow with the flat of the blade, catching the man across the side of the head. The Korean shuddered. Blood began to stream from the gash the spade had opened.

Undeterred, the Korean came at Lyons again, avoiding the next swing of the spade and sweeping in with his blade.

The edge caught the sleeve of Lyons's padded coat, cutting through to tear the flesh of his forearm. Backing off, Lyons took his time and launched another swing with his spade, this time edge on. It landed squarely, biting into his adversary's left shoulder and sinking in almost to the bone. The Korean screamed in rage, but instead of stepping back, he went for Lyons, snarling against the pain that followed the blow. He cut for the throat, just missing as Lyons leaned away from the blade. There was no escaping the inevitability of this conflict. One way or another someone was going to end up dead, or severely injured.

Lyons had no intention of ending up buried in some unmarked grave in this miserable place. He launched a deadly swing with the spade that carried with it every ounce of strength in his shoulders and arms. The blade, its edge keened by use, chopped into the side of the Korean's neck, opening a wide gash that peeled back and gushed blood in a torrent. With his main artery severed, the Korean gave a terrified scream, staggering back from Lyons, blood pumping out in a furious stream that soaked his coat and spattered the ground at his feet. He stumbled blindly about, lost in his new world of pain and terror, his fellow prisoners backing off, any earlier thoughts of anger dissipated. The sight of their fellow inmate reduced to a bloody wreck made them aware of their own vulnerability. They shrank away in seconds, leaving Lyons on his own. The Korean was on his knees, his life washing away in the rain. As Lyons turned to go to Rinaldi's aid, the man responsible toppled facedown in the mud.

Rinaldi was unconscious. The back of his skull had been shattered where it had smacked against the piled stone. When Lyons gently probed, he could feel the deep depression where the bone had caved in. His fingers came away red. Rinaldi's face was deathly white and his breathing almost nonexistent.

Behind Lyons guards were shouting, pushing the prisoners away from the scene.

Rinaldi's breathing became labored. Trickles of blood ran from his ears. His lean body went slack in Lyons's grip, and his breathing stopped completely.

"Sorry, Chuck," Lyons said.

"Very touching," a familiar voice said.

Lyons turned to see Captain Yun standing close by.

"You happy now?" Lyons asked. "One of us is dead. That only leaves me."

"You make it sound as if I want that more than anything."

"I'm going to disappoint you, Yun. Unless you shoot me for killing one of your prisoners."

"You are a good worker. As you explained to me before, why waste the life of a productive prisoner? You may carry on. I need you to make up for the two men we have lost today. So. Time to return to work."

Yun walked away, pulling his heavy coat around him. He issued commands to the guards, and Rinaldi and the Korean were moved out of sight. Lyons, under the gun of another guard, was ordered back to work.

He crossed to where he had dropped his spade. Bending to pick it up, Lyons saw something in the mud beside it. He realized it was the Korean's blade. He scooped it up in his hand as he lifted the spade, pressing the muddy blade hard against the wooden shaft, and straightened. The guard stayed with him until they were back at Lyons's work site. Then the guard backed off and resumed his stance some distance away so he could watch the other prisoners, as well. Lyons bent to his work, digging out more of the site. He kept the blade where it was, gripping it tightly so it didn't slip. It was some time later when he had to put down his spade and help lift a large chunk of rock from the site that he was able to hurriedly stuff the blade down the side of his work boot.

That night, back in his solitary hut, Lyons examined the blade. It was a tapered length of steel, about seven inches long, coming to a point at the blade end. The Korean had spent some time honing the edges of the cutting blade. They were still ragged but there was enough sharpness to make a formidable weapon. Lyons tore some strips off one of the blankets and wound them around the handle section, then cut some thinner strips to bind it in place. It gave the handle a better grip.

When he had completed that, he checked the cut on his arm. The blood had congealed over the gash, which turned out not to be as deep as Lyons had thought. He didn't have anything to treat it with so he left it alone. He lay down and tried to sleep. The way things had gone, it was time he made his move. Killing the Korean prisoner had been a necessity, but the others weren't going to view it that way. There was going to be a lot of resentment among the other prisoners, and sooner or later that resentment was going to come Lyons's way. He couldn't fight off the whole camp. Lyons decided he was going to be better off away from the camp and the construction site, out on his own.

And to hell with Captain Yun.

LYONS WAS ISOLATED by the rest of the prisoners the next morning. They avoided him completely. He took his meager breakfast alone, which suited him fine. He sensed their hostility. They watched him from a distance, and being who he was, Lyons didn't give a damn.

In the truck going to the site, Lyons was made to sit with guards flanking him either side. It made him smile. The guards hated him as much as the prisoners, but they were under orders to make sure he came to no harm.

At the site Lyons went straight to his section and started work. In the distance he saw Captain Yun, accompanied by Yat Sen Took, supervising the lifting of some heavy equipment. They were involved for some time, but when the task had been completed they came across to where Lyons was working and stood watching him.

"I hear you experienced a little difficulty yesterday," Took said.

"Nothing I couldn't handle."

"So Captain Yun has been telling me."

"Something to talk about over your rice and fish."

Took smiled. "Actually, it was rice and pork. Very tasty."

"Isn't that a little like eating your own?" Lyons said.

Yun stiffened with barely repressed anger. All Took did was smile even more.

"You see, Yun. After everything he has been through, he still retains a sense of humor."

"I will remember that when I cut his Yankee throat," Yun said.

Lyons refrained from making any more comments. He wasn't about to step over the line today. If he was going to make his attempt at getting out, it wouldn't do him any good enraging Yun. The man was liable to do something out of sheer frustration.

AFTER RETURNING to the main site, Took paused.

"Yun, I believe our Russian friend, Gagarin, may have been correct about this American. He has shown no inclination toward relenting, nor has he offered us any deals to save himself. Perhaps my judgment was clouded by the fact he interfered with the Alaskan project. It would have been useful if he had revealed information. He has not, and now we are reaching a critical stage in our new project I don't have the patience to concern myself with him any longer."

"That means?"

"Come along, Yun, you know exactly what it means. From tomorrow his status will be the same as any other prisoner. He is yours to do what you want with.''

They walked down the concrete ramp that led to the entrance of the underground site. The armed guards at the door stood to attention as Took and Yun stepped inside. Behind them the door slid shut on oiled rollers. In a separate bunker a powerful generator ran full-time. It provided the unit with all the electrical power it needed. There were three more identical bunkers where three more generators were on standby in case of emergencies. The generator provided the electricity that powered the strip lights illuminating the concrete passageways.

At the end of the passage Took pushed open a door that led into a security area. Television cameras located around the site fed them pictures of the scene outside. Took and Yun passed through the security area and exited the door leading to the main area of the unit. A number of doors opened onto rooms used for a variety of purposes. Took was interested in only one at the moment.

Inside the room was an array of computers, electronic equipment Took had little knowledge about. His computer skills were only a step above basic. He watched as Jerome Berkoff busied himself with the installation of the recently delivered hardware. He had given Duong Chin a list of his needs, and the Chinese had organized the acquisition very quickly. Berkoff had gone to work immediately, unpacking the equipment and assembling it. He had worked through most of the previous night and had taken off no more than a couple of hours for a snatched rest before starting again.

Berkoff glanced up as Took and Yun entered the room.

"So?" Took asked.

"It is all here," Berkoff said. "Once I have it assembled, I can install the programs and then I can begin."

"Is there anything you need in the meantime?"

"No." Berkoff glanced around the room with its plain walls and ceiling and its concrete floor. "A little decoration wouldn't go amiss. I never did take to the minimalist look."

Took nodded. "I understand. But we constructed this purely for a particular function. At this stage making it homely wasn't important."

"You succeeded, then."

"Seriously, Mr. Berkoff, do you have any idea how long?"

"Before I can start looking at the disks? Three, maybe four days."

"So long?"

"I have to know when I insert those disks that the configuration on these computers is one hundred percent ideal. I can't afford to have any problems. If I get a glitch in the system, it could trigger the self-destruct sequence."

"They are that sensitive?"

"Oh, yes," Berkoff said. "Remember we are dealing with a Raymond Gilman program here. The man is no fool, which is why the Americans hired him to write the Slingshot database. The destruct sequence he set if anyone tries to copy the disks is only a kid's thing to him. His encryption is something else. It's going to have traps and tricks, subroutines, blind alleys. When Gilman devises an encryption, he does it differently than anyone else. Nothing is as it seems. To him it is a very clever game. The program is the work. The encryption is the fun part for Gilman.''

''Then doesn't that make it less of a problem?'' Took asked. ''If he treats it as a game, surely it cannot be so hard to…''

''Maybe I used the wrong word,'' Berkoff said. ''Gilman isn't creating the encryption as a game per se. Not as we would interpret game. He does it against himself. The man is so gifted he invents encryptions that make grown men weep because of their complexity. To him, Gilman, they are simply mind games to stretch *his* imagination.''

''I will take your word for it, Mr. Berkoff. Perhaps we should leave you to your work. If you require anything, please let me know.''

Berkoff had already returned to his equipment.

Outside Took glanced at Yun. ''Well, Yun, after that conversation we are either very stupid, or this man Gilman is incredibly smart.''

''I didn't understand much of it myself,'' Yun replied.

In truth he wasn't really interested in Took's obsession. Yun was thinking ahead. To the next day when he would have the pleasure of informing the American that the rules had changed and the game had moved on. Now Yun was the master, able to do what he was best at.

Playing with men's lives.

# CHAPTER TWELVE

"Ahead and to the right," Manning said. "Pretty sure I saw buildings. Metal structures."

McCarter took the helicopter down, swinging it around so they were head-on to whatever Manning had seen. The snow had eased, giving way to a thin rain that created a fine mist, still obscuring clear vision.

"Hey, Gary's right," James called from the cabin behind McCarter. "See, there."

McCarter nodded. "Looks like the image Aaron picked up when we spotted Carl."

"So we need to keep heading north," Manning said. "If we stay on course, we should fly over the camp before we hit the new site."

"Talking of hitting things," McCarter said, "I think I've figured out which is the fuel gauge."

"And?" Manning asked.

"And we seem to be getting low on fuel. So hitting things might be nearer than you think."

Manning checked the map again. He did some quick mental calculations. "We need at least another couple hours' flying time to reach the site."

"I hear you. I'll see what I can do. This bloody crate is gobbling fuel. Must need a service and new plugs."

"Some chance," Encizo said. "Great, we'll be doing some more walking, huh?"

Manning, who was keeping a constant check on the ground, tapped McCarter on the shoulder.

"Looks like some movement down there. Couple of vehicles. Troops spread out in a line. Taking a guess, I'd say they're looking for us."

"Well, they'll have to run bloody fast to keep up," the Briton said and took the helicopter higher.

A range of low, thinly timbered hills stood dead ahead. McCarter crested the trees and then dropped the Mi-2 into the valley that stretched ahead of them. They flew for a half hour, then the valley broadened out onto rugged terrain, with little to distinguish it. The land wasn't exactly barren. It just had an inhospitable look to it.

"The Jolly Green Giant would have a hell of job growing his corn out here," James observed. "Looks pretty rough."

"Which is why they chose to build a labor camp on it," Encizo said.

The outline of the camp came into view. McCarter eased the chopper across so they could overfly the place. Seen from the air they could get a sense of the camp's desolation. It wasn't just the high fences and watch towers. The interior was bleak, harsh and gave off an air of hopelessness. The compound was a quagmire of mud. The huts were crude, basic structures that would offer nothing but the basest protection. There were armed guards in sight, but few prisoners. Near the main gate was a collection of trucks and smaller vehicles.

"Makes you want to drop a couple of missiles on the place." James said. "Nobody's that bad they should be kept in a place like that."

"Cal, the rights and wrong don't even come into it," Encizo said. "The bastards who send people here are no different than the ones in Cuba who sent me to El Principe. They're not in the rehab business. These places are for punishment. For taking away everything a man has and leaving him nothing. Pride, dignity, free speech. The ones who do this are frightened men who get scared when they hear those words. It threatens their positions of power. So they take the good men, put them in places like this and strip their souls."

The camp fell behind them. Under Manning's guidance McCarter altered course slightly, bringing them around to the northeast. Once they were clear of the camp, McCarter reduced height again. Despite the weather, they were able to see wheel marks where heavy trucks had traveled from the camp and in the same direction they were flying.

Twice they saw small troop patrols. Armed soldiers on foot. At one point they spotted a small military vehicle. It was mired down to the axles, its crew struggling to free it from the mud that had the vehicle in its grip.

"How we doing for fuel?" James asked some time later.

"Getting pretty low," McCarter said. "You'd better decide what we want to take with us. Anything we can't use, strip out the firing mechanism and throw it out. No point leaving anything behind these blokes can use against us."

James and Encizo set to the task. When they had completed it, they slid open the hatch a few inches and began to drop out the removed mechanisms.

"We'll leave the machine gun until we go ourselves," James said. "We might need it yet."

*Aboard the U.S. Navy Carrier*

"THEY'RE OVERDUE," Grimaldi said.

Blancanales and Schwarz were with him eating breakfast.

"Take it easy, Jack," Schwarz said. "A deal like this is never going to run to the minute."

Grimaldi swirled coffee around in his mug. "I know that. But it doesn't feel right."

He pushed to his feet and zipped up his jacket. "I'm going to check the Lady," he said, and walked away.

"That guy is walking on hot coals," Blancanales commented. "He won't be happy until he has Phoenix wrapped up nice and cozy."

"He worries."

"Yeah, I know. What? You saying we don't?"

Schwarz grinned. He refilled his coffee mug and raised it in Blancanales's direction.

"To all those who care."

Blancanales shook his head. "Crazy mother," he said. "We going to get Carl back?"

"Damn right we are. We have to."

"Yeah, right. But let's face it. He could be dead. No pretending otherwise. It *could* have happened."

"Only if we think that way, Pol. Right now Carl's alive. I know he is because the minute we start thinking anything else, we lose him."

Schwarz's words echoed through Blancanales's mind. He knew his partner was right. They had to stay faithful to the thought. Giving up wasn't an option.

Lyons was still alive. Still alive…and they would find him….

*North Korea*

THE ONLY GOOD THING about that day was the fact that the snow eased off towards midmorning. The rain was still there, and a chill wind blew in from north. The ground underfoot, wet and muddy, would start to freeze later if the temperature dropped. That made the work even harder, having to hack through the semifrozen surface layer. Carl Lyons worked with a vengeance, loosening the muscles that had ached with stiffness after another night of half sleep in his cold, damp hut.

He kept an eye open for the appearance of Captain Yun. He had a feeling there was a change about to take place. If so, he wanted to be ahead of it. Lyons had noticed an atmosphere around the site from the moment the trucks deposited him and the other prisoners, a mood of excitement among the usually sullen guards. As if something was about to happen. It wasn't that there were more of them, rather that they were alert. He wondered if some important dignitary was making a visit. The North Koreans liked to make big when they achieved one of their goals. The site might be playing host to someone of importance.

The event in itself, if there was one, held no interest for Lyons. The only thing it might do would be to take the attention of the guards off the prisoners to a degree, which might provide him with his opportunity to escape. If he was wrong and there was no special event, he was still going to try. One way or another, however it worked out, Carl Lyons intended to sleep out that night.

He had his extra blankets and he had his knife. A weapon of sorts. Maybe not the Colt Python or a combat shotgun, with a few fragmentation grenades just to balance things out, but he wasn't exactly in a position where being choosy made much difference. The thought crossed Lyons's mind that he might acquire a weapon on his way out. If the chance offered itself.

Captain Yun did appear at one point during the morning. He showed little interest in Lyons, or any of the prisoners. The man seemed distracted. When he showed, it was in the company of the Chinese and his minders. They were involved in some kind of heated discussion. As they stood talking, the AS365 helicopter appeared and made a hurried landing. Yat Sen Took and the Russian climbed out, swathed in thick coats. They joined the others, carried on their discussion for a while, then returned to the underground complex.

The more he saw, the more intrigued Lyons became. There was definitely something in the wind but what he couldn't figure out. He returned to work, this time studying guard movements and trying to form some kind of scheme that would get him in a position where he might make his attempt. He needed to be near the trucks, which were on the perimeter of the site, close to the concrete wall that surrounded it. He couldn't go over the wall, or through it. So his best chance was going to be when they completed work and were taken to the trucks to be driven back to the camp. It was always dark when they headed out. That would give him cover and the opportunity to gain some distance before any kind of pursuit could be mounted. When he considered that, Lyons realized that his best chance would be *after* they had been driving for a time. The farther he was from the site, the better chance he would have.

His thoughts returned to Captain Yun. His plan for escape depended a great deal on how the Korean acted toward him. Yun would delight in tormenting Lyons, and if the American reacted it would give Yun the chance to punish him. If that punishment was some kind of incarceration, then Lyons's plan would have to be postponed. Something he didn't want. His need to get clear of the site, the camp and all that went with it had become the single most important objective in his life at that point.

Midday came and went. Lyons was fed along with the other prisoners. He devoured his share down to the last drop. If there had been a way for him to get more, he would done so. Once he broke from captivity, he would be cut off from the regular food he got.

As he returned to work, he saw Took standing alone near the entrance to the underground complex. The man was staring off into the distance, oblivious to the fact he was getting soaked by the falling rain. For a brief moment their eyes met across the gap between them. Then Took returned to the ramp that led back to the complex.

"ANYTHING YET?" Took asked, shrugging out of his coat. He picked up a towel and scrubbed it through his hair.

"The helicopter was sighted earlier by foot patrols," Yun said.

He was seated behind a desk in the main control area, drumming the fingers of one hand on the top. The situation seemed to be affecting him more than it did anyone else.

"How can these damn Americans hide from us? They kill the crew and steal their helicopter. Twice they have been seen, but now they have vanished. Where are they?"

He stood, almost knocking over his chair, and strode to an area map pinned to the wall. He indicated various points.

"They took the helicopter here. From the sightings, they are plainly trying to reach us." He jabbed at the map in irritation. "They don't know the country that well, so they are not going to wander off course too far. So they should be in this area somewhere."

"When we first apprehended them," Took said, "I took away the GPS unit they had. That would have enabled them to pinpoint this site exactly. Now they have to depend on their own judgment. Surely, Yun, we should be able to catch them."

"I will lead the hunt myself," Yun said. "These Yankees will not leave here alive or dead."

Gagarin appeared in the doorway. "Have they been sighted yet?" he asked.

"Yun has just promised me they will never the leave the country," Took said. "He will command the search personally."

"Good luck, my friend," Gagarin said. "A word of caution. Do not underestimate these Americans. They are extremely proficient."

Yun pulled on his heavy topcoat, buttoning it tightly. He strapped a belt and holster around his waist.

"And so are we." he said. "We will see how proficient they are when I have them digging alongside Comrade Took's pet American."

Gagarin watched him leave, a wry smile on his face.

"I hope for his sake he gets what he wants. Personally, Took, I do believe you should make security arrangements around here."

"The guards have already been alerted to the possibility of sabotage. You still expect them to show up, don't you?"

"If they don't, I'll have come a long way for nothing. One thing you should know about me, Took. I do not like being made a fool of twice by the same people.''

''At least we have that in common. Have you seen Chin this morning?''

''He's with Berkoff.''

DUONG CHIN STOOD at a distance watching Jerome Berkoff work. The German had been up most of the night, taking a few hours off before returning to his computers. He was almost ready to start checking through the operating systems, having installed them in the past hour. He sat at the keyboard of the main computer, his eyes fixed on the large screen. Data scrolled across the monitor. Berkoff made a final entry, then sat back, stretching to ease the kinks from his aching back.

''Now we wait,'' he said.

''What are you doing now?'' Chin asked.

''I have just instructed the computer to run a self-diagnostic routine. It will check every phase of the installed program section by section, then double-check. This part will take most of the day. I wrote this program myself. It is an improvement on the normal diagnostic checks.''

''And after that you will be ready to break the encryption?''

''I have the other equipment to check as well. Remember, once I attempt to enter Gilman's encryption, nothing must left to chance. One slip and we lose everything.'' Berkoff swung his chair around to face the Chinese. ''I always believed the Chinese were the masters of patience. Please do not spoil the illusion of inscrutability, Chin.''

Chin laughed, genuinely amused.

"I would never do that, Jerome. I understand how much of a romantic you are.''

Took came into the room. In answer to his question, Berkoff repeated what he had told Chin.

"Progress indeed.''

"And how is Captain Yun faring in his quest for the Americans?" Chin asked.

"About to leave,'' Took said. "Not entirely a happy man. I really believe he is starting to take all this as a personal matter.''

"If he lets himself become distracted, he will only make things harder for himself,'' Chin said.

"Do you want to tell him that?''

Chin crossed his hands over his stomach, shaking his head.

"I'm sure Yun is a capable officer. It's not my place to interfere.''

YUN SETTLED into the seat of the all-terrain vehicle. He instructed the driver to move off. As the vehicle rumbled toward the open gate, with two trucks of troops falling in behind, Yun couldn't resist a glance back over his shoulder.

His American prisoner was visible, his back bent as he shoveled the sodden, freezing dirt into a wheelbarrow. The man seemed to have a frenzy for work this morning. His breath hung in the cold air above him as his powerful arms hauled up the heavy dirt, repeating the process over and over almost without pause.

Yun turned to face front again. He reached for the radio's handset and made sure he had contact with the base behind him and also the other trucks. He picked up the map he had brought along, checked the locations he had marked. Giving orders to his driver, he sat back and prepared himself for the day ahead.

# CHAPTER THIRTEEN

*Stony Man Farm, Virginia*

Huntington Wethers scanned the readout and nodded in satisfaction at what he saw.

"We're getting a clear image now," he stated. "That band of snow has worked its way out. All we got now is rain and a temperature drop. It's going to be very cold where the guys are."

"Okay," Kurtzman said, "let's run some scans of the area and see if we can pick up anything. Barb, you want to talk to Jack? Tell him the weather's improving a tad. He's been chewing the airwaves like a wild man."

Price smiled. "You know Jack. He doesn't like standing around. I'll give him a call."

Before Price could move away, Katz appeared.

"You won't believe this," he said. "I checked through some of Hal's government contacts. The movement of high-spec computers is always of interest to the security community. Allows them to assess if any foreign regimes are purchasing equipment that would only be of use in certain applications."

"And did you find what you were looking for?" Price asked.

"I can't prove it to the letter," Katz said, "but computer equipment, equal in design and specification to the type Raymond Gilman used, was purchased via an agent in Germany for initial shipment to a holding warehouse in Frankfurt earlier in the week. It stayed there for a day before it was put on a flight to the Philippines."

"Getting close to home."

"The added interest is that the computer company has been used before by Jerome Berkoff. I know it's a tenuous connection but if it's correct it suggests the North Koreans may well have the equipment Berkoff needs to carry out his code breaking."

"Going on the time scale, the equipment would be in North Korea by now," Kurtzman said. "Berkoff would have to set it up and install his hardware. Probably need some time to run full diagnostics to clear out any bugs before he starts trying to break the encryption."

"You mean he won't be up and running yet?" Price asked.

Kurtzman nodded. "Gilman's encryption will be extremely complex. To him it'll be as simple as writing his own signature. To everyone else it will be like a maze turned on its side and placed in a dark room. Knowing the way he works, he'll have built in all kinds of traps and blind alleys. When Berkoff starts his break-in, he has to know his system is completely stable. Any deviation could trigger one of Gilman's little tricks. Hit a false one and the whole thing could just corrupt.''

"Sounds a bit like defusing a bomb," Katz said.

"Good analogy," Kurtzman said. "The principle is similar. Triggers. Different wiring. Cut one, it sets off a detonation sequence. Others could be just dead ends. Miss the right one, and there's no going back."

"Berkoff has to be good, then?" Price said.

"Better than good. He has to have a similar mindset as Gilman. And Berkoff does."

"Let's hope the guys reach that site before he gets too far into his code breaking," Price said.

THE SAR SATELLITE SWUNG on its axis under Wethers's command. He keyed in the instructions that told the satellite to scan a particular area. Wethers picked up on the last location they had scanned and started a step-by-step progression, moving north. As soon as he had the image set, Wethers activated the record device so that they would be able to analyze everything the satellite picked up.

Keying in the command that requested automatic advancement of the scan, Wethers leaned back in his seat. There was little for him to do at this precise moment. The SAR would follow the course he had set. His contribution was to simply observe and be ready to pinpoint anything the electronic eye picked up.

The scan was traversing east and west of the main path, seeking anything that might indicate movement of troops or vehicles. Information gathered had to be looked at and broken down into useful data. Images could be captured and enlarged, specific sections magnified for close inspection. At a stage such as the one Stony Man was going through, nothing would be overlooked. The most insignificant observation might prove to have great importance at a later date.

Wethers picked up on movement. He leaned forward and tapped in the zoom command, the satellite's camera sharpening the image as it enlarged it. Soon he was able to observe North Korean troops moving over the bleak, undulating terrain. Snow on the ground was being washed away by the rain still falling. Now that the snowfall had blown itself out, the image the satellite sent back had a sharper quality to it, and Wethers felt almost a part of the scene he was watching.

"Aaron, catch this," he said, transferring the image to Kurtzman's monitor, as well.

"Location?" Kurtzman asked.

"Northwest of the camp. I counted at least twenty."

"Log it," Kurtzman said.

"Already done."

Kurtzman stared at the monitor screen, willing it to show him where Phoenix Force was. The lack of communication increased his concern even though he knew that once in the field circumstances often denied any kind of contact with home. Knowing that didn't make him feel any better. It added to his frustration. He swung his chair around and wheeled it across to the coffeepot.

"Keep scanning, Hunt. Find them."

*North Korea*

"THAT SHOULD DO IT," McCarter said. He stood back and surveyed their camouflage work on the helicopter.

They had landed two hours ago, the Mi-2 sucking on fumes as the fuel supply was exhausted. McCarter brought them down in the lee of a timbered hill. Once on the ground they set to concealing the helicopter as best they could. They used low tree branches and foliage to break up the Mi-2's profile. The snow was still falling when they landed, so the light covering of white helped to hide the aircraft's outline. Manning opened the engine cowling and cut all the wiring he could find. He also loosened and removed any parts he was able, taking them into the trees to dump them.

Before they disabled the radio, James switched on and ran through the frequencies, seeking Dragon Slayer's band. He knew Grimaldi would be monitoring the band spread in case they attempted to contact him. Despite his best efforts, James was unable to lock on to Grimaldi's frequency. The Mi-2's built-in radio had a limited spread, and all he picked up was heavy static and a couple of Korean transmissions. Once he had decided he wasn't going to contact Grimaldi, James switched off. He yanked out all the cables, then put the butt of his M-16 through the front panel.

"No go," he said as he climbed out.

"We'll have to wait until we can signal Jack to

come and pick us up," McCarter said. "He'll sit and wait for us."

With the helicopter covered, they moved out. According to the calculations they had worked out, they were still on course for the site. It lay a good way ahead of them, and it would be dark in less than an hour. There was no way they would reach the place while it was still light.

The snow had stopped falling by the time they set off. The rain was still with them, thin and chilling. They were aware that the temperature was starting to drop. The soft ground underfoot would freeze as the lowering temperature took hold.

They spotted troop movements twice before the light started to fail. Always in the distance, but they knew that the Koreans wouldn't stop looking for them. Phoenix Force presented a potential threat, and the Koreans would maintain their vigilance.

THE ONSET OF DARKNESS alerted Lyons to the fact that his intended escape attempt was coming close. He maintained his work effort, while still keeping a sharp eye out for the guards.

The order to cease work was given earlier than usual. The guards moved in and watched as the prisoners returned all their work tools to a sturdy wooden hut, which was then locked. After that had been completed, the prisoners were herded together and marched to the waiting trucks. Lyons hung back and allowed the others to overtake him. No one seemed concerned. He was, to all intents, still isolated from the rest of the prisoners. Keeping his head down, Lyons shuffled along until he reached the last truck in the line. The guards waited as the prisoners climbed in, then took their places. Lyons, sitting near the rear, had one of the guards beside him. He had hoped this might happen because having a guard with him when he exited the truck was vital to his escape plan.

The trucks started up and lurched into motion. Tires fought hard to gain traction on ground already turning solid due to the lowering temperature.

The prisoners huddled together for collective warmth, jolted around by the swaying motion of the truck. The chill rain blew inside the truck and added to the misery of those riding in it.

Lyons saw the work site vanish from sight in the oncoming dark. He had to allow some more time before he did anything. Breaking out too close to the site would only add to his problems. It was a difficult time. Lyons wanted to make his move but had to rein his enthusiasm until the trucks had driven a good distance.

Hoping his judgment was realistic, Lyons decided they had been driving for at least forty minutes. Looking beyond the tailgate he saw that it was full dark. There was very little light from the moon, obscured by the heavy clouds and the misty rain. This was as good a moment as he was going to get.

The guard beside Lyons stirred uncomfortably. He was as wet and cold as the prisoners, not enjoying the ride, and his attention had wandered as the seemingly endless ride went on. He muttered to himself, shifting the AK hanging around his neck by its webbing strap.

Lyons leaned forward, head down on his chest, feigning sleep. He let his hands drop between his legs and felt for the knife tucked down inside his left boot. He felt the solid shape of the weapon.

The truck hit a deep rift and bounced, jolting everyone around. Prisoners slithered across the wet bed of the truck, knocking into one another. The truck's driver hit the gas pedal, and the engine roared as he piled on the power to pull them out of the depression. The truck lurched again, then swayed from side to side on its poor suspension. The guard beside Lyons half rose from his seat, yelling at the driver. He was still expressing his anger when Lyons pushed upright, turned to face the guard and hit the Korean chest high, wrapping his arms around the man as they struck the side of the truck and went over.

Lyons kept the guard underneath him, the Korean absorbing most of the impact when they landed. In the darkness the steep slope next to where they struck was invisible. Lyons felt the earth slip away and then he and the guard were rolling down the slope at an increasing rate, bodies bumping and scraping over the hard ground. The descent seemed to go on forever—then it abruptly ceased as Lyons and the Korean came to a bone-jarring stop.

The Korean kicked out, catching Lyons in the side, knocking him clear. Lyons, ignoring the pain from the fall, rolled to his feet, reaching down to snatch the concealed knife free. He moved in as the Korean, half-risen, tried to clear his AK. Lyons hit the man with a body slam that took them to the ground again.

They rolled, each struggling to gain the advantage. Cold water soaked them as they slid over the bank of a stream. The struggle went on for a short time, up to the moment when Lyons cleared his right arm, then thrust the blade of his knife into the Korean's side. The padded clothing the Korean wore slowed the blade. Lyons leaned his full weight on it, and the knife sank in to the handle. Beneath him the Korean let out a shuddering moan, his body arching up off the ground. Lyons twisted the blade, feeling flesh tear. Warm blood bubbled from the elongated wound, washing over Lyons's gloved hand. The Korean struggled frantically as the serrated edge of the blade tore at internal organs. Jamming his left hand against the Korean's throat, pushing down hard to stop the man shouting any warnings, Lyons pulled the blade free, drew his arm back and plunged it in again, this time aiming for the heart. His second thrust was on target. As the jagged steel penetrated the heart, the Korean's panicked scream came out as an uneven sound. Lyons gave the knife a final push, sawing it back and forth until the Korean became still.

Lyons lay for a moment, panting. The exertion had winded him. His body was bruised and battered from the fall. Pushing upright, he bent over the dead Korean and freed the AK. He searched the body for extra magazines and found only one. He shoved it into the folds of his padded jacket. Reaching down, he pulled the knife free and pushed it back down inside his boot. Just before he moved away, he pulled off the padded cap the Korean wore and put it on.

The cap had earflaps, and he pulled these down and used the cloth ribbons to secure the cap.

Peering into the gloom, Lyons checked out his surroundings. He could make out the high, steep slope he had come down. He turned and crossed the stream, making for the open ground beyond. He could make out a dark stand of skinny trees and made that his first objective. Once he reached the trees, he dropped to a crouch and checked out the way he had come.

He could hear the distant rumble of truck engines and tried to work out if they were moving or just idling because the vehicle had stopped. With the soft hiss of the rain and the buffeting of the wind, it was hard to establish what he was hearing.

Lyons pulled his coat tight around him. He was on his own now, free at least from the camp and the brutal regime that ran it. Captain Yun was going to be a disappointed man. Lyons knew he wouldn't let it go. It would be a matter of pride to the Korean to recapture Lyons—or kill him in the attempt.

He checked the AK, making sure it was cocked and locked. If they wanted him, let them come. However this turned out, the sons of bitches would know Carl Lyons had been around.

# CHAPTER FOURTEEN

Yun stared at the handset, his face suffused with rage. He had just received a message informing him that the American prisoner had escaped. To add further complications, the man had killed one of the guards and taken his weapon.

The American was on the loose and armed.

He ordered his driver to stop, flung down the handset and climbed out of the all-terrain vehicle, pulling up his coat collar against the chill rain. He walked away from the truck and stood gazing out across the moonlit landscape. His anger stemmed from a combination of tiredness and a lack of any progress. Reports coming in from his other patrols had been exactly the same. The American strike team had vanished from sight. No one had seen a thing.

He wondered how this could be. Something struck a chord at the back of his mind. Was it something Gagarin had said? That the Americans were extremely proficient. Perhaps the Russian had been right and he, Yun, hadn't accorded the Americans the respect they deserved. He raised his face to the dark sky and let cold rain wash over his face. The chill snapped him out of his somber mood. There was little they could do now. The night would hamper any kind of search and might lead to a reversal, with the Americans doing the chasing. They were few in number, able to move about quickly. Yun decided it was time to stop for the night. He would return to base, allow his men the opportunity to change into dry clothing and eat. Then they could get some rest before morning, when they would resume their search.

In the meantime the Americans would have to stay out in the wilds, unprotected and exposed to the severe cold. Perhaps they wouldn't feel so superior after a freezing night in the open.

Yun returned to his vehicle and instructed his driver to return to base. He picked up the handset and spoke to his patrols, ordering them all back to base.

By the time they reached the site, the news of the escaped prisoner was on everyone's lips. Yun gave his orders to the shivering troops, then made his way below. He went directly to the room he was using and dried himself off, tidied his appearance and then made his way to the main control center.

Took was there, along with Gagarin. They told him that Duong Chin was with Berkoff. Yun helped himself to some hot tea and sat down.

"Some days are better than others," Gagarin said quietly. "Our American friend has taken us all by surprise."

"Perhaps I should have seen this coming," Yun said. "That one was never going to accept imprisonment."

"The American spirit," Gagarin said. "They are never comfortable being denied their freedom."

"So we have a prisoner on the loose, as well as this American team," Took said. "Perhaps it is a forerunner to an invasion. Soon we will be overrun by these damn Yankees."

"Took, concentrate on your missile program," Gagarin said. "Leave the Americans to Captain Yun. I am sure he will deal with them very shortly. Right, Captain?"

Yun nodded. "Tomorrow the search will resume. They cannot hide forever. Not in this terrain and certainly not in the temperatures we are experiencing."

"A caution there, Captain. They did survive in Siberia. These men are no beginners."

"Thank you for the warning," Yun said. "Now, is there any chance of a meal?"

"IS THIS HIGH LIVING, or what?" Calvin James said.

He dug his fork into the tin he was holding and scooped out the remains of its contents. He wolfed down the cold chicken stew. Reaching for his canteen, he took a drink.

"Sorry, lads, but I couldn't get a table anywhere," McCarter said. "You know how it is without reservations."

They were dug in under a sagging overhang, water dripping all around them. It had become colder as the night wore on. They were uncomfortable, but they were surviving.

"Anybody want a dry cracker?" Manning asked, holding out the pack he had just unsealed.

"I'll have one," Encizo said.

"Somebody tell me what time it is," James said. "I'm too damn lazy to look at my watch."

"Twenty after eight," Encizo said. "Just a nice time to be leaving home for a night out with a pretty lady. Go for a meal. Dancing, and after…"

"Yeah?" James said.

"Hey, figure the rest out for yourself."

"I'll use my imagination," James said.

He reached into his backpack and pulled out a rolled-up sleeping bag. The bag was waterproof and had a heat-retaining inner lining.

"We're going to need plenty of imagination when we find this missile site," McCarter said.

"No master plan?" Manning asked.

"We don't have any idea what we'll find when we get there," the Briton said. "Probably a full battalion of Korean troops and a tank squadron."

"We could do with some satellite intel," Encizo said. "David, we might have to risk breaking silence and talk to base."

"I was thinking along those lines myself," McCarter said. "If they can spot troop movements for us, we may have an easier time getting through."

"We going to move before it gets light?" Manning asked.

"It could get us closer before the Koreans start searching again," McCarter said. "When they start searching in the morning, they'll most probably move out from the site. If we get inside that initial perimeter, it could give us a clear time to establish ourselves before they come back."

"Sounds good in theory," Encizo said.

"Ideas always do," McCarter agreed. "Problems start when you try to make the bloody things work in reality. I'm trying to give us an advantage. We don't have a lot going for us right now. So we have to make the best of what we do have. Mobility. We're small in number. We have a specific target. It should work for us."

"Now can we get some sleep?" James asked. "These pep talks of yours really make me tired, David."

"Did you ever think that maybe this isn't your line of work?" McCarter asked.

"Every day, man. Every damn day." James grinned and pulled the hood of his sleeping bag over his head.

THE HOURS SINCE his escape had blurred into an endless period of enforced loneliness for Carl Lyons. Alone and friendless in a brutal environment, he was nevertheless determined to stay free and to survive.

He kept moving. He was cold and wet, and the temperature was still falling, so he couldn't afford to stop and allow himself to rest. If he gave in to the temptation, he was finished. Falling asleep out here, with little protection other than the clothes he wore and his additional blanket wrap, would be fatal. Curling up and giving in to the need for rest and recuperation would be his final act. Once the lethargy of exhaustion washed over him, he wouldn't care about anything. He would slip easily into that state of semiconsciousness from which there would be no waking.

Lyons realized just how easy it would be to do that. Welcoming the false comfort. Imagining he was warm and safe as the lowering temperature froze his mind and body until he went into that dreamless sleep prior to death...

"No way! No fucking way!"

The sound of his own voice startled Lyons. He hadn't realized what he was doing until his anger kicked him out of the stupor. He shook his head, blinking his eyes.

"Dammit, you haven't come this far to lie down and die!"

He stared around him, peering into the gloom of night. He could barely make out the form of the landscape. He had no idea how far he had come since breaking away from the dead Korean and heading away from where he had left the truck. All he did clearly know was the need to keep moving. Not to slow down or give in to the weariness engulfing his battered body. He knew well enough that he desperately needed rest. Hot food and drink. But he knew just as definitely that those things were well beyond his reach out here in this semifrozen wilderness.

He had paused a number of times, checking his back trail in case the Koreans were following. He had seen nothing, heard nothing. That was no guarantee they weren't out there. He accepted that the Koreans were no novices. Existing in this harsh land would have made them a tough breed. And capable of tracking a lone man across their own backyard. He was a stranger here, planted on this alien terrain by a quirk of fate that had caught him in the wrong place at the wrong time. Now he was on the run. A fugitive from his captors. A moving target to be cut down by any soldier who got him in his sights. Lyons was under no illusion. His life meant nothing to the Koreans. He was more of an irritant than a threat.

To Captain Yun he represented a challenge to his authority. Yun would see this as a game. He wanted Lyons dead, and would be delighted if he was the one who pulled the trigger. Their relationship had been brief, but in that short time the lines had been drawn. In many respects they were alike. Neither would give an inch. Each had his own agenda. Yun's was to take down this foreigner who had stood up in front of the entire prison camp and defied him. Lyons was a little more practical. He just wanted to stay alive and return home. If he was forced to fight for that right, he would do it without a second's hesitation.

Lyons kept on his course, head down to avoid the sting of the cold rain that was starting to turn to tiny ice crystals on his clothing. He could feel the beard on his face starting to ice up. The cold penetrated his clothing, and he could feel the material beginning to stiffen. His arms held tight against his chest, covering the AK. He didn't want the weapon freezing up and refusing to fire if the need arose.

The ground underfoot was turning harder with the passing of time. The thin ice forming on the surface made walking difficult, and Lyons stumbled more than once. Other times he fell, bruising his already battered body. Each time he struggled to his feet again, fighting against the voice inside his head that insisted he stay down. He lurched upright, muscles screaming against the strain, pushing forward, into the darkness, concentrating on staying on his feet, cursing himself for his weakness, and sometimes just letting his inner rage come out in a muttered monotone. He couldn't recall what he said, didn't even know at the time he uttered the garbled litany. His mind was separate from his actions, a tiny flame of intelligence that struggled with itself, part wanting him to quit, the other resisting because he was Carl Lyons and it had no intention of giving in.

He struggled up some long slope, reaching a straggling line of skeletal trees. The bare limbs flailed in the wind, making a hissing sound, and Lyons stopped in their meager shelter for a time. He leaned against one twisted trunk, letting its solid form support him. The moment he started to feel comfortable, he pushed himself away from the tree and stumbled on. He followed the rim of the slope for a way, then started down the far side. The way was steep and rough. Lyons fell a number of times, crashing through the brush, scraping his hands and face against the thorny foliage.

He was on his knees, slitted eyes peering through the shadows. He made out the outline of what he thought might be a building. He couldn't be sure. Blinking against the rain that stung his eyes, he stared at the object. The brief gleam of a light showed, then vanished. Lyons decided he had been imagining it. There was nothing there. Only the night and freezing rain.

He regained his feet again, still hugging the rifle

hard against his body, and moved on. He walked maybe twenty feet before his feet became entangled in something and he fell forward, crashing against something that splintered under his weight. Lyons hit the ground with a jarring thump. His head smacked against the earth, and the impact stunned him. He felt the AK spill from his frozen fingers. He made a feeble attempt to find it, but the weapon was lost in the darkness. He tasted blood in his mouth where he had banged it when he fell.

Lyons fought to get up, pressing his hands against the ground, but this time even his iron will failed him. The strength was gone. He sank back to the ground, rolling on his back. He lay staring up at the cloud-heavy sky, feeling the bitter rain on his face.

Shadows moved in, covering him. Lyons had the sensation of floating. The dark night sky turned above him, shadows flitting back and forth. There was a swirl of soft light, a wash of comforting heat that drew him to its source. He yelled, but there was no sound. He tried to move his arms and legs, but they refused to respond. He didn't understand what was happening. The sensation rose and covered him, shutting out everything except the warmth and the soft light, and Carl Lyons knew no more.

## CHAPTER FIFTEEN

David McCarter worked his way out of his sleeping bag, feeling the bitter cold strike through his clothing. It was still dark, the sky heavy with clouds that held back much of the light from the moon. There was enough to give him a chance to see what lay ahead of them. He pushed to his feet, arching his back to loosen stiff muscles. Moving away from the overhang he stepped into the open, feeling the bite of the wind against his face. It took a moment for him to realize that the rain had stopped. The temperature had plummeted while they slept, so they still had that to face.

He stood beside a twisted tree, its branches dragging on the ground, and stared across the undulating terrain. Ahead of where they had chosen to rest, the land started to rise in a series of jagged hills to a low mountain range. To McCarter the landscape looked hostile. It was as simple as that. He wasn't impressed with this part of North Korea at all. Not that Phoenix Force ever had much choice of locations. They went where the mission dictated, and more often than not the places they conducted their business weren't on the tourist maps.

McCarter turned to wake the rest of the team. They shrugged off sleep and quickly packed away sleeping bags and any other equipment they had used. With their backpacks in place and weapons checked, Phoenix Force prepared for the upcoming phase of its mission.

"You had any more thoughts about contacting Stony Man?" Manning asked.

McCarter nodded. "The Koreans know we were in the area. So we're not exactly going to tell them anything they don't know."

He had taken the cell phone from his backpack. McCarter slid it from the protective case and switched on the power. The phone had been fully charged before they left Stony Man, and the level showed high when McCarter checked it.

"Here goes nothing," he murmured as he pressed the speed-dial Stony Man number that was an encoded feature of the phone. He listened as the soft electronic feedback told him the signal was being sent to the orbiting communications satellite. There was a long pause as the number was accepted, then transferred to the distant locator. Moments later McCarter heard the connection ringing. The receiver at the other end was picked up and Barbara Price's familiar tones reached him.

"Phoenix calling home," McCarter said.

"You guys okay? We were starting to worry."

"That's nice to know. Things got a little messy out here. Our contact was caught. We're having to find our own way. We need some feedback. Satellite surveillance."

"We'll come back to you."

"Let our taxi know we may be delayed, but we still need him."

"Got you."

McCarter cut the call and put the cell phone on stand by.

"Short and sweet," James said.

"Let's hope it gets us what we want," McCarter said. "Saddle up, mates, it's time to go."

James took the point, the others falling in line behind. They moved out from their cover and began the trek that would bring them to the missile site. There were at least three hours left before the light began to intrude. If they were able to use that time effectively, they would be a great deal closer to their target by dawn.

*Sea of Japan*

THE MOMENT HE RECEIVED the call from Stony Man, Jack Grimaldi informed Blancanales and Schwarz. He found them in the cabin that had been assigned them while they were on board. The Able Team duo took the news calmly. There was one question that had to be asked, and it was Blancanales who voiced it.

"Anything about Carl?"

Grimaldi dragged off his baseball cap, running a hand through his thick hair.

"Stony Man didn't mention him. Look, guys, Phoenix has been on the move since they hit North

Korea. With their contact being taken out of the picture, they're on their own out there.''

''I guess,'' Blancanales said.

''We haven't given up on him yet, Pol,'' Schwarz said.

''None of us have,'' Grimaldi added.

Blancanales acknowledged what they said. Inside he was still angry. Mainly because there was nothing he could do to save his friend. He had to sit out his time on this multimillion dollar warship, equipped with all kinds of weaponry and technical gizmos, while Carl Lyons remained in captivity somewhere in North Korea. If Blancanales had his way, the whole of the carrier's hardware would have been directed at the country. He knew it was an irrational thought the moment he created it, but right there and then he didn't give a damn. Blancanales would have done anything to get Lyons back.

Anything?

He leaned against the bulkhead, staring into the distance as he reconsidered his wild thoughts. No matter how he felt about Carl Lyons, there was no profit in allowing his deep feelings to push him off track. That wouldn't do anyone any good, least of all Lyons. He had to maintain his objectivity. There were bigger things at stake, and they took priority over everything else. Until the mission itself had been resolved there wasn't going to be much to be done about Lyons.

''So we wait?'' he asked. ''Nothing we can do to help the guys?''

''Not until they activate their signal device,'' Grimaldi said. "Our job is to extract them once the mission is complete. Or unless they have to abort."

"Let's hope it doesn't come to that," Schwarz said.

"Is that North Korean ship still tailing us?" Blancanales asked.

"She's still around," Grimaldi said. "Damn thing's like a bug you can't swat."

Schwarz stood and pulled on his weatherproof jacket.

"I'm going to take a walk topside."

"Hey, no shouting rude words at the Koreans," Blancanales said.

"As if," Schwarz said, and left.

"Jack, how do you rate this?" Blancanales asked.

"I reckon the guys are going to have one hell of a fight on their hands once they reach that site. With all respect to Stony Man, the best high-tech backup in the world isn't going to be much use in the middle of a down-and-dirty firefight. And that's what it's going to be, Pol."

*North Korea*

YUN ROSE EARLY. He washed and dressed, then made his way to the control room. He found Took already there, talking to Chin. The only one missing was Gagarin.

"How is Berkoff progressing?" Yun asked.

"Better than expected," Chin said. "He completed the first phase of his diagnostic checks an hour ago.

Everything appears to be fine. He's resting now. He will move to the next operation once he returns.''

Yun ordered one of the privates to bring him food and a hot drink. While he waited he spoke with his sergeant, giving the man his orders for the troops.

"So, Yun, will you have more success today?" Chin asked.

"I hope so," the Korean replied. "The weather has settled, according to my sergeant. If that is the case, we will have better visibility. Clearer weather will also make it harder for the Americans to hide. Hopefully we will have them in our hands before nightfall.''

Took cleared his throat. "Does that include our escaped prisoner, too, Yun?''

"I hope so," Yun said. "I certainly hope so.''

HE WOKE SUDDENLY. Momentary panic had him back in his cell. The stone walls closing in on him. Someone banging on the locked door.

Lyons opened his eyes. He was lying down, staring up at an angled roof that was constructed from wood. He wasn't back in his cell, nor was he in the crude hut at the labor camp.

So where was he?

He sat up. Too quickly and he flopped back as a feeling of giddiness washed over him. He lay still, waiting until his senses had calmed down. Now he could smell something. Food. Maybe even the distinct odor of tea. There were sounds, too. Nothing alarming. Simply the noise made by someone moving around. The rattle of utensils.

When Lyons moved the second time, he did it slowly, raising himself to a sitting position. He was lying on a thin mattress, covered by blankets. He was warm and dry. There was a certain degree of stiffness in his joints and the odd ache. He recalled his journey through the freezing night. The times he had fallen, his body bruised and scraped from his contact with the hard ground.

And then...?

How had he gotten here? To this place?

He stared around. The interior of the dwelling was sparse by his standards. A wooden house, equipped with a smooth wooden floor. Little furniture apart from a low table and some random items for storage. On one wall was a large framed photograph of the Korean leader, smiling down with a benevolent expression. Here and there touches of color from decorations hanging from the rafters.

Movement caught Lyons's eye. He turned and came face-to-face with the old man. Small and lean, dressed in baggy gray pants and a dark tunic, soft-soled shoes on his feet. The Korean studied Lyons, his bright, dark eyes darting back and forth as he looked the American over. Lyons couldn't work out the man's age. His brown face was lined, his thinning hair graying. He could have been anything between sixty and ninety years old.

The Korean had a bowl in his hands, which he held out to Lyons. There was steam rising from the bowl. Lyons took it. It held some kind of meat-and-noodle mixture, and to Lyons's empty stomach it smelled good. The Korean handed him a wooden spoon. Lyons took it and began to eat. He was so immersed in eating that he didn't realize the Korean had remained watching him, only now he had squatted on his heels, bringing him to the same level as Lyons. When Lyons raised his eyes to look at him, the Korean inclined his head and smiled approvingly. He gestured with his bony hands for Lyons to keep on eating. When Lyons finished the contents of the bowl, the Korean stood and moved to the far side of the hut, bending over what Lyons took to be the cooking stove. He returned with another dish. This contained steaming rolls of vegetables and chopped meat wrapped in thin casings. They were spiced and hot enough to scald Lyons's fingers. He ate them carefully. The Korean nodded, then brought Lyons a delicate china cup holding hot tea. It was faintly perfumed. The Korean brought himself a cup of the tea and he squatted again.

Lyons held the cup and gestured at the Korean.

"Good," he said. "Good."

The Korean replied at length. Lyons nodded his own head and repeated his earlier "good." He was trying to figure why the Korean had helped him. Why had he plucked Lyons from the dark night and brought him here? The reason became apparent when the Korean pointed to the clothing Lyons was wearing.

He touched the padded coat and the pants, making disapproving gestures with his hands. He spoke again, then realized there was no understanding. He went away and came back with a piece of rough paper and a stick of charcoal. Placing the paper on the floor, he began to draw something. Lyons watched, fascinated. When he had finished, the Korean lifted the paper and showed it to Lyons.

The Korean had sketched a crude illustration. Despite that, Lyons recognized the guard towers and the high fences. It was a drawing of the labor camp. The Korean had even managed to draw the huts and stick figures of prisoners. There were armed guards and skeletal dogs.

The Korean touched the drawing, then pointed his finger at Lyons, who nodded.

"Yes. I was in there."

Lyons repeated the gesture, touching himself then the drawing. He waved his hands in front of the drawing, shaking his head.

The Korean indicated the drawing and then touched his thin chest. He repeated the gesture, but Lyons knew what he was saying. The Korean had been in the camp himself.

"Bad place," Lyons said.

The tone of his words translated themselves for the Korean. He spoke in his own language, the strength of his feelings coming through.

They drank more tea. As they sat there, daylight began to penetrate the cracks in the walls. The Korean went around and blew out the lamps that had provided light during the darkness. He beckoned Lyons to join him, and they squatted together in front of the small stove that provided heat and cooking facilities. The stove burned wood, and the Korean placed more logs on it. Soon the heat reached out and filled the hut with its warmth.

Carl Lyons might never have realized the comfort to be obtained from such a simple pleasure if he hadn't experienced the harshness of captivity. It was only as the heat from the simple stove wrapped itself around him that he realized he had almost forgotten what it meant to be warm. He had become accustomed to the cold and the lack of amenities. They had become the norm. His body had adjusted to the severe conditions to the point where it hadn't mattered any longer. Being cold and wet, half-starved and subjected to brutal treatment had been his world. Now that he had removed himself from the environment, Lyons could see how easily he might have become like Rinaldi. So used to the regime that nothing else mattered. The will to return to his former life might have withered away, turning him into one of the shuffling prisoners he shared the camp with.

At least now he could make his own choices.

Even though, brought down to basics, those choices comprised little more than fight or die.

Not that such a choice was too bad. Carl Lyons liked life to be uncomplicated, and with something like fight or die, he recognized his options and could go straight to the game.

## CHAPTER SIXTEEN

The Phoenix Force commandos made their contact earlier than they might have anticipated. It was almost full light. The last shadows were shrinking, allowing the team to observe its surroundings. During the last few hours before dawn, they had moved on a steady course in the direction of the missile site. Their trek took them along the rugged foothills of the mountain range McCarter had seen. They moved through a series of deep gorges, with the near vertical rock faces rising on either side. The foothills resembled sharp sawtooths, jagged serrations with clumps of trees and foliage clinging precariously to the formations. The ground underfoot was difficult to cross in some areas, with loose rock hidden beneath grassy coverings. Streams, full from the recent rain, foamed and rushed between the rock faces.

The Stony Man commandos were moving in line ahead, each man assigned to a different viewpoint to give them as much coverage as possible. They were moving through terrain that gave all the advantage to the hunters rather than the hunted. The landscape offered an endless selection of cover. A soldier could have been hiding behind any one of a hundred places and remained unseen until the last possible moment. The team was aware of that, but there was little they could do. They were four, and it restricted their ability to do more than make a cursory check of the terrain before they moved on.

McCarter wasn't happy about the situation. Both from the way it left them exposed, and also because he was unable to do a damn thing about it. Being in control of the situation was always preferable, but there were times when circumstances prevented that. This was one of those times.

Their predawn move had brought them much closer to their target. McCarter was hoping they had gotten within the search perimeter and that the search parties were beyond them now, spreading across a wider section of territory. He could have been wrong. For all they knew, the Koreans might have worked out that theory and were keeping their people closer to home.

He didn't let the negative thoughts hold him back. McCarter wasn't one for dwelling on depressing thoughts for long. He much preferred to stay optimistic until proved wrong.

As with many combat situations, matters were in a fluid state, with sudden and dramatic changes liable to occur within a heartbeat.

Phoenix Force was just moving across a wide stream, heading for the far bank, when a loose formation of Korean troops came over the top of the slope that bordered the stream. The Koreans were talking among themselves, almost casual in their manner. A number of them were carrying canteens in their hands, ready to fill them from the stream. Only two out of the six-man squad had their rifles in their hands.

One of them began shouting, bringing his AK into firing position. He triggered shots in Phoenix Force's general direction, his bullets kicking up geysers of water from the stream.

In the split second of recognition between the two groups, Calvin James, in the point position, pulled his M-16 to his shoulder and returned fire. He directed his shots at the Korean who had opened fire, taking out the man. The Korean stumbled as the 5.56 mm round burst through his chest. He tumbled down the slope, ending up in the icy water of the stream. Before the first man hit the water, James had triggered twice more, catching his second target as the man put his AK to his shoulder.

Close on James's reaction the others brought their own weapons on line.

Manning saw one of the Koreans reaching for a radio slung from his shoulder by a leather strap. The man was attempting to call in that they had encountered the invaders. The Canadian snapped his own AK to his shoulder and hit the Korean with three fast shots. The soldier staggered under impact of the bullets, his chest erupting bloody fragments. He fell facedown, his body slack, and Manning knew the man wasn't going to get up again.

McCarter and Encizo took on the three remaining Koreans, crouching in midstream as the trio scrambled for their slung weapons and opened fire. The

Phoenix Force pair traded a brief flurry of shots that ended with the Koreans down on the slope. As the sound of the firefight drifted away, the team remained on alert in case there were any other Korean troops in the vicinity.

"Rafe, go take a look over that slope," McCarter said. "Gary, check our back trail."

The pair moved off, leaving McCarter and James to check out the casualties. The Koreans had all taken fatal shots. It was a testament to the instinctive response Phoenix Force had made under fire. They took that extra moment to gain target acquisition rather than let loose with random fire. It made the difference.

James searched each body for additional magazines for the AKs they carried themselves. There were enough for a couple of extras for each of them.

"What we really need to know is if this was an isolated patrol, or whether they're part of a larger group," McCarter said. "Either way we need to get the hell away from here before their mates come over the next hill."

"Maybe we'll find out," James said as Manning appeared and made his way toward them.

"Couldn't see any other movement," Manning reported. "Doesn't mean there aren't more hiding behind every rock."

He took the additional magazines James handed him.

Encizo pushed through a clump of thorny growth, shouldering his M-16.

"Another group," he said. "Too far away to

have heard the shooting. And they are moving away from us.''

"Good," McCarter said. "So we might still get the chance to reach the site while the main force is out looking for us.''

They moved off, picking up their original line of travel.

As the day brightened around them, the persistent cold remained. Every breath they took hung in the frosty air. The chill air stung their skin. There was no relief from the harshness of the Korean climate. Their only defense was to keep moving to maintain the body temperature and not allow the cold to slow them.

Over the next hour Phoenix Force kept a steady pace. The only difficulty they faced was the dramatic nature of the landscape. The undulations and the deep fissures. The steep drops and the sheerness of the rock formations that made up the foothills of the mountain range. On a number of occasions they were forced to backtrack and find a fresh approach to some barrier, simply due to the fact that it would have been impossible to climb.

Reaching a high point, they took the opportunity to both rest and take a long look across the terrain ahead. It was during this break that McCarter's cell phone began to vibrate. He took it from his pocket and heard Barbara Price's voice.

"Satellite scans of the area show some activity in a number of areas around this new site. Look like troop movements. Some vehicular traffic. They seem to be concentrating in specific sections moving away from the site.''

''Any assessment on the site itself?''

''Work is still going on.''

''Did you pass my message to taxi driver?''

''Yes. He understands the situation and can't wait to hear from you.''

McCarter smiled. ''I'll bet. Come back if you come up with anything else.''

Manning, using a pair of small, powerful binoculars he'd carried in his pack, took the opportunity of making an all-points check of the surrounding landscape. He did isolate some movement off to the west. Focusing in, he sharpened the image and watched a patrol of eight to ten armed soldiers covering the ground slowly as they searched. His observation had the group moving in a westerly direction. As he made his directional checks he saw a smaller patrol, five men and a small vehicle, off to the south. His check of the north and east produced nothing. He spent more time checking those areas, again coming up empty.

''It's almost like they're doing exactly what we want them to,'' the Canadian said to McCarter. ''There's something odd about it, David. I don't like it when things run to pattern. Especially when that pattern is pretty well off the wall.''

''Give me the glasses,'' McCarter said, and took a look himself.

He watched the distant figures as they moved across the landscape. As he watched, the patrol changed direction and McCarter realized they were coming around to the north. A quick check of the other patrol confirmed what he had already noticed. This patrol was making a wide loop that would eventually turn them north, as well.

"Maybe we were too bloody clever," he said. McCarter slid down the bank, evaluating what he had just witnessed. "The crafty sods are coming in behind us. Heading north the same as we are."

"You think they've spotted us?" James asked.

"No. I think whoever is controlling these people has figured out what we're up to. And he's closing the gate behind us. Looks like we're all heading for the site now."

"And there I was thinking it was getting to be a drag," James said.

McCarter pushed to his feet. "Time we upped the pace. We need to hit that site before the whole of that search party gets back."

CAPTAIN YUN COMPLETED his round of contacting the separate groups. They had reached the limit of the outer search, and Yun had brought them all into line. His final order had been for them to change direction and head north. In the direction of the site. Since he had led his troops out from the site during the final hours of darkness, his mind had been playing strategy games as he tried to put himself in the position of the Americans.

Their objective was the site. It had to be. The computer disks Took guarded so zealously were the prize in this game. However they achieved it, the Americans wanted those disks. They would make an attempt to locate and destroy them. Of that he had no doubt. Yun wanted to catch them before they reached the site. There was too much at stake if they actually gained entry to the site and reached the underground complex. A firefight down below would be catastrophic. There was too much electronic equipment that might easily be destroyed if the Americans took the fight into the complex. There was too much at stake to let that happen. The Americans had to be stopped out here. If a confrontation took place in this open landscape, the effects wouldn't touch the site and Took's precious missile and computer complex would remain unharmed.

The time and effort, not to mention the cost, of the complex was a massive investment for the Korean administration. Its sole purpose was to eliminate the American Slingshot system. If they succeeded, then Korea would stand head and shoulders above the entire region. Her status would leap to the top, and the states that had bought her missiles before would now have no reason to hold back from purchasing the latest in ballistic technology. With the U.S. shield taken down, the Americans would have to back away from making any further threats, or sending in their military where it wasn't wanted. Slingshot, already creating a great deal of unrest around the world, would be destroyed by the Korean missiles before it actually came on-line. That destruction would bring sighs of relief from millions. It would also show how advanced the Koreans were in being able to launch and deploy her missiles in space. The only matter needing to be resolved was the breaking of the encryption code on the disks. Once Berkoff had achieved that, there was nothing to stop the strike against the American satellites.

Nothing apart from the American strike force running free somewhere in the area. They presented a genuine threat to the continuation of the project. *If* they did manage to breach the security around the site and get to the computer facility, there was a chance they could succeed. Yun wasn't naive enough to believe it couldn't happen. It was unlikely, but then Yat Sen Took had believed his nuclear weapon would destroy the American radar site in Alaska and had been proved wrong. Every situation had its negative side. It was foolish to see only the one you wanted. Closing your eyes to the negative wasn't the answer. Admitting there was an alternative scenario to every action kept the senses alert. Shutting them down because one refused to see the other argument was the act of a foolish person. As much as he wanted to defeat the Americans, Yun also accepted that he might not stop them—which only made him more determined.

AS THE MORNING WORE ON, Lyons became more restless. He had found the AK, which the Korean had wiped dry and hung from a wooden peg on the wall. Taking the weapon, Lyons stripped and cleaned it. The Korean watched with great interest, his bright eyes following Lyons's every move. Later he removed himself to the stove and made more tea for them. They squatted on the floor and drank it like two old friends, despite being unable to converse because of their different languages.

Lyons wanted to show his gratitude to the Korean. If the man hadn't heard him floundering around in the darkness and brought him inside the hut, Lyons might have died. The fact hadn't escaped the American, and he realized he had been lucky both for being found, and also fortunate to have been discovered by an ex-prisoner who understood his need to escape. The problem, as before, was the lack of communication.

Lyons took his time preparing to leave. Only when he was ready did he turn to the Korean and hold out his hand. The Korean stared at it, then reached out himself. His thin hand was swamped by Lyons's larger one.

"Thanks," Lyons said. There was nothing else he could say.

The Korean bobbed his head and pumped Lyons's hand.

*"Annyŏnghi kaseyo."*

Was it good luck? Goodbye? Lyons had no idea, but he sensed the Korean's gentle tone and took the expression as one of concern.

*"Annyŏnghi kaseyo,"* he repeated, and the Korean smiled.

Lyons had watched the sunrise from the door of the hut earlier, establishing directions, and he began to move east as he left the hut and climbed the slope that would set him on his way.

When he reached the top of the slope, checking

that there were no hostiles in the vicinity, he turned to take a final look at the hut.

The Korean was still there, and he raised a hand in a final wave when Lyons did turn. He returned the gesture.

*Annyŏnghi kaseyo.*

He would find out what that meant when he got back. It was important to him that he did.

# CHAPTER SEVENTEEN

Duong Chin stood watching as his helicopter touched down. The hatch slid open, and six dark-clad Chinese stepped out and crossed over to join him. These were operatives from his covert squad, highly trained men he had chosen himself from the Chinese military. He trusted these six more than he would have trusted the entire North Korean army, though that particular thought was something he kept entirely to himself.

"Belowground is the complex where this site is run," Chin explained to his group. "You all understand why we want this project to work?"

"Yes, sir. If the American satellite system is put out of action, it restricts their missile capability."

"Simply put but adequate, Lim. There's a great deal more to this. Political, as well as strategic. Suffice it to say anything that weakens the American military function can only be good for us."

"Orders, sir?" Lim asked.

"Say little to these people. Understand that the Koreans are bordering on the paranoid. They regard most things as being a direct threat to them. I have explained that you are here to protect Berkoff above everything. Not that it isn't true. But I want you around if these damn Americans show up. This Captain Yun doesn't inspire me too much. The man has his troops running around the countryside looking for this American group. Up to now they haven't found a thing. Actually that is not accurate. They have found the helicopter the Americans stole to fly here.''

Lim smiled. ''We understand, sir.''

He looked around the site, assessing the area.

''Plenty of cover for a team once they get inside the perimeter.''

''Too much cover for my liking,'' Chin agreed. ''I'll take you inside. Remember, you are here to watch over Berkoff. Be polite. Be respectful of our Korean brothers in arms. Above all, keep alert.''

''We heard that Gagarin is here,'' Lim said.

Chin smiled. ''Yes, he's here. The Russians he is working with have similar feelings to ours for once. Slingshot would place the Americans in a position of power that would not go down too well. The Russians have enough internal problems without the Americans being able to lord it over them. Also Gagarin has a personal need to become involved with the demise of these Americans. They embarrassed him over the Alaskan project.''

''With the militia group?''

''Yes. That was a mess. Too many chiefs and not enough Indians, I believe our colorful American friends would say. These matters are best dealt with by those who have a sympathetic understanding of the overall problem.''

Chin led his group underground. They located Yat

Sen Took, and Chin made his low-key introductions. Took watched as the Chinese took their places outside the room where Berkoff was working.

"Thank you for allowing me to provide this additional protection. Understand, Took, that we have invested a great deal in bringing Berkoff here. My concern is for his safety in case the Americans breach the site. Hopefully Captain Yun will apprehend them long be fore that happens. If not, we can't risk Berkoff being disturbed. Even killed."

"Yun does not have the same attitude," Took said. "He is a soldier and he thinks like one. The escape of his American prisoner is also on his mind. It may distract him. Something that should not happen at a time like this."

"Exactly, my friend. My people will look after Berkoff. Their thoughts will not be interrupted by anything else."

Chin entered the room where Berkoff had established himself. The German was sitting at the main desk, watching data scroll across one of his monitors. He glanced up as Chin appeared.

"To save you asking, I have had a slight delay. One of the hard drives displayed an error, so I had to replace it. Which meant I needed to reload a section of the system data. It set me back about four hours. Nothing to be concerned about."

Chin smiled. "Jerome, when you are involved in anything, I don't worry. You have never let me down before. Why should it be any different this time?"

Berkoff gave the Chinese a long look. "If I didn't

know you better, Chin, I would have to take that as a compliment.''

''I must watch what I say, then. You will start to believe I have gone soft.''

''So how are things in the real world?'' Berkoff asked.

''A little unsettled,'' Chin said. ''Our Korean friends are having some local difficulty with this team of Americans they believe are here to neutralize this site. Which is why I have brought in some of my people to make sure you are not disturbed.''

''Concern for my safety, too. Or are you just protecting your investment?''

''Jerome, are you trying to make a point? Have I ever done anything to make you believe your safety does not come first?''

''Ever the professional, Chin.''

Berkoff turned back to his monitor as a soft beep alerted him. He tapped in instructions, and the screen showed lines of machine code.

''Good. The configuration is nearing completion. As soon as that has completed, I will be ready to start looking at those disks.''

''And?''

''And then the real work begins. Chin, when I begin looking at the encryption, there must be no disturbances. I need to concentrate fully. No visitors. No interruptions. If I make the slightest mistake, the disks will corrupt. Make all your people understand. I get one chance at this.''

Chin nodded. ''I will make sure everyone is informed. If anyone disobeys, I will shoot him myself.''

Berkoff knew Chin well enough to realize the man was serious.

"If you do, make sure you use a silencer," Berkoff said. "Gunshots make me very nervous."

"Jerome, inform me the moment you require isolation," Chin said, and left the German to his work.

Outside Chin had a brief word with his people. They had stationed themselves near the door of Berkoff's room and along the passage in both directions. He moved on to the control room, where he found Gagarin studying the monitor screens fed from the outside cameras. The Russian was checking each screen thoroughly, leaning over the shoulders of the Korean operatives.

"Looking for something in particular?" Chin asked.

Gagarin glanced around. "I was just confirming something."

"Yes?"

"This whole site is a mess," the Russian said. "Piles of building materials. Mounds of earth. Equipment. Storage tanks. Ideal for a small team of infiltrators. Plenty of cover for them."

"True."

"Does Took understand this? Or Yun?"

Chin shrugged. "Took is not a soldier. He is more of an administrator. His skill lies with missiles and guidance systems. Nuclear weaponry. Look at the foolishness with the American prisoner. He should have executed the man the moment he took him pris-

oner. Did he really believe the man was the head of
the CIA or something equally bizarre? People like
that do not venture into the field.''

''I think Took became a little too involved with
him. He convinced himself the man had valuable information locked away inside his head. And I think
he wanted some kind of revenge for his injury. There
was little I could do as a guest. So I allowed him his
fantasy. My main interest, as it still is, was in the
American strike force. I knew they would come after
the Alaskan fiasco. Once the Americans discovered
that the disks had been passed to the Koreans, they
had to make an attempt at retrieving or destroying
them. And that would give us the chance to destroy
*them* once and for all.''

''Until Captain Yun became involved,'' Chin said.

Gagarin smiled. ''We shouldn't be too hard on
Yun. He is doing what he was trained for. Unfortunately he fails to understand how these Americans
work. They are not a squad of soldiers who obey
direct orders and follow a man in charge. These men
are seasoned in combat of all kinds. Evasion is second nature to them. And they are capable of great
improvisation. Look what happened when Took captured them. They escaped. Then they commandeered
a helicopter and used it to bring them closer to this
place. Yun sees them simply as an objective to be
surrounded and destroyed. While he is conducting his
maneuvers, the Americans will be moving around
him and getting ever closer to the site.''

''So we must be ready for them,'' Chin said.

''Yes,'' Gagarin agreed.

MIDMORNING.

The weather was holding. Still extremely cold, but no more rain. The sky was a pale ice blue, with a few scrappy white clouds. The cold air was sharp and clear, and a strong breeze moved across the landscape.

Phoenix Force was still skirting the foothills. The mountains rising to their left and ahead had white snow on their higher slopes and peaks. The mountain range was indicated on McCarter's map, and it told him they were still moving in the right direction. The ground underfoot was rough and made walking difficult for prolonged periods. Added to that the team was constantly on the lookout for any of the Korean search force.

They had spotted only one more group, a good way off and moving toward higher ground. McCarter ordered his teammates to cover, and they stayed until the patrol had vanished from sight.

At least an hour had passed since that moment, and Phoenix Force had been moving ever since. McCarter glanced at his watch and called a halt.

"Ten minutes. Whose turn is it to stand watch?"

"Yours," Manning said.

McCarter pulled a face. "You sure?"

James and Encizo joined Manning and they chorused a "Yes."

"You buggers ganging up on me again?" the Briton asked.

"Yes, sir." Encizo grinned.

McCarter moved to a position where he had a clear field of vision. He laid his AK on top of a rock and unclipped his canteen. Taking a slow swallow, rinsed his mouth and spit out the water, then he took a small gulp of the water, which had remained cold due to the low temperature.

The Briton hung his canteen back on his belt and picked up his rifle again. Settling with his back to a rock, McCarter assumed his position and scanned the surrounding terrain. He was looking for anything, visual or otherwise, that might suggest they weren't alone. It didn't have to be extreme, just a telltale sign of the presence of others.

There were countless ways the opposition might give themselves away. Sometimes nothing more than a faint sound. The chink of equipment on rock. The rustle of clothing. The click as someone eased off a safety or drew back a cocking bolt. Close examination of the ground could give away the fact that someone had passed by recently. The scuff mark left by a boot sole on a clean rock surface. Perhaps a damp boot print because the owner had recently walked through water, or over wet earth. There were more obvious signs. A cigarette butt thrown down and left still smoking. Traces of food.

If the Koreans *had* been here, they had moved on without leaving a single trace of their former presence.

McCarter stirred restlessly. What the hell was he doing wasting time and effort on what might or might not have been? The Koreans probably hadn't been anywhere near this damn place. It was time to get moving again. To give his mind something more constructive to deal with, he glanced at his watch. Four minutes to go. He could have started the others off now, but he had promised them ten minutes. They deserved the break.

He turned his attention to the sky, watching the clouds drift by. McCarter looked north. Far off he could see a bank of darker cloud. They were still in the far distance. He judged they would be overhead by nightfall. Maybe another storm. More snow? Rain? He really didn't want to find out.

*Stony Man Farm, Virginia*

"WEATHER'S MOVING IN on them again," Carmen Delahunt said.

On her monitor the satellite weather scan showed cloud banks moving down from the Chinese–North Korean border area.

"Looks like more strong wind and rain," Delahunt added. She captured the image and recorded it, printing off the data.

Price crossed over and took the printout. She picked up one of the Computer Room phones and hit the speed dial for McCarter's cell phone. When he came on, she reported the forecast.

"I've been doing some amateur weather forecasting myself," he replied.

"How is it at the moment?"

"I think the expression 'bloody freezing' covers it," McCarter said.

"I wish we could give you better news. And backup."

"Don't make it too easy for us, Barb. Thanks for the update. Time we moved on."

"Getting close?"

"Close enough."

McCarter put the phone away. He stared at the compact instrument. Here they were in the wilds of North Korea, and he was able to speak to Stony Man as if they were behind the next rock. Somewhere overhead, in the bleak chill of space, a silent satellite moving in its orbit was the link between Phoenix Force in the field and their command center nestling in the mountains of Virginia. For a few seconds it made McCarter feel isolated and lost. He shrugged off the sensation, squaring his shoulders as he pushed away from his resting place and turned to rouse the rest of his team.

*U.S. Navy Carrier, Sea of Japan*

"JUST THOUGHT YOU'D LIKE to know our escort is still around," the captain informed Grimaldi.

"I don't really need to know that."

"I've been giving it some thought," the captain said. "Maybe we can do something when you get your call. I've been thinking about it, talking it over with my guys. What you need is some kind of diversion. Something to make the Koreans look the other way."

"It would be handy," Grimaldi said.

The captain grinned. "And would give my crew something to do. They've been lazing around for too long. Leave it to the Navy, Mr. Pierce. We'll figure something out for you.''

''Thanks,'' Grimaldi said.

''No sweat. You just give me the call when you're ready to rock and roll. We'll do the rest.''

### North Korea

LYONS WAS TRYING to keep on the move. As time wore on, he completed his plan of action. If he kept on moving east, he would eventually reach the coast. Once he had the sea in front of him, he would look for a boat. If he could steal something substantial, he might be able to make for Japan. He wasn't sure how far it was to the coast, but as long as he actually had a destination in mind it gave purpose to his situation. However long it took didn't matter. Just as long as he made it in the end. One way or another Lyons had to get out of the country. He had no intention of dying there.

He recalled his promise to Captain Yun—that if they ever crossed paths once Lyons escaped, he would kill the man. The Able Team leader hadn't forgotten that, and as much as he would have liked to have kept that promise, he decided he would forgo the pleasure if denying it to himself allowed him to escape from North Korea. He figured he couldn't have everything.

Toward noon he found himself in the shadow of a mountain range, with jagged foothills spreading across the way he was moving. Lyons followed the foothills, aware that the striations of rock and the wiry vegetation spreading around him would offer cover if the need arose.

That need came when he heard the rumble of a truck. He clambered over jumbles of shattered rocks that had slid down the slopes at some time past. Dragging himself into the closest hollow between the rocks, he listened for the approaching vehicle.

It came in from his right, a truck similar in design to the ones he had been transported in lately. There were two uniformed soldiers in the cab and five more on the open flatbed behind. It rumbled by him, swaying on weak springs as it bumped its way over the rough ground. As it passed, Lyons could even hear the squad riding in back talking. He leaned out as it moved away, his AK ready in his hands. Smoke trailed from the exhaust, drifting in the wind. The truck peaked a slope and vanished down the other side. Lyons waited as the sound of the engine began to fade. Then he heard the brakes groan.

The first thing he thought was that they had spotted him and were jumping off the truck to search for him. He dismissed that notion. They hadn't seen him. His place of concealment had been too good for them to have noticed him in passing. If they had, the chattering soldiers would have given themselves away. They weren't that good as actors.

Using the rock formation as cover, Lyons moved up the slope until he reached the top, where he was able to see the truck and the soldiers who had been riding on it.

They were moving ahead of the vehicle, spreading out as they sought cover of their own in the rocks and foliage. As Lyons watched, he saw the soldiers checking their weapons and adjusting them for range. The man in charge was giving orders. One of the North Koreans had a Chinese Type 56 rocket launcher, and a number of spare missiles were laid out on the ground beside him.

Lyons's curiosity was aroused by the identity of the enemy the North Koreans were preparing to confront. He checked out the area around him and saw a way up the slope that would still keep him from being seen by the Koreans. He eased to the left of his position and started up the slope. He found the going hard and began to realize he was weaker than he might have admitted. His recent incarceration and treatment had depleted some of his strength. The knowledge only made him more determined to push on.

As he climbed the slope, Lyons's mind was focusing on who the North Korean's enemy might be. South Koreans? An antigovernment group? His train of thought ran along the lines of if they were enemies of North Korea, then maybe they could be *his* friends. It was illogical in a way, but at that point in his life Carl Lyons needed friends. He was loath to admit the fact, but if he could make contact with someone able to help him out of this country, he didn't really care who they were.

He reached a point that placed him well above the waiting North Koreans. Easing to the lip of a ledge, Lyons was able to look downslope and to the undulating terrain beyond.

He saw a small group moving single file out of a

section of the foothills. He counted four in number. He was able to make out the camou clothing they wore and the fact they were well armed. They had their backs to him, so he was unable to get any suggestion of who they were.

Lyons turned to check the Koreans and saw they were, to a man, bringing their rifles into target acquisition. Even the man with the rocket launcher was lining up his weapon.

Something caught Lyons's eye. He took a fleeting moment to check what had attracted him, unsure at first why he was interested. Then he realized what it was. The man walking point was taller than any Korean that Lyons had ever seen. So was one of the others in the group. The other two, while not short, were below the height of the tall pair.

Lyons's tired mind stirred as he gazed at the group. Familiarity began to assert itself. It slowly dawned on Lyons that he might know these people, and the point clicked home in the second that the tall point-man halted suddenly, raising his left hand and turned to speak to the others.

The man's black skin forced the answer to Lyons's lips as recognition dawned.

He was looking at Calvin James.

And that meant Phoenix Force.

# CHAPTER EIGHTEEN

Lyons didn't wait to see if he was hallucinating. He knew he wasn't. He also knew the Koreans weren't going to sit around playing guessing games. They had their target lock, and they were going to use it.

He saw the soldier with the rocket launcher rise slightly from his kneeling position, angling the weapon around for a clearer shot at the four men below him.

Checking that the AK was set for single shots, Lyons pulled the weapon to his shoulder. He picked the guy with the rocket launcher, knowing that if he did fire, the missile would take out Phoenix Force in one explosion. Lyons drew a breath, held his aim and then stroked the trigger.

The target arched backward as the bullet cored between his shoulders, punching a bloody hole on its way out. His reaction pushed the tube of the launcher skyward so that when his finger jerked back on the trigger, the missile rose in a vertical blur, the back blast from the tube scorching the Korean's lower legs.

The moment he had fired Lyons shifted aim and

began to cut loose in the direction of the other Koreans. He caught one in the left shoulder before return fire drove him back to cover, chips of splintered rock stinging his face. He moved to the far side of the rock he was concealed behind, ignoring the whine of bullets bouncing off the front face. Leaning out, he triggered more shots, seeing his bullets throw geysers of earth into the air.

THE BLAST from the off-target rocket launcher brought Phoenix Force directly into the fight.

They scattered, turning their weapons in the direction of the eruption of the gunfire. Some of the Koreans kept their weapons on Phoenix Force while others started to exchange shots with whoever was concealed in the rocks above them.

Gary Manning dropped to the ground, hauling himself behind the scant cover of a low rock, resting his AK on its top. He tracked the barrel back and forth until he caught a glimpse of one of the Koreans showing over the rise of the slope above them. Manning held the target and eased back on the trigger. The AK cracked sharply, sending its bullet on its way. It lodged in the Korean's skull, just above his left eye. The impact kicked the soldier's head up and back so that the Canadian's second shot caught him in the throat.

James and Encizo had both chosen the same spot for cover. They reached the dip in the ground by taking an uncoordinated dive, landing on the inner slope and slithering to the bottom. Behind them they heard the vicious snap of bullets chewing at the rim of the dip, showering them with fragments of frozen earth.

"That hurt," James grumbled, flexing a bruised shoulder.

"Better than a damn bullet," Encizo said.

The Cuban rolled on his stomach, wriggling up the slope, and returned fire, pushing the Koreans back from their own firing line.

James plucked a 40 mm HEDP round from his webbing and snapped it into the grenade launcher fixed to his M-16. He pushed up beside Encizo and laid the weapon on target.

"Let's see how those mothers like these cherries," he said, triggering the launcher.

The M-433 round soared toward the Korean emplacement in a graceful arc, detonating with a sharp crack. It struck just below the lip of the spot where the Koreans were concealed. The impact threw a burst of earth skyward. One of the Koreans caught part of the explosion in his chest. He was thrown over by the force of the blast, his shredded chest bloody.

David McCarter, braced against the side of a large boulder, fired off shot after shot, raking the slope with constant fire. The ground at his feet became littered with shell casings. His unrelenting fire kept the attacking force occupied and gave the unknown shooter above the Koreans time to fix his aim and pick off more targets.

The Koreans found that their intended ambush had backfired. Suddenly they were caught between two forces. One above and one below. They responded with the maximum effort, but the abrupt change in the setup took them by surprise. The hunters became the hunted.

Carl Lyons took out the remaining pair as they attempted to retreat to their truck. They had his position and fired on him as they climbed the slope. Lyons maintained his partial cover, swinging out enough to use up the last shot in his magazine. The slugs from the AK punched in hard, driving the soldiers to the ground, where they lay in ragged bundles.

He ejected the empty magazine and replaced it with a spare. He snapped back the bolt, loading the rifle before he slumped down behind his rock, exhaustion catching up with him.

Ten minutes passed before Lyons heard the sound of Phoenix Force coming up on the defunct Korean position. He heard their voices before he saw them.

McCarter, James, Encizo, Manning. They were voices he hadn't heard in a long time, and they sounded almost to good to be real.

"Whoever you are, show yourself," McCarter ordered.

"Yeah, come on out," James yelled.

CARL LYONS PUSHED to his feet and emerged from behind his protective rock, the AK held snug against his hip. He was still in a defensive mood, not entirely trusting to anything just yet. He half slithered down the loose slope until he was on a level with the four men who stood staring at him as if he had grown a second head.

No one said anything. They all just stared at one another.

"This is a first," Lyons said finally, just to break the silence. "McCarter speechless."

"Bloody hell, Carl," McCarter replied. "You sound as bad as you look."

It was only when McCarter spoke that Lyons realized how rough his own voice sounded. He hadn't been speaking a great deal, and the harsh treatment he had experienced had affected his voice. Now, as he listened to the words he uttered, he sounded like a wizened old man.

"Here, man, take a drink," Encizo said, pushing his canteen at Lyons.

He took it and swallowed some of the chilled water, letting it trickle down his taut throat. He was aware that the others were studying him closely and remembered what he was wearing.

"It's the latest fashion from Pyongyang," he said, "so hands off. Christ, what I had to do to get this."

Out the corner of his eye Lyons saw that Manning had moved away from the group. No one had said anything. Manning had simply taken it on himself to stand watch, his eyes scanning the terrain around them. Lyons knew he was back with his own kind. If he had been capable of it, he would have felt good. But his mind was still in its fugitive state, and he wouldn't feel satisfied until things moved on.

"Okay, so tell me why you're here. And don't give me any bullshit about this being a mercy mission to pull my ass out of the fire."

"Still full of charm, I see." McCarter grinned. "We're here because the Koreans got hold of system disks that will allow them to access Slingshot's orbiting satellite ring. If they break the encryption code, they'll be able to blow the satellites out of orbit and close Slingshot. Our information suggests they have a computer expert at this site they're building. His job is to break the encryption. Ours is to stop him and destroy the disks.''

"Sounds reasonable.''

"If time allowed after the main mission, we were going to look for you.''

Lyons stared at McCarter. The Briton held his gaze.

"I don't lie to friends, Carl.''

"Okay. How're you getting out?''

"Jack's waiting with Dragon Slayer on a carrier out on the Sea of Japan. When we're ready for extraction, I activate a homing device and he comes in to fetch us.''

"And here I've been hiking all around this fucking country looking for a ride,'' Lyons said testily.

"He gets better fast, doesn't he?'' Encizo commented.

"I wish,'' Lyons said.

It had to have been a first for any of them. To actually hear Carl Lyons admitting he was less than 110 percent. They didn't need to ask why. A quick look at his gaunt, unshaved face revealed every bruise and scrape. His lips were cracked from exposure. It was obvious to them all that his body would be in a similar state beneath the filthy, crude clothing he was wearing. They knew something else. He wouldn't quit. No matter how badly he felt, Carl Lyons would go that extra mile and then some.

"What do you know about this missile site?" Lyons asked.

"Only what Stony Man fed us. Why?"

"Where the hell do you think I've been lately? Disneyland, North Korea?"

"You were in there?" McCarter asked.

"Digging with the best," Lyons said.

"I hate to ask, but do you feel up to a return visit?"

Lyons didn't even hesitate. He even managed a crooked smile, despite the pain it caused to his sore lips.

"Why the hell not!"

LYONS SAT IN THE CAB beside McCarter, who drove the truck. The others were perched on the flatbed. They had collected all the unused ammunition clips from the Koreans. Encizo had gathered up the rocket launcher and the extra missiles.

Under Lyons's direction McCarter turned the truck in the direction of the missile site. The Able Team leader had the Briton's map on his knee, tracing the directions.

"We should be about here," he said. "Take us a couple of hours to reach the area."

"What do they have in the way of defenses?" McCarter asked.

"Fair number of troops, but I figure most will be out looking for you guys. And me."

McCarter glanced at him. "They figure you're that special?"

"A certain Captain Yun does. We kind of crossed swords while I was in his camp and at the site."

"I'll bet."

"The guy has some kind of hard-on for me. I got stubborn and wouldn't play his game. So he sees it as his duty to put me under."

"Well, I can see his point of view, Carl. You almost got me pissed off a couple of times."

Lyons managed a croaky chuckle. It didn't last long as he stared out through the windshield, recalling events of the near past. McCarter sensed Lyons's mood and left him alone for a while.

Then he asked, "Rough time."

"Yeah. One way of describing it. That camp was a bad place, David. Give me all the excuses in the damn world, and it doesn't justify what those poor bastards are going through. Bad enough to do it to the enemy in a war, but to your own people? Just because they have the guts to say no."

James banged on the roof of the cab, then leaned in at McCarter's window.

"Off to the west. Single vehicle."

McCarter glanced in the direction.

"I see it."

He put his foot down, pushing the truck to its maximum speed, which wasn't great. The hard suspension gave them a bumpy ride over the rough ground. Manning, James and Encizo were forced to hang on to whatever they could find.

The distant vehicle stopped. There was a pause, and then the whoosh of a rocket launcher told them they were under fire. The missile landed some twenty feet behind the truck. A second missile landed closer, showering the rear of the truck with debris.

"This isn't good," James complained.

"Ask David to stop," Encizo said. "Let that bastard get a little closer."

James relayed the request, and McCarter rolled the truck to a stop. Encizo jumped to the ground on the side of the truck away from the enemy vehicle. He rested the loaded rocket launcher on his shoulder, leaning against the flatbed to steady his aim. The Cuban held the approaching vehicle in his sights.

"Don't wait too long, my man," James advised.

"Have faith," Encizo replied.

"I have faith," James said. "I just don't want to fill my underwear with it."

The Korean vehicle began to slow and then it turned broadside on to them. It was an all-terrain-type vehicle, and they could all see the outline of a rocket launcher poking out of one of the side windows.

James drew a long breath.

Even Manning was disturbed enough to glance at Encizo.

"Anytime you're ready, Rafe."

Encizo seemed to hold for even longer. Then the rocket launcher roared. A tongue of flame burst from the tube's rear. The missile leaped out of the muzzle and streaked in the direction of the enemy vehicle. It struck midway along the body. The all-terrain vehicle blew apart in a ball of orange fire. Smoke bloomed skyward. Debris was flung in all directions, scattering across the ground. A smoking wheel and tire rolled for yards until its momentum ceased and it dropped.

McCarter waited until Encizo was back on board, then dropped the truck in gear and set off again.

"I have the feeling we might pick up other guests on the way in," Manning commented.

"Let them come," Encizo said. He patted the rocket launcher. "We are ready to receive them."

THEY WERE CLOSE to the site by early afternoon. No other vehicles or soldiers had appeared. McCarter found that more worrisome than if there had been hordes of them following.

He pulled the truck into the cover of trees and undergrowth, cutting the engine. Climbing out, McCarter took the binoculars and went with Lyons to a spot where they could look down on the site.

"Give me a rundown, Carl," he said as he scanned the distant site.

Lyons conjured an image in his mind, remembering the layout of the site.

"Whole place is surrounded by concrete walls topped by razor wire. Walls are around eight feet high. Main gate is the only way in or out. Opens by sliding from right to left."

"What's the gate made of?"

"Heavy timbers strapped with iron."

"Okay. What about security?"

"Guard towers on either side of the gate and around the perimeter walls. Eight in total. Each tower has two guards and a machine gun. They also have a searchlight. A number of pylons around the site are topped by more searchlights.''

''If we go for a night attack, we need to black out those towers. Where does the power come from?''

''Couple of big generators are located at the far end of the site. Near the east wall. They run on gasoline, not diesel. I guess that's because diesel freezes easier than gas. There's a hell of a gasoline storage tank that feeds the generators.''

''What about the buildings?''

''I never got too close to them. They kept me on digging duty. Everything is built low profile, which means the complex will be underground. There's the main structure and next to it is a smaller building with radio masts. A radar dish.''

''Let's backtrack,'' McCarter said. ''These generators. Were they running during the day?''

''No. They had them on when we arrived each morning. As soon as it got light, they were cut until it got dark again.''

McCarter smiled. ''So that means the underground complex has its own power supply. They need light all the time down there. And to run computer and electronic systems.''

Lyons leaned his back against a tree trunk, running a hand across his face.

''We get inside and take out the exterior power, then move on to the main complex?''

''Put the communication center out of action, too,'' McCarter said. ''We need to prevent their sending out any messages once we hit. Likely we should take that out first, then go for the fuel tank. Blow that we'll cause some fuss.''

"What have you got planned, David?''

"Right now? Not much.''

"First thing we need to do is get inside,'' Lyons said. "I did some watching while I was in there. The gate stays shut most of the time. They don't get many visitors. Longest time it's open is when the prisoners are trucked in and out.''

"Maybe that's our time,'' McCarter said.

He studied the layout again. The terrain approaching the site was rugged, dotted with patches of vegetation and outcroppings. McCarter spent some time observing the guard towers. The machine guns were turned inward because they were intended to intimidate the prisoners, rather than repel an attacking force. It was unlikely the Koreans expected any kind of external threat. Not on their own territory. The construction of the towers consisted of a box where the guards stood, at each of four corners to support a basic wooden roof. The construction would prevent the machine guns being swiveled to fire on anyone outside without being manually carried and turned about. It was a small point but one worth remembering.

McCarter and Lyons returned to where the others waited. McCarter detailed what he and Lyons had discussed, then outlined his thoughts and laid it open for discussion.

"If we can get close to the gate and wait for it to open,'' McCarter said, "it gives us the best chance to get inside.''

"Be cutting things damn close," James said.

"Carl," he continued, "when the trucks leave, are there many guards around?"

"They load in the prisoners, then leave them to the guards in the trucks. Remember these site guards are outside all day, as well as the prisoners. All they want to do is get under cover and dry off. Maybe get something hot inside them. The guards in the towers oversee the trucks leaving."

"Could leave us a way in if we're fast," Encizo said.

"The communication center will be our first target," McCarter said. "Can you take it out with that launcher, Rafe?"

"I've got five chances," Encizo said.

"Okay. We get inside and Rafe handles the comm center. Cal, you run interference for him. Keep the opposition off his back."

"No problem."

"Gary, the generators need taking out pretty fast once Rafe hits the comm center. And then the fuel tank."

"I can lead Gary to the generators," Lyons told him.

"All right," McCarter said. "I'll go for the fuel tank."

They dug out the personal communication sets and slipped on the lightweight earphone-microphone sets, clipping the power packs to their belts. Once they had them in place, they ran a check to satisfy themselves the communicators were on-line.

"Sorry we don't have a spare," McCarter said.

Lyons shrugged. "I'll stick with Gary."

"Once we start the ball rolling, the main objective is to get inside the complex and find those disks," McCarter said. "If anything gets in the way, deal with it. As far as I'm concerned, all options are off. We go in bloody hard. I'm not going to make a fuss about it, but we all know the background. If we lose out, Slingshot could get wiped before it even comes on-line."

"What about Jack?" James asked. "We might need his backup pretty sharp."

McCarter nodded. "I'm on that."

He pulled out his cell phone and keyed the number for the Farm.

"Barb? Tell Jack to wind up the Lady and be ready. I'll be activating the device in a few hours. You have a location for this site so he can work out how long it'll take him to reach us. If everything goes to plan, he'll spot us a long way off."

"Okay. I'll talk to him. How's it going?"

"Right now it's quiet. By the way, you can pass a message to Able. We picked up an old friend on the way. Tell them he's a bit rough around the edges but apart from that he's as rude as ever."

"I'll tell them. They're with Jack as backup, so they'll be happy for the news."

McCarter cut the connection and put the phone away.

"Taxi ordered, ladies. I suggest we do a weapons check and get ready for a bit of sneaking through the long grass."

*Stony Man Farm, Virginia*

"HOW THE HELL did they manage to find Carl?" Brognola asked when Price gave him the news.

"I didn't ask," Price said.

"Who cares?" Delahunt said. "Long as he's alive."

"Yeah." Tokaido grinned.

"Hey, I only asked," Brognola said.

Price established contact with the carrier and asked for Grimaldi.

"Your signal should be coming through in a few hours," she told him. "I'll get the satellite location for the site through to you. I'll give you a chance to work out flying time."

"We're ready here," Grimaldi said.

"Are the others around?"

"Not right now. Why?"

"Got some news they might like to hear."

*U.S. Carrier, Sea of Japan*

GRIMALDI FOUND Blancanales and Schwarz at a workbench in the belowdecks hangar where Dragon Slayer was housed. They were checking their gear and weapons. He strolled up to them with three bottles of Coke he'd picked up from one of the drinks machines. They took the chilled bottles, staring at him with curiosity.

"Just heard from Stony Man. We should be getting the signal from Phoenix in a few hours."

"And that's a reason to celebrate?" Blancanales

asked. "Nice thought, Jack, but we're not exactly setting out for a picnic."

Schwarz saw the grin on Grimaldi's face.

"Give, Jack. You look like a pageant queen who just got the first prize."

"Yeah, I almost forgot. Phoenix picked up a hitchhiker on the way. Some dropout who goes by the name of Carl Lyons."

Blancanales and Schwarz didn't say a word. They looked at Grimaldi, then at each other. Blancanales lifted his bottle and took a long swallow. He let out a sigh and turned away. Placing the Coke bottle on the bench, he returned to checking his gear.

Schwarz glanced at Grimaldi.

"Thanks, Jack. That's one piece of news we never expected to hear right now. How is he?"

"I didn't get much. Sounds like he's up and running. Barb didn't have a lot to tell me. He's beat up a little but still crusty."

Blancanales turned at that, his face split by a wide smile.

"I knew it," he said. "Leaves us to worry, then comes back still grumpy. That guy will never change."

Grimaldi emptied his bottle and dropped it in a trash can.

"Time to open up the Lady and get her ready. We could have a long night ahead of us."

# CHAPTER NINETEEN

*North Korea*

The night was closing in as Phoenix Force reached to within two hundred yards of the outer wall. Shadows were lengthening, aiding their slow approach. They had been maneuvering their way along the ground, coming in from the west side of the site. The gated wall faced south, so they had that to move across to get close to the gate when it was opened. The rough terrain had concealed their movement. Carl Lyons's information had proved to be accurate as far as the tower guards were concerned. The soldiers spent their time watching over the prisoners working within the walled site. On a few occasions one of them would turn to stare out across the outer reaches of the landscape. When they did, they seemed to be looking far out, not checking the ground close to the site. Lyons suggested they were checking for any signs of the patrols. Despite the guards' seeming carelessness, Phoenix Force chose to assume there might be a threat and acted accordingly. They spent much of the time motionless, only moving when they were absolutely certain it was safe.

Their approach was unhurried. Even though they were under a time limit, they ignored the urge to move faster. One slip now and they would have found themselves under the guns of the Koreans, exposed and with no defensive positions to use.

As they set out on their approach, McCarter made a final call to Stony Man, informing them of what they were about to do. Barbara Price had told him that Grimaldi's estimated flight time from the carrier to the site would be around two and a half hours. It was the only information McCarter needed. As soon as he finished his call, he took the homing device and activated it. McCarter watched the pulsing red light. The signal would reach out and be picked up by Dragon Slayer, telling Grimaldi it was time to go. He tucked the device into a small pocket on his camou jacket and zipped it up. It was up to Jack Grimaldi now.

THE HARD GROUND was icy cold. Every shrub, every rock they came in contact with was the same. Each time they were forced to lie still and wait added to their discomfort. As the afternoon wore on and the temperature began to drop, their body heat was reduced, too. It made moving off again that much more difficult.

McCarter made sure he kept up a dialogue with each of his team. He used the comm sets they wore to check on them every few minutes. If he failed to get an instant response, he would keep on talking to the particular man until he did. He was too aware of the problems associated with freezing temperatures, the desire to simply stay still and let the cold fool the body into believing it was actually comfortable. The slow onset of hypothermia often induced a feeling of well-being. If the victim wasn't roused and brought back to a rational frame of mind, the comatose state would eventually lead to death.

Gary Manning, who was partnered with Lyons, had no opportunity to fall into that state. Lyons, still acutely aware of his own lucky escape from the very same thing, made certain the Canadian stayed alert. His voice was never far from Manning's hearing, and his constant rebukes kept Manning awake.

As darkness began to envelop the site, the lights on top of the guard towers and the pylons came on. Bright arcs of light pushed the darkness aside. Some fell outside the walls, diffused and not as sharp.

Phoenix Force was at the base of the south-facing wall by this time, hugging the shadows where the light failed to reach. For the first time in hours they came together, strung out against the rough concrete barrier. They could barely make out one another's faces in the darkness.

"That gate will be opening anytime," Lyons said. "They only keep it open for a few minutes. Long enough for the trucks to move out."

"How is it opened?" James asked. "I mean manual or powered?"

"Electric-powered rollers," Lyons said, "operated from one of the guard towers."

"Let's move, then," McCarter said. "Everyone

okay on what they're going to do once we're inside?''

He received affirmative responses from them all.

*"Go!"* McCarter said.

They crouched and moved along the base of the wall, their objective the heavy wooden gate. Reaching it, they split into teams, Manning and Lyons crossing to the far side, where they dropped into the shadows, hugging the concrete. McCarter, James and Encizo stayed where they were. Lyons had given them all the positions of their particular targets.

The sounds of truck engines being started reached them. Once the engines caught, they were revved hard to warm them up. The big gate began to slide open on metal rollers. Beams of light showed as the truck headlights were switched on. The lead truck jerked forward, almost stalling before the driver gained control. The vehicle moved toward the opening as the gate slid fully open. It filled the gap, pushing through, swaying dangerously.

The gap between truck and concrete wall was no more than a couple of feet. It presented a risk to anyone trying to slip through, but Manning and Lyons, almost on their knees, gambled and won. Breathing in thick exhaust fumes, the pair pushed through, hiding in the shadows against the inner wall. Lyons led the way to concealment behind stacks of building materials. He pointed out the dark shape of the large generator that provided power for the exterior functions of the site.

"Lead the way, Carl, this is your home ground," Manning said.

"Don't remind me," Lyons muttered as he moved ahead.

The second truck was emerging from the open gate when James's voice filled McCarter's earphones.

"Vehicles approaching."

McCarter glanced over his shoulder, and saw the bobbing pinpoints of light in the distance.

"Patrols coming back?" Encizo said. "That's all we need."

"Inside now," McCarter snapped. "Let's go."

They slipped around the edge of the concrete wall and crawled through the gap as the second truck rolled by them. Bunching together at the base of the wall, they moved in behind the support legs of the guard tower, flattening on the ground.

"Let's hope they close that gate before they spot those vehicles coming in," McCarter said.

Almost in answer to his wish the gate began to close the moment the second truck had cleared the gap.

"Rafe, take out that bloody comm center," McCarter said. "Gary, blow that generator the minute Rafe does his stuff. We spotted vehicles heading this way. Cut the power, and they won't be able to open the gate."

Manning acknowledged, "Just setting charges now. I can detonate them from a distance."

"I'm heading for that gas tank," McCarter said. "See you at the party."

He turned and moved off, vanishing in the shadows, leaving Encizo and James to handle their part of the operation.

James eased to one side, his eyes scanning the site while Encizo fed the first of his missiles into the launcher. He checked that it was activated, then set the launcher on his shoulder, leaning against one of the tower legs to steady his body. He settled the launcher, sighting on the distant comm center. He aimed at the base of the cluster of tall aerials. His finger eased back on the trigger, and the launcher exhausted flame and smoke. The missile struck at the base of the aerials and exploded with a sharp crack of sound. Encizo didn't check whether he had scored a solid hit. He concentrated on loading a second rocket. When he raised his head to take aim again, he saw the aerials falling. This time he sighted on the comm center itself. The second missile arced across the gap and slammed into the wall of the building, tearing a ragged hole as it detonated.

James brought his AK into play as armed men, alerted by the flash of Encizo's launcher, turned in their direction. Autofire crackled, bullets slicing the air. With his usual calm James returned fire and saw men go down. He expended a full magazine, his shots cutting back and forth as he held the trigger down on full-auto.

Beside him Encizo fed a third rocket into the launcher and put it into the comm center again. The squat structure was almost razed to the ground by this final strike, smoke billowing from the rubble.

GARY MANNING HEARD the blast as Encizo hit the comm center for the third time. He and Lyons had moved back from the generator, taking cover behind a stack of heavy planks. Manning activated the remote detonator in his hand. He extended the aerial and pressed the button. The explosive packs he had fixed to the generator blew with sharp cracks. The large unit was severely damaged as the explosions split it open. The static motor that powered the generator blossomed with flame as its fuel line burst and the core of the generator itself shattered. Following the blast of the detonations, the power plant died. The lights went out on all the guard towers and the pylons.

MCCARTER HAD the gasoline tank directly in front of him. He moved from one piece of cover to another, pausing, then proceeding. He heard the explosion as Encizo's missiles struck the comm center. Two more blasts followed, interspersed by autofire. As the Briton moved on, he heard additional explosions as Manning's charges took out the generator. The site was plunged into darkness. McCarter dropped down behind a pile of rubble, his AK held across his chest. Behind him more autofire rattled, muzzle-flashes briefly throwing light into the darkness. He could hear shouted commands in Korean. Without warning, one of the guard towers opened up, sending machine-gun fire across the site. Bullets whined off unseen targets. McCarter pulled himself low as stray shots whacked the earth close by.

The recognizable dull thump of James's 40 mm grenade launcher reached McCarter's ears. He turned his head and caught the flash of the explosion as the HEDP round shredded the tower box into silence.

Using the moment, McCarter ran on, staying low until he was halfway across the site. In his earphones he could hear the occasional exchange between Manning, James and Encizo. As he stepped around the final obstacle between himself and the gas tank, a uniformed figure blocked his way. McCarter caught the gleam of a gun barrel as the Korean swung it to bear on him. The Phoenix Force leader had no time to raise his own weapon, so he let his momentum carry him forward. He hit the Korean with a full body slam, the impact knocking the man off his feet. He crashed to the hard ground, winded by the blow. McCarter reversed his AK and slammed the butt into the fallen man's face. He hit hard, once, then again. Bone splintered under the impact. The Korean expelled a strangled gasp, his body arching against the pain, then slumped motionless.

McCarter stepped over the body, reaching the massive gasoline tank. It rested on a steel cradle that held it a few feet off the ground. A feed pipe ran from a valve, snaking across the site to where it would eventually join up to the now destroyed generator. Moving around the tank, McCarter located another valve. This one had no pipe attached to it. A metal wheel was fixed above the valve pipe. He grasped the wheel and began to turn it. The threads were tight from lack of lubrication, and it took a great deal of effort to start it moving. Once McCarter had broken the initial stiffness, the wheel loosened. After a half turn he smelled gasoline. Opening the valve farther, McCarter heard the splash of gas as it trickled, then rushed from the outlet pipe. He kept turning until the valve was fully open and the gas was gushing out. It pooled on the ground, then began to spread, pushed by the sheer force of the escaping liquid. The force behind the jet of gasoline told McCarter there was a high volume inside the tank. He backed away, moving so that he was well clear of the main flow.

Once he was at a safe distance McCarter took a grenade from his harness and pulled the pin. He threw the grenade underhand, into the gap beneath the gas tank. The moment he tossed the grenade McCarter turned and distanced himself from the area.

The grenade's explosion ripped a gash in the underside of the tank, allowing even more of the fuel to escape in the seconds before the fumes were ignited by the detonation. The already spilled fuel ignited, as well, greedy fingers of flame rushing along the gasoline where it had flowed. The site was lit up by the massive flare of the burning fuel. When the main tank burst, spewing liquid fire across the site, chaos reigned in the first few minutes.

YUN'S FIRST INDICATION of trouble came when he and his patrols were a quarter mile from the site. The first of the missiles to take out the comm center aerials showed as a brief flash. Two more followed. There was autofire, as well. And then the sudden explosion in the vicinity of the generator was followed by all the lights going out.

"Quickly, get us back there," Yun ordered his driver.

After all they had been through during the day, Yun didn't need this kind of occurrence on his return.

The American commandos had eluded him. And even while they stayed out of his reach, they had managed to wipe out two of his squads and steal another vehicle. Later in the day one of Yun's vehicle crews had been destroyed by a stolen rocket launcher. And now, it seemed, the Americans had broken through to breach the site.

Above the crackle of gunfire Yun heard a grenade blast. The sky lit up as the gasoline tank exploded. Even from where he was outside the site, Yun saw the huge ball of flame rise into the night sky. Fiery tentacles of raw fire reached across the site.

Yun's driver brought the all-terrain vehicle to a shuddering stop at the closed gate. Some distance from the gate the trucks carrying the prisoners back to the camp had stopped. Prisoners and guards were staring at the flames showing behind the walls. They were also able to hear the crackle of gunfire coming from inside.

"Get the gate open," Yun roared at the guard tower, then realized it had been hit by a grenade. He turned to call up to the guard tower on the opposite side of the gate, then changed his mind. He remembered the gate could only be opened from the tower that had been demolished. It was only after a few seconds he realized that due to the power having been cut off, the gate couldn't be opened anyway.

"Get the vehicle up to the wall. See if we can climb over from the roof."

The driver, well aware of Yun's capacity for unreasonable rages, didn't argue. He swung the all-terrain vehicle around and placed it parallel to the wall. He climbed out of the vehicle and onto the roof. He found he was able to reach the top of the wall easily.

"There's razor wire on the top, Captain."

Yun made the man climb down. "See if you can find some kind of cutters. Maybe in the truck tool-boxes. We have to get inside. Those Americans are killing our comrades."

# CHAPTER TWENTY

*U.S. Navy Carrier, Sea of Japan*

The moment the signal was activated, Grimaldi contacted the carrier's captain. While the Stony Man pilot and Able Team climbed into Dragon Slayer, the carrier's crew moved to their stations prior to the commencement of the diversion operation.

With Dragon Slayer fully operational, Grimaldi sealed the hatches. Behind him Blancanales and Schwarz, suited up and armed, settled in their seats. There was a slight bump as the elevator started to rise, taking the combat helicopter up to the flight deck.

Grimaldi activated the onboard computer and watched the monitor illuminate with a terrain map, showing their course once they made land. The data bank fed in the information, including the location of the signal device McCarter had activated. Leaning forward, Grimaldi changed fuel intake from the main tanks to the auxiliary tanks. He would use these for the flight in and dump them once their destination was reached.

"Mr. Pierce," the captain's voice greeted Grimaldi through his headset, "I hope you enjoyed your stay with us."

"No complaints, Captain."

"We aim to please. In a few seconds our diversion will start. Give it a couple of minutes and you can take off."

"Thanks."

"Good luck, Mr. Pierce. We look forward to seeing you after your mission."

The deck elevator stopped. Dragon Slayer sat poised for takeoff, her rotors blurred as Grimaldi held her in readiness. Beyond the carrier the sea was running with a strong swell. The late-afternoon sky held the threat of more bad weather. Grimaldi didn't worry about that. The Lady handled bad weather without a problem.

In the far distance he could see the Korean ship. Like the carrier it was moving slowly, riding the movement of the water. The sight of it irked Grimaldi. It was like having an itch he couldn't scratch.

From somewhere along the hull of the carrier, thick white smoke began to coil into the air. It rose in dense formations, caught by the wind, and was sucked in across the flight deck. As Grimaldi and Able Team watched, the smoke intensified until it obscured their vision of the distant Korean ship. The carrier was putting up a smoke screen, using its onboard defensive capabilities to mask Dragon Slayer's departure. Darker smoke was added to the white, and then a number of the carrier's own helicopters rose into the air and flew off in different directions, circling the side of the carrier between it and the distant Korean vessel.

"I think it's time we left," Grimaldi said.

He kicked in the power, working the controls, and lifted off the deck. Dragon Slayer moved to the far side of the carrier, and Grimaldi dropped the aircraft to just above sea level once he was clear of the carrier. He held the combat chopper on a course that matched the carrier until the rolling bank of thick smoke had formed a curtain in its wake.

"Keep your hands inside the car at all times," Grimaldi said, and opened up Dragon Slayer's reserve power.

The twin turboshaft engines howled, and the sleek black helicopter sped away from the carrier, heading out to sea. Grimaldi held his course for at least ten miles before he eased the chopper around and began a return to land in a long, low-altitude sweep that took it well out of visual range of the Korean ship. Wave hopping all the way, Grimaldi kept his fingers crossed that his low profile would bring him in under Korean radar.

"We fool them?" Blancanales asked through his headset.

"If we haven't, we'll see soon enough."

They made it to the coast in less than a half hour, Grimaldi keeping the helicopter close to the ground. He followed the course of the shoreline for a time until the computer automatically altered course and set them on a direct path for the site.

With Dragon Slayer locked on course, Grimaldi was able to run an in-flight weapons check. He activated the 30 mm chain gun and rocket pods. A small monitor flicked into life, showing the full complement of missiles housed in the underwing pods. Grimaldi switched on his IHDDS helmet and made sure the connection was open that allowed him to aim via movements of his head and eyes. The slaved helmet was linked to the weapons system. It allowed him faster reaction time during combat situations. Those vital seconds could mean the difference between life or death, something that Jack Grimaldi was extremely sensitive about.

The helicopter's radar scanned the way ahead, feeding back the data that allowed Dragon Slayer to follow the contours of the landscape. Low-profile flying kept the speeding craft below ground radar. The highly sophisticated equipment worked faster than any human pilot. It meant the pilot had to have great trust in the machine intelligence that sometimes took over from him. One slight error by the machine would mean instant destruction. Grimaldi's faith in Dragon Slayer never wavered for a second. His input into the helicopter's development had conceived a machine built around his skills and personality, and the machine's performance proved his worth once it was in the field.

Grimaldi watched the sky, searching for any signs of any incoming aircraft. He saw nothing. Dragon Slayer's radar was sweeping in all directions, backing up his checks with its electronic surveillance. He knew, too, that Stony Man would be using satellite scans to monitor the area and would pass along anything they sighted.

Nothing.

The pilot remained alert. In the high-speed world of air combat, situations were liable to change in seconds. An enemy aircraft could appear as if from nowhere in the blink of an eye. With heat-seeking missiles the opposition could remain detached and even invisible, sending its projectiles from a safe location. Close combat was a lost art. Distant kills were the stuff of modern warfare.

The first hour merged into the second. The light was fading fast now. Electronic flying would ease the strain on Grimaldi, his dependence on the machine growing as the daylight fell away and plunged him into a shadow world. The helicopter's windshield canopy dotted with rain. The drops were smashed against the screen, streaking it. Grimaldi hit the button and set the wipers in motion. The rain increased in intensity. Grimaldi checked the outside temperature and saw it was plummeting fast. Ice would begin to form on the outer surfaces, frosting the screen. He activated the heat unit to maintain a clear screen.

He ran a diagnostic check from the computer. The helicopter had the capability to run full system and operating checks. Grimaldi let it scan, seeing the results on one of the small monitor screens on his console. The computer ran a checklist, ticking off each component as it was assessed. When the full scan had been completed, Grimaldi was able to see that Dragon Slayer was fully operational.

His radar screen showed clear.

No pursuit.

Grimaldi pondered the situation. Maybe their entry

into Korean territory had gone unnoticed. The diversion provided by the carrier had worked as it had been intended, giving Dragon Slayer a clear run. A possibility was that the Korean radar defenses weren't as high-tech as might have been thought. Grimaldi wasn't going to get solid answers to those questions, so he decided there was no use in worrying. If anything did happen, he would deal with it. Right now his job was to provide a ride home for Phoenix Force. That was his priority, and unless something drastic happened, that was exactly what he would do.

THE ERUPTION OF SOUND penetrated even the thick concrete of the complex—a number of explosions, the distant rattle of autofire.

Yat Sen Took bent over the row of TV monitors. Those located outside the complex showed a confusion of color and movement. He witnessed the gasoline tank explosion, saw the huge ball of flame that swelled up from the storage area. The leaping flames were the only source of illumination now that the exterior power had been cut.

"Where is that idiot Yun?" he said. "Is he still running around the countryside while we are under siege?"

Gagarin appeared, casting a cursory glance at the monitors. He allowed himself a shadow of a smile, keeping the expression from Took. The Korean was barely holding himself in check.

"I cannot believe this," Took ranted. "We have

an army of millions, but we fail to stop this group of American assassins.''

''Took, an army is no good to you if it's stationed hundreds of miles away. We deal with these Americans with what we have.''

He pulled back his jacket to expose a shoulder rig holding a SIG-Sauer P-226. Slipping the handgun from its holster, Gagarin checked the weapon. It was fitted with a 20-round extended magazine. The Russian had two extra magazines in a holder on the other side of the shoulder rig.

''You obviously came prepared,'' Duong Chin said as he joined them.

''One of the reasons I came here was because I *knew* these Americans would show up,'' Gagarin said. ''And this time they will not leave.''

''We have to protect Berkoff,'' Took said. ''He must complete his code breaking.''

''Precisely why I flew in my protection squad,'' Chin said. ''Between us we have to be able to stop these damn Americans. Or die trying.''

''A sense of humor appears to be developing,'' Gagarin said.

''I must be spending too much time in your company, Nikolai.''

Chin turned and left them, making his way through the passages until he reached the room where Berkoff was working. After a word with his people, Chin entered the room.

Berkoff glanced up. He blinked his eyes.

''Can I hear gunfire?''

"Nothing for you to worry about," Chin said. "Ignore any disturbances. Is there any progress?"

Berkoff allowed a thin smile to curl his lips.

"I am ready to start looking at Gilman's encryption. The computers are fully up and running. No bugs. No problems."

Berkoff picked up the plastic container that held the two small, gleaming disks.

"Now I start to work."

"Excellent," Chin said. "Whatever happens beyond this room, ignore it. My people are on guard outside. They will prevent your being interrupted."

Berkoff returned to his computers, forgetting Chin was even in the room. The Chinese took his leave. Outside he spoke to Lim.

"Berkoff must be protected. If things become too unstable, we take him and the disks and we leave. Understand?"

Lim nodded. "May I ask about Took and the Russian, Gagarin?"

"In the event we have to evacuate this site, we will only concern ourselves with Berkoff. Took will probably go down with his damn complex. As for Gagarin...I don't know. He has his own agenda. The American strike force. He is determined they will die here. If he becomes involved with them, it could allow us our time to leave."

"The helicopter is on the far side of the site, beyond the wall. The pilot is under instruction to maintain it in readiness for a quick liftoff."

"Good."

"Do you want any of the team to go with you?" Lim asked.

"Maintain your position for the moment. If I need help, I will let you know."

Lim nodded.

Chin made his way along the concrete passages until he was back in the control room. Took was still there, his expression that of a man who believed his time had come.

"Took, if Yun is not here, the soldiers out there need a commander. They need to be told what to do."

"Me? I am not a soldier. Yun is supposed to be handling this. My work is with the missiles and the satellite system."

"The way things are going, you ought to think about finding yourself a gun," Chin said. "If those Americans get in here, all your clever knowledge won't do a thing to help you."

The Chinese turned to the Koreans operating the TV setup.

"Do you have weapons?"

They nodded.

"Find them and get ready. Never mind watching those screens. Cover the approach passage from the door."

He turned back to Took. "Where is Gagarin?"

"He said he wasn't going to wait down here for them to come looking for him."

"I take it the communications have been destroyed?"

"The masts are down and the radar dish."

"Very efficient. We cannot call for help. So we are on our own, Took. Like it or not, my friend, you are going to have to fight if you want to save this place."

"Where is Yun?" Took demanded. "What is the fool doing?"

CAPTAIN YUN HEARD and saw the explosions. His anger turned him into a wild thing. He screamed at his soldiers to find a means to get into the site. One of them came running, carrying one of the rocket launchers. He had two missiles.

"Blow down the gate," Yun ordered. "I want a way in. The rest of you be ready to attack."

The soldier took up his position, the launcher over his shoulder. He took careful aim, pressed the trigger and sent the missile into the gate. The explosion rocked the structure. When the smoke cleared, they saw that the gate had been badly fractured but hadn't been breached.

"Again," Yun bellowed. "If you fail, I will kill you myself."

The soldier loaded the remaining rocket. He moved a little closer, steadying his aim, and triggered the launcher. The rocket struck home, the blast filling the air with jagged splinters of wood and spinning the gate off its runners. It crashed to the ground inside the walls.

"Go!" Yun screamed. "Find these Americans and kill them. I want every one of them dead."

# CHAPTER TWENTY-ONE

The gate to the site shattered and fell inside the opening. As smoke cleared, Yun's soldiers moved in. The captain was at the rear, urging them on. They were met by a scene of total chaos. The site was lit by the orange glow of the burning gasoline. It threw patches of light and dark across the hellish scene. Figures moved back and forth, standing out as black silhouettes against the raging fire. Spilled fuel had lit other fires among the piles of earth and building materials.

Yun paused in the opening, his pistol in his gloved hand as he surveyed the site. His anger was mingled with a degree of embarrassment. He accepted that he had been fooled by the Americans. They had eluded his patrols, inflicting damage on the way, and now had beaten him back to the site. He knew that this could mean the end of his military career, and maybe even his life. The Korean regime had little tolerance for those who failed in their duty, and Yun's failure would cost dearly in both financial and national-security terms.

His mind worked frantically as he sought a solution, some way out of this catastrophic mess. Yun began to call out orders, desperately attempting to bring the soldiers under some kind of control. They seemed to have fallen victim to a panic attack, running back and forth as they tried to locate the American force. The problem appeared to be the ability of the Americans to hide themselves within the site—due mainly to the piles of construction material and earth—and from those hiding places continue their attack on the exposed Koreans and the site itself.

The explosion of another grenade added to Yun's frustration. He realized that the target had been one of the covered missiles. The grenade blew a ragged hole in the outer casing of the missile, rendering it inoperative. Yun felt a twinge of desperation start to coil in his stomach. If the missiles themselves were damaged, the project timetable would be delayed even further. He stared around him, unsure what to do. The scenario was becoming more chaotic with each passing moment, and Yun was fast realizing there was little he could do about it.

REACHING THE HEAD of the ramp, Gagarin paused, pressing hard against the concrete wall, his autopistol in his hand. He also had an AK slung from his shoulder, picked up from the armory on his way to the ramp. Peering over the edge of the side wall, he looked out over the site. What he saw created a moment of sheer admiration.

The site was on fire. The breached gasoline storage tank burned like a blown oil wellhead. The hundreds of gallons of fuel had become a boiling mass of flame. Leaked fuel had run off in all directions, starting other fires that had spread widely. The flames cast an orange glow across the site.

Autofire crackled from locations around the site. Every now and then grenades exploded, causing more damage, more confusion.

How had the Americans done all this in such a short time?

There was a short-lived moment when he felt like running out to join them. Then sanity took over, and Gagarin reminded himself why he was here. His task, apart from keeping an eye on the Slingshot project, was to do what he could to eliminate the American commando team. He admitted it was going to be difficult. They were spread out across the site, creating as much damage as they could, while most probably working their way toward the entrance to the underground complex. And they appeared to be succeeding. The Korean troops, with little in the way of leadership, were scattering in chaos. Most of them probably had no idea exactly what was going on, so their first instinct would be toward their own survival. If Yun failed to bring them together and have them perform as trained soldiers should, then the Americans were going to have a relatively easy task ahead of them.

Gagarin drew back from the head of the ramp as a couple of stray bullets struck the concrete above his head. He felt the sting of chipped concrete against his cheek. There was no point in getting himself shot by remaining where he was. His place was down below, at the bottom of the ramp, where he could wait in comparative comfort. If the Americans did breach the complex, they had to pass this way first.

And he would be waiting for them.

With his back to the wall Gagarin sank into a crouch, listening to the sounds of combat, and waited for his time to come.

*Aboard Dragon Slayer*

"CAN'T HEAR ANYTHING yet," Blancanales said.

Grimaldi checked his readouts. "We need to be closer before we can speak to them," he said. "Those headsets won't reach us this far out."

"Jack, how long now?"

"Ten, fifteen minutes."

"Can't you kick in the turbocharger or something?" Schwarz asked.

Grimaldi chuckled. "If we go any faster we'll meet ourselves coming back."

"What did he say?" Blancanales asked.

"I think he's been watching *Star Trek* again. Warp speed and time travel."

"Maybe it can tell us if there are any Korean unfriendly aircraft around," Blancanales said.

It was dark outside the helicopter, the rain spattering against the windows.

"We're still clear," Grimaldi said.

"Does anyone get the feeling this is all going very smoothly?"

Schwarz glanced at his partner. "You getting a touch of the old-lay blues?"

"I've been happier," Blancanales admitted.

YAT SEN TOOK'S feeling of isolation was compounded by his helplessness. There didn't seem to be a thing he could do to affect the situation. From his position within the complex, in the security area, he was able to view the escalation of destruction via the TV cameras. He watched in horror as the stark images allowed him to see the site falling apart before his eyes. The raging fire stemming from the shattered fuel tank showed no signs of burning itself out. The hundreds of gallons of gasoline had spilled out and spread across the site, pooling and streaming down hollows and into excavations. The blazing liquid seemed to have taken on a life of its own. Took saw flowing streams spill over the concrete surrounds of missile pits, where the launchers lay beneath canvas covers. The gasoline found its way into every crevice and section, then flared as the traveling flames reached it. The concrete pits became infernos as the gasoline burned, the hungry flames finding the intricate mass of cable work that provided power to the launching towers and cradles. Fluid pipes, compressed-air hoses, Electronic junction boxes. They were all there as part of the mechanism that would have been used to move, lift and raise the programmed missiles into their prelaunch positions. Took imagined the delicate parts charring, melting, pipes bursting to allow the fluids to leak out and probably add to the flames.

He wanted to do something. Anything.

Yet he knew in the same moment that there wasn't a single thing he could do.

The Americans had started a sequence of events

that would leave a trail of destruction across the site. Even if they were shot, or caught and executed, the damage was already done. It was going to take a great deal of reconstruction to put it all back as it had been. And that meant lost time. Time that would give the Americans the opportunity to bring Slingshot on-line. Once they did that, any attempt to destroy the satellite ring would be seen as a purely hostile act against them. And once the system was up and running, any missiles sent to destroy it would be dealt with by the selfsame system.

Took felt a sudden severe twinge of pain in his left hand. He pressed his right hand over the heavily bandaged wound, holding it tight against his body. The pain surged, agonizing in its intensity, and he clenched his teeth against it. Every now and then the wounds ached, though never as severe as now, and he wondered if it was simply his body reacting to the extreme tension he was feeling. Took sat down, staring at the monitor screens again, trying to take his mind off his hand. The things he saw only increased his discomfort. Took tore his gaze from the screens. Standing by and watching would achieve nothing. If he wanted to save his project, he needed to act positively. If Captain Yun was incapable, then he, Yat Sen Took, *would* have to take over. Duong Chin had been right. It was up to him do something.

Took pushed away from the screens. He made his way to the armory and picked up an autorifle. He clamped the weapon against his side, holding it there with his left arm, and fed in a magazine with his good hand. He cocked the weapon. Wrapping the sling strap around his bandaged hand, he used his thumb and good fingers to grip the rifle, slipping his right around the grip.

He made his way along the passage, heading for the exit ramp. Nearing it, he came in sight of Nikolai Gagarin. The Russian was armed with a rifle, as well. He turned as Took approached.

"Took, where do you think you are going?"

"I have to take command of the troops. They have no one to follow."

"And you think you can do that?" Gagarin seemed amused at the very thought. "Took, you're no soldier. What the hell do you know about combat?"

"What does that matter? Have you seen what is happening out there? Those Americans are destroying my site. They have to be stopped."

"By you? Don't be a damn fool, Took. You step out there and you'll be dead inside a minute."

"At least I am not hiding in the shadows. I thought you would at least understand."

"Took, there's a difference between understanding and throwing away your life on useless gestures. As much as I want this project to succeed, I am not going to walk out there and get my head blown off. Believe me, Took, it could happen."

"Maybe. But I am willing to take that risk."

"Your choice," Gagarin said.

Took nodded. "Even in Korea we still have that freedom."

Gagarin watched the slim figure walk away from

him, moving toward the exit ramp and whatever Fate
had in store for him.

THE SOUND of the conflict grew louder in Took's ears
as he climbed the ramp. Before he was halfway up,
he was able to see the fiery glow that hung over the
site. Auto fire rattled sporadically. The dull thump of
small explosions sounded. Men were shouting. Despite the confusion, Took felt sure he could hear
Yun's voice.

He wondered whether he had misjudged the captain. Perhaps Yun *was* taking command, organizing
his men into some kind of cohesive force ready to
take on the invading Americans. Until he was certain,
Took decided he had to stay with his decision.

He had reached almost to the head of the ramp.
The sound of bullets slapping against the concrete
walls registered as ugly sounds, and Took realized he
was about to step into a dangerous situation. The
need to protect the site forced him on. He couldn't
turn back now. The words he had spoken to Gagarin
came rushing back. Damn the Russian! If he hadn't
been at the bottom of the ramp, Took wouldn't have
been forced into explaining his motives. Retreating
now would make him look foolish. He moved a few
steps farther up the ramp. Now he could see the
raging furnace that had once been the gasoline storage tank. The flames were boiling up from the steel
vessel, with the flooded fuel creating fiery trails
across the ground. Took recalled what he had seen
on the monitor screens and turned to look in the

direction of the missile pits. They were ablaze with spilled fuel.

His spirits sank at the sight.

And then his anger rose, directed at the American commando team, and the urge to destroy them became overwhelming.

Yat Sen Took gripped the AK and hurried to the head of the ramp. He looked right and left, searching for the enemy, but they were too well hidden from sight and he was left standing in the open, brandishing his rifle.

He had no target, nothing to vent his anger on.

He had nowhere to go right at that moment, and had only his own rage to feed on. The fact he had committed himself to this futile act was the only thing on his mind when a stray bullet struck him in the back of his skull, impacted against the bone and mushroomed into his brain. He felt only the initial blow before his world blew apart in a burst of numbing pain. He saw light, then dark as his body tumbled forward. Yat Sen Took hit the ground with a sodden thump, convulsing for a few seconds before he died.

"DO YOU HAVE your radio with you?" Duong Chin asked Lim.

"Yes."

"Be ready to call in the helicopter."

"It is beyond the north wall. I checked earlier and there is enough empty space for it to land."

"If this conflict escalates beyond control, I am not going to wait here to be slaughtered," Chin said. "We will take Berkoff out with us. We can relocate him in one of our safehouses back home, and he can continue his work. If these damn Koreans can't provide a safe haven, then we will do it ourselves.''

"A pity we didn't receive the disks at the start," Lim said. "We would have been spared all this play-acting with the Koreans."

"Lim, are you suggesting I have not been entirely truthful with our Korean comrades?"

"I believe we have played along with them while they were able to provide the necessary backup. At their expense and effort."

"Lim, with thinking like that, you will go far."

"I will call the pilot now. Have him be ready the moment you give the word."

## CHAPTER TWENTY-TWO

Gary Manning, crouched in the cover of stacked metal drums, spoke into his microphone.

"I have the entrance ramp in sight. About twenty feet from my right. Any takers?"

"Just keep your eye on those guard towers," McCarter replied. "They're just itching to let fly with those machine guns."

"They would if they could see us," Encizo said.

As if on cue, one of the towers opened up, the stuttering crackle of machine-gun fire echoing across the site. The stream of bullets clanged off metalwork and ripped chunks from concrete ramps. The burst was long and noisy, but achieved nothing. Without their powerful searchlights, the towers were depending on the burning gasoline to show them a target. That wasn't working well, as the flames from the ignited fuel were erratic and caused as much shadow as they did light.

"See how they like this," Encizo muttered.

His launcher spit flame, and a rocket sailed across the site. It struck the offending tower about halfway down, blowing away two of the support legs. The tower slowly toppled, dumping machine gun and operators on the frozen ground.

"Hey, guys," James said through his headset, "let's move in. This damn rain is freezing me."

"Come on," McCarter said. "Where's the opposition?"

His three teammates each passed along their estimates of Korean positions throughout the site. Where the Koreans were out in the open, moving back and forth as they searched, Phoenix and Carl Lyons had gone to ground, burrowing beneath anything they could find. Below the level of the illumination offered by the burning gasoline, the Phoenix Force commandos were able to change position at will, staying out of sight when needed and exposing themselves only when it became strategically necessary.

They knew this couldn't last forever. Once the Koreans organized themselves and began inch-by-inch coverage of the site, Phoenix Force would find the situation reversing itself. In the meantime they were moving closer to the entrance ramp and creating as much confusion as they could.

"Rafe, how many of those rockets do you have left?" McCarter asked.

"Last one is in the tube," came the answer.

"Go for that wooden hut over by the south wall. Should make a bit of a show. Soon as she blows, we head directly for the entrance ramp."

"You got it," Encizo said.

He turned the launcher in the direction of the hut. It was a long shot from where he was positioned, but the Cuban had the feel of the launcher now. He took

his aim and stroked the trigger. The launcher jumped
on his shoulder as the missile left it, streaking across
the site. It struck the hut and exploded, shattering the
flimsy construction. The ball of flame from the blast
was followed by the disintegration of the hut and its
contents. The air was filled with shattered fragments
of board. Dust and debris flew in all directions.

"Let's go," McCarter snapped.

THEY EMERGED from their places of cover, dragging
themselves from beneath a pile of wood, shaking off
the dirt that had covered them, blending them in with
the pile of earth they had used. As one, the men of
Stony Man Farm broke cover and sprinted for the
entrance ramp.

Gary Manning covered his section ahead of the
others, almost losing his balance as he stepped onto
the rain-slick concrete. He dropped into a crouch,
hard against the side wall, his AK abandoned now
for the M-16 he carried. With calm precision the
Canadian employed his skills as the team sniper,
loosing single shots that either found their target or
drove the intended target to cover. The steady crack
of his weapon held back any of the Koreans who felt
confident enough to take him on.

Close behind came Carl Lyons, ducking and weav-
ing as he made for the comparative cover of the ramp
walls. He rolled the last few feet, pulling himself
around, and started to trade shots with the Koreans.
He fired each shot with an expression of cold fury in
his eyes. Lyons was repaying a debt. A shot for every
hour he had spent in captivity under Took's com-

mand and then the labor camp and the missile site. He held a grudge that had to be worked out of his system, and he wasn't going to give an inch.

Encizo and James moved in from the far left, swinging in around the edge of the ramp wall, firing as they came.

The last man in was David McCarter. He had held back to provide covering fire for his team, close but still vulnerable. That vulnerability cost him. As he made his final dash for the protection of the ramp, a Korean bullet scored his right thigh, near the hip. The passing force of the bullet knocked him off his feet and he hit the ground, rolling the last few feet with further shots chipping at the ground around him.

Willing hands reached out to drag him into cover. James and Encizo eased him against the wall. McCarter was cursing steadily, his tone low but intense.

James made a quick inspection of the wound. The bullet had shredded McCarter's fatigues and gouged the flesh beneath. The wound was ragged around the edges and bleeding freely. While the others maintained their standoff, James pulled a pressure pad from his medical kit and pressed it over the wound.

"Hold it there," he told the still muttering Briton.

James found a bandage roll and wrapped it around McCarter's thigh, fastening it securely.

"Have to hold you for now," he said.

McCarter reached out and caught hold of James's arm.

"Doc, will I have a scar?"

"You're okay." James grinned and picked up his M-16.

"Look here," Lyons said.

He had spotted the body lying on the ground a few feet from where they were gathered. The first thing Lyons noticed was the bandaged left hand. He turned the body over. Despite the ugly exit wound in the man's skull, Lyons had no problem recognizing Yat Sen Took.

"Isn't that the guy who...?" Encizo asked.

"Invited me to spend some time with him in sunny Korea," Lyons said. "That's the son of a bitch."

McCarter pushed to his feet. He glanced down the ramp leading to the complex.

"Cal, you got any of those grenades left?"

James nodded.

"Put one inside that opening," McCarter said, "in case someone's waiting for us."

James fed one of the HEDP rounds into the launcher on his M-16. He turned and fired it down the ramp. The grenade bounced off the concrete at the base of the ramp and detonated with an echoing blast. The entrance to the complex filled with smoke and debris.

"Cal, you and Rafe stay here. Keep those buggers out there off our backs for as long as you can."

"You got it," James said.

"Let's move," McCarter said to Manning and Lyons.

They made for the bottom of the ramp, hearing the last of the debris patter to the concrete.

They reached the bottom of the ramp, leaving

James and Encizo to take their positions at the head of the ramp. The pair had ample ammunition for the weapons they were carrying. Each carried grenades, and James still had a number of M-433 rounds for his grenade launcher.

"THEY'LL KNOW we're coming now," Manning stated.

"So let's not disappoint them," McCarter said, and led the way into the passage.

The M-433 had thrown its powerful blast into the passage, catching Nikolai Gagarin as he tried to back away. The Russian felt the concussion of the detonation. He was no more than eight feet from the epicenter of the exploding round. The force tore into him, searing and destroying his flesh and bone. It picked him up and smashed him back against the concrete wall, his pulverized flesh smeared against it. What remained of Nikolai Gagarin lay at the base of the wall. The only item not harmed by the explosion was the SIG-Sauer pistol he had been carrying. It lay on the blood-spattered floor, inches away from the tatters of his right hand.

Phoenix Force separated, staying close to opposite walls of the passage. Lyons was just behind Manning on the right. McCarter, limping slightly, held the left side. Up ahead, where the first fork in the passage showed, they picked up whispered words. There was the click of a bolt being cocked. McCarter held up his left hand and they all stopped.

Behind them they heard the crackle of autofire from the position James and Encizo were holding.

A voice was raised ahead of them. Shadows flickered on the wall of the left fork in the passage. A slim Korean, carrying an AK, ran into sight. He came on a few feet before he spotted the three men waiting for him. If he had retreated, he might have moved back around the corner without being harmed. Instead he brought up the AK and fired a burst, filling the passage with bullets that bounced and whined off the concrete.

Manning and McCarter dropped to a crouch, raising their weapons. They were behind Lyons, who remained standing and returned fire with the Korean. The Able Team leader's shots were placed dead center, coring into the target chest high and spinning him off his feet. The Korean crashed to the concrete floor of the passage, trailing a fine mist of pink. Before the corpse struck the concrete, Lyons ran forward, reaching the fork in the passage to peer around the curved wall. He saw the Korean's partner, waiting, his own weapon half raised. Lyons leaned out, tracking his AK onto the man, and fired a short burst that knocked the gunner off his feet and slammed him to the floor.

McCarter and Manning joined him. Lyons glanced at them. He ran a hand over his unshaved face, shaking his head.

"I look like shit. I feel like shit. I can still beat you two," he stated.

"We could always take him back to that camp," Manning said.

They took the left fork and moved on, aware that they were on a downslope that was leading them deeper underground with each step.

The gunfire behind them began to fade. They could hear it, but it was muffled now by the cold, rough concrete surrounding them.

"Berkoff is going to be well protected," McCarter said. "He's their only hope for the code breaking."

Autofire crackled, directed at them. Bullets scored the concrete walls, leaving white marks behind.

"These guys don't give up," Manning observed.

"Neither do we," McCarter replied.

JAMES AND ENCIZO WERE keeping the Korean troops back. Their position allowed them wide coverage of the main site, presenting them with the opportunity to spot any attempted assault before it got under way.

They were drawing return fire from the Koreans, but due to the extended walls that flanked either side of the ramp, there was no way of acquiring good target locks.

James saw Encizo tapping his headset.

"Problem?"

"I don't know," Encizo said.

His voice coming through James's own headset was accompanied by a background crackle, then what sounded like a distant voice.

"Maybe something from the others," James said. "Poor transmission coming from inside that complex."

"Hell, no," Encizo said. "I know that damn voice."

James listened to the voice on his own headset, a grin forming on his lips.

"Hey, flyboy, where are you?"

"We see your fires," Jack Grimaldi told him. "You guys need any help down there?"

# CHAPTER TWENTY-THREE

Grimaldi had picked up the burning fuel within moments of hearing Phoenix Force communicating via their headsets. He had started to talk to them, though it was a couple of minutes before anyone responded.

"Yes, we do need help, buddy," James replied to his question.

"I'm coming in from the east," Grimaldi said.

"Stay on that heading," James said. "It should bring you directly at our position. We have a bunch of unfriendlies trying to dislodge us from the entrance ramp to the complex. Maybe you can persuade them to back off."

"Let me do a flyover and see where you guys are."

Checking the stub-wing tanks, Grimaldi saw that the fuel level was low. He had enough fuel in the main tanks for both maneuvers at the site and for the return flight. He cut the fuel from the wing tanks and changed to the main tanks, then released the wing tanks. Dragon Slayer lifted as the additional weight was lost.

Grimaldi pushed up the pace, dropping lower so

he could assess what lay below. Dragon Slayer swept in over the site's east wall. Scanning the site, the Stony Man pilot saw the burning fuel tank, the rivers of flaming fuel that had spread out from the heart of the blaze. The site itself was like any construction site in the world, with materials and equipment scattered around, piles of excavated earth. Grimaldi saw figures moving in and around the area. As Dragon Slayer flew over the site, he made out the shape of the main structure, which was low to the ground with its concrete construction glistening in the rain. He identified the entrance ramp and spotted two figures crouched behind the cover of the side walls, one of them giving a brief wave as the helicopter swept by.

"Looks like they've got themselves in a tight squeeze there," Blancanales said.

"We'll loosen it up for them," Grimaldi said.

He banked the helicopter, making a wide turn that would bring them back in from the west.

"Heads down, guys, it could get noisy," he warned James and Encizo.

Dragon Slayer swept in with a whine of power from her engines. Grimaldi held his thumb over the firing button of the 30 mm chain gun, leveling out as he came in over the concrete structure again. When he touched the button the chain gun erupted, flame spouting from the muzzle as it loosed off its deadly fire. The 30 mm shells struck with devastating effect, gouging earth and concrete alike, puncturing anything that came within its range. Figures scattered before the marching line of shells.

"Watch out for the guard towers on the walls," Encizo warned. "They have machine guns."

Grimaldi arced the combat chopper around and came in from a different direction. He flicked on the powerful spotlight recessed under Dragon Slayer's nose, using it to pinpoint his targets as he sought the towers. The 30 mm shells shredded the support legs, toppling the towers and their chattering machine guns.

Passing along the south wall, Grimaldi and Able Team were able to see where the main gate had been blown from its tracks. Before he turned again, Grimaldi saw the two trucks that had contained the prisoners on their way back to the camp. The trucks were empty now, the prisoners having taken the opportunity to break free once their guards had been ordered to storm the site. Grimaldi saw a reason to deprive the Koreans the means of any pursuit, and used the chain gun to put the trucks out of action. The 30 mm shells tore the trucks apart. The second vehicle burst into flame as the ravaging shells ignited the fuel tank.

Swinging in over the site, Grimaldi took Dragon Slayer directly over the head of the ramp, hovering no more than a few feet off the ground. He arced the chain gun back and forth, laying down a hail of deadly fire while Blancanales and Schwarz dropped to the ground to reinforce Phoenix Force.

"Hey, guys, I'll be around," he said.

"You better be," Blancanales warned. "We bought return tickets."

"Check out the area to our right," James said. "Missiles under cover. Launch cradles."

"Affirmative. Just blow the whistle when you want to move out."

Dragon Slayer rose into the dark sky above the site, Grimaldi seeking the targets James had described. It didn't take him long. The launch pits were well illuminated by the burning fuel that had spilled into them. He made out the long shapes of missiles, waiting on their wheeled cradles. Turning Dragon Slayer, he activated the missile pods, then loosed a couple of heat seekers. They struck the cradled missiles and reduced them to masses of tangled, smoking metal.

Taking Dragon Slayer on a sweep over the north wall of the site, the Stony Man pilot caught a glimpse of an AS365 Dauphin commercial helicopter parked a short distance away. The chopper's rotors were idling slowly. Grimaldi got the distinct impression it was waiting for someone who might be leaving in a hurry.

He brought Dragon Slayer around and back over the wall to cover the site. The image of the helicopter stayed with him.

DUONG CHIN HAD SEEN the swooping dark outline of Dragon Slayer on the monitor screens. It appeared the Americans had brought in reinforcements. The fleeting images of the combat helicopter confirmed Chin's earlier misgivings. The site wasn't going to survive. And the longer he allowed Berkoff to remain here, the less chance there would be of accessing the Slingshot disks. Chin made his decision.

It was time to make a strategic retreat.

If Took and Gagarin wanted to stay, it was their choice. As far as Chin was concerned, this episode was over. A stubborn determination to hang on to the last moment would only result in their deaths.

Chin moved quickly. He used his radio to contact Lim.

"Move Berkoff now," he ordered. "Make certain you bring the disks. Take him to the north fire exit and wait for me. If any of Took's people get in your way, deal with them. Understand?"

"I understand," Lim said.

LIM ENTERED THE ROOM where Berkoff was working. The German swung around in his seat, scowling.

"I asked not to be disturbed. Where is Chin?"

"We have to leave. Now. Comrade Chin will join us shortly."

"Leave?" Berkoff yelled. "I am just beginning my code breaking..."

"The site is under attack. If we remain, we could die. We are leaving to return to Beijing. Understand, Mr. Berkoff, there is no argument here. We cannot remain any longer."

Berkoff sighed. If Chin had decided they had to leave, then it would happen. The Chinese was no fool. He wouldn't risk their lives if he thought it was dangerous to remain.

"I need a few minutes to come out of the system. At this stage I can't risk doing anything that might harm the disks."

Lim nodded. "Do it, then. I will stay with you."

As Berkoff returned to his computer, Lim spoke

into his radio, informing the rest of his team they had to prepare to leave. He warned them to be alert for any sign of the American commando team.

CALVIN JAMES MANAGED to contact McCarter over his headset. The reception was spasmodic, the thick concrete walls blocking part of the signal, but even so James managed to inform McCarter that Grimaldi had arrived and that Able Team was now with them.

"Jack's doing a pretty good job of beating up the Koreans on the surface. He keeps making passes and laying down 30 mm fire."

"Maybe you guys want to back off a little," McCarter said. "Get inside under cover."

The contact broke then, with only a soft hiss issuing from James's headset.

"You hear that?" he asked the others. "Okay, let's back off. Get inside."

They moved down the ramp and through the entrance.

The floor was littered with debris from the grenade blast, and to one side of the passage they saw the grisly remains of Nikolai Gagarin.

It was Schwarz who spotted the steel door on its rollers. He located the control box and knocked on the power. He jabbed at the buttons and was finally rewarded by the door starting to close. The moment the door was secure, Encizo switched off the power.

"We need a presence here," James said, "in case those jokers out there break through, or open this door from the outside."

"Fine by me," Encizo said. "I've done enough walking the last couple of days."

"I'll stay with Rafe," Blancanales said.

"Okay."

James glanced at Schwarz. "You set?"

Schwarz nodded. They moved off along the passage at a trot, weapons held in the firing position. Some yards along they spotted a side passage. James spoke into his headset and raised a faint McCarter.

"You guys in the main passage?"

"Yes."

"We picked up on a side passage just along from the entrance. We'll check it out."

"Okay."

James and Schwarz entered the side passage which ran in a straight line for about twenty feet then opened on a flight of steps leading deeper into the complex. The steps dropped roughly twenty feet, bringing them to another level of the complex. Directly in front of them a steel door stood ajar. Schwarz stood to one side covering James as the Phoenix Force warrior edged the door open, swinging it wide.

James looked in on a long, narrow room through main wall, which was a glass panel. Inside the room was a long control desk and a number of swivel chairs. No people were in sight. Beyond the glass James could see what were obviously the launch pits for the missiles. The steel-structured missile cradles were visible, sunk into the concrete floor. Dripping tongues of flame were seeping through from the sections aboveground, and James recalled seeing the upper pits ablaze with gasoline that had flooded into them from the breached tank. Smoke was fogging the launch pits as the burning gas attacked cabling and hoses.

Schwarz peered into the room, realizing what they had found.

"We should leave this place as we found it," he said dryly.

"I guess so."

James plucked a pair of grenades from his webbing. He handed his M-16 to Schwarz while he took the pins from the grenades. Stepping inside the room, James placed the grenades, a few feet apart, on the control desk, then turned and quickly stepped out of the room, pulling the steel door shut behind him.

Schwarz was already climbing the steps, James hard on his heels, when the grenades detonated. Smoke blew out from around the steel door, and they heard debris from the twin blasts slamming against the inside of the door.

"Take more than a new fuse to fix that," Schwarz said.

They returned to the main passage and continued along it, passing the body of the Korean Lyons had shot. They found themselves at the fork. When they eased around the left passage entrance, they saw the second body.

"Looks like they passed this way," James said.

They moved back and took the right passage, which brought them to the security area, deserted now. The flickering monitor screens showed them the exterior of the site. On one screen Dragon Slayer could be seen sweeping back and forth, flame issuing from the muzzle of the underslung 30 mm chain gun.

"Heads up," Schwarz warned.

He had picked up on the sound of hard-soled boots on the concrete floor of the passage that led out from the far side of the security area. A trio of uniformed figures came into view, weapons up. The moment they saw James and Schwarz they opened fire.

The Stony Man commandos dropped to the floor, rolling apart as autofire raked the desks above them. Monitor screens imploded as bullets shattered them. Glass and slivers of plastic filled the air. The room rattled to the loud chatter of gunfire.

"Jesus Christ!" Schwarz yelled.

He dragged himself under the closest desk, feeling concrete chips pepper his legs as the shooters altered their aim. Pushing his MP-5 forward, he triggered a burst at their exposed lower limbs. Flesh and bone shattered as the sustained burst tore through them. One man fell on his side, screaming in pain, and brought himself directly into line with Schwarz's continuing burst. The 9 mm bullets ripped into his upper chest and head.

Calvin James had continued his floor movement, wriggling in behind the desk, ignoring the debris showering him. He pushed up into a kneeling position, his M-16 tracking in on the remaining shooters. He triggered quick shots into the upper bodies of the two men, already distracted by Schwarz's leg shots. They toppled over, chests punctured by the hard-driven 5.56 mm bullets.

Scrambling to his feet, Schwarz moved to the passage that had produced the three Koreans. He had barely leaned his head around the corner of the wall when an autoweapon opened up. Bullets gouged the concrete, and Schwarz felt hot splinters lash his cheek. Moments later he felt warm blood course down the side of his face. He pushed the muzzle of his MP-5 around the edge of the wall and triggered a burst along the passage.

"Let me," James offered.

He stood on the other side of the passage, slotting an HEDP round into the underslung launcher. Lifting the M-16, he triggered the round down the passage. It exploded with a hard sound, smoke billowing thickly. Stepping into the passage James and Schwarz ran along the passage, peering through the smoke. They made out hazy figures moving about. Someone yelled in Korean. James opened up with his M-16, laying down a heavy burst, his shots taking out the survivors of the grenade blast.

Beside him Schwarz's MP-5 added its sound, 9 mm slugs finding targets.

They reached the end of the passage and found a number of bodies. Two of them weren't in uniform. They weren't Korean, either.

They were Chinese, dressed in black.

"Who the hell are these guys?" James asked.

"Whoever, they dealt themselves in on the wrong game," Schwarz said.

Up ahead they heard autofire.

"That could be David and the others," James said. "Let's find out."

# CHAPTER TWENTY-FOUR

McCarter pushed back the nagging pain in his thigh. He knew that in the best possible circumstances he should have been resting, having a medic stop the bleeding and bandage it properly. Only he was in a combat situation, chasing around looking for a pair of bloody computer disks, hoping to get his hands on them before some German cyber genius cracked the encryption code.

They had reached a T-junction. The right showed an empty passage. To the left was a short passage ending in a door, with another passage cutting off to the left again.

Three black-clad Chinese, armed with Uzi submachine guns, were guarding the door.

"Berkoff?" Manning asked.

"The Chinese protecting their investment," McCarter said. "So there's our target."

Lyons fed a fresh magazine into his AK and snapped back the bolt.

"We going to talk all night?" he asked.

"No," McCarter said. "Just let's make sure we do this right."

They broke cover, spreading across the passage, raising their weapons to cover the three Chinese.

The door to the room opened, and a fourth Chinese stepped out, a tall, broad-shouldered man beside him.

The man had pale hair, shoulder length.

It was Jerome Berkoff.

The Chinese with Berkoff was facing the three Stony Man commandos. He had an Uzi in his free hand and he raised it and opened fire, pushing Berkoff to one side as he did.

A burst of 9 mm bullets struck the walls of the passage as the Stony Man warriors dropped to the floor.

The Chinese with Berkoff—Lim—shouted instructions to his three guards. They began to raise their own weapons.

From behind McCarter, Manning's and Lyons's autoweapons began to fire.

One of the Chinese guards was hit in the chest, driven into the wall behind him, bloody holes in his chest. His convulsed body rebounded from the wall, and he crashed facedown on the floor.

The other two Chinese loosed short bursts before they turned and followed Lim, who had propelled Berkoff down the left-hand passage, out of sight.

As McCarter and the others scrambled to their feet, they were joined by James and Schwarz.

"Let's move," McCarter snapped. "Those blokes have Berkoff. And he'll have the bloody disks."

They headed for the side passage. As he passed the open door of the room Berkoff had exited, James glanced inside. There was an impressive array of computer equipment in the plain room. James took a grenade from his webbing, popped the pin and tossed the grenade inside the room, pulling the door shut before he went after the others.

When the grenade exploded within the confines of the small room, the blast destroyed the electronic equipment and blew a hole in the outer wall, filling the passage with dust and concrete.

CHIN WAS RETURNING to the computer room when he saw Lim, Berkoff and the two surviving Chinese heading his way.

"They are behind us," Lim told him.

He took out his radio and spoke to the pilot of the waiting helicopter.

"We are on our way out. Bring the helicopter inside the wall and wait for us where we agreed."

Chin led them along the passage to the emergency exit he had located when he had first checked out the complex. This one would allow them to exit close to where the helicopter would pick them up. He went up the short flight of steps and broke the seal on the drop bar that opened the steel door. Chin placed his foot against the door and pushed it open. Boxed-in concrete steps led upward. They would emerge at ground level.

"Hurry," Chin yelled.

Berkoff stepped through the door, hugging a flat plastic case close to his chest. He saw Chin staring at him.

"Yes, I have the disks with me, Chin. You really think I dare leave without them?"

"I never doubted you, Jerome. Not for a moment."

The Chinese pushed Berkoff ahead of him, and they began to climb the steep rise of steps. Lim and his remaining men followed.

THE EMERGENCY-EXIT door was open. Lyons pushed his way to the front and checked the steps leading up to ground level. He ducked back as one of the Chinese opened up, 9 mm bullets slapping the concrete at the foot of the steps.

"We go in there and they can pick us off one by one," he said.

McCarter spoke to Blancanales and Encizo via his headset.

"Berkoff and his Chinese minders are making a break, taking an emergency exit that comes out on the north side of the complex. Any chance for an intercept?"

"We'll see what we can do."

BLANCANALES MOVED to the control panel and activated the door mechanism. By that time Encizo was in contact with Grimaldi.

"Jack, can you clear a path for us?"

"You have a bunch of hostiles at the head of the ramp. I'll clear it for you."

Blancanales and Encizo drew to the side of the door as it rolled open. Autofire clattered from the top of the ramp, bullets chipping the concrete.

The glare of Dragon Slayer's spotlight hit the ramp, pinpointing the Koreans who were directing their fire at the entrance to the complex. Moments later the chain gun opened up, traversing the width of the ramp and silencing the enemy guns. Swinging the helicopter around, Grimaldi laid down heavy fire across the site, driving back any other opposition.

"Make it a go," Grimaldi said to the waiting Stony Man commandos.

Blancanales and Encizo powered up the ramp, reaching the top, with Dragon Slayer hovering overhead, looking for all the world like a huge black bird. As soon as Grimaldi saw them, he tipped Dragon Slayer's nose to cover them as they skirted the outside of the complex. The very presence of the combat chopper held back any attack.

The AS365 helicopter was just rising above the north wall of the site. As Blancanales and Encizo rounded the end of the building, they saw figures moving into sight from the head of the steps.

"We have them spotted," Blancanales yelled into his headset, trying to make himself heard above the rotor noise of the AS365 and Dragon Slayer. The rotor wash from the pair of choppers was whipping up debris from the ground and driving the rain into his face.

The rattle of autofire cut through the noise. Bullets gouged the earth to one side of the Stony Man pair. They parted company, each returning fire.

The fair-haired man at the head of the group ducked low as he made a dash for the AS365 as it swept in over the site, coming in only a few feet above the ground.

"Berkoff," Encizo said.

He cut off to intercept the German. He had discarded his AK in preference for the MP-5 slung across his chest.

Blancanales turned his own MP-5 on the Chinese who had cleared the side of the building. His burst caught the tail man, spinning him off his feet as the 9 mm slugs took him in the side. The man went down, scrambling to regain his balance. The Able Team commando hit him with a second burst, the shots stitching the Chinese across the upper chest. He collapsed to the ground and stayed down.

DUONG CHIN CLOSED UP behind Berkoff. The German was starting to panic, seeming ready to turn back for the protection of the complex.

"This is crazy," Berkoff yelled. "They will kill us."

"No, Jerome. Once we are in the helicopter, we will be safe."

"This wasn't in our agreement."

"Things change. Now go!"

The crackle of autofire threw Berkoff. He glanced around, seeing the flames against the night sky illuminating the site, the menacing outline of Dragon Slayer hovering in the background.

"No! I won't. They will shoot you down once we are in the air."

Berkoff turned without warning and moved to push past Chin. The Chinese reached out and snatched the plastic case holding the disks, shouldering Berkoff out of his way.

"Then go where you want," he said, and continued on toward the helicopter.

Berkoff was left stranded, with nowhere to go if he didn't follow Chin to the helicopter. He was roughly pushed out of the way by the other Chinese as they made for the helicopter.

"THE LEAD CHINESE GUY just took a package from Berkoff," Encizo yelled into his microphone. "I'm betting it was the disks."

"Don't let him get on board," McCarter snapped back.

They were moving in to cut off the fleeing Chinese.

Manning paused to shoulder his M-16. He picked up on Chin as the Chinese reached out to grab hold of the open hatch. The M-16 fired a single shot. The 5.56 mm bullet struck Chin in the right shoulder, the impact knocking him against the AS365's fuselage.

Calvin James, hanging back, snapped in the last of his M-433 explosive rounds into the launcher. He brought the M-16 to his shoulder and fired off the grenade. It struck the helicopter just short of the tail rotor and tore the unit clean off. The blast spun the aircraft and it slewed sideways, tilting. Before it struck the ground, the flailing rotors swept directly into the path of Lim and his teammates. Lim and the man close behind him were struck at shoulder level, the keen edge of the rotor decapitating them both. The helicopter's deadweight rolled it, and the mass of the fuselage pinned Duong Chin beneath it up to his waist. He gave a terrified scream as his body was crushed, blood spurting from his mouth in a crimson torrent.

The surviving Chinese turned toward Phoenix Force in a moment of pure defiance, his finger already on the trigger of his SMG. He hadn't noticed Schwarz, who was standing a little way off. The Able Team warrior had been covering the Chinese group all the while. Schwarz fired before the Chinese could complete his action, dropping the man on the ground.

McCarter moved to the wrecked helicopter. He crouched beside the bloody body of Duong Chin and picked up the plastic case that had slipped from the man's fingers. He opened it and breathed a sigh of relief when he saw the two disks inside. He tucked them inside one of his pockets and closed the zip. As he began to stand, he smelled leaking fuel from somewhere in the AS365.

"Let's get out of here," he said. "Jack, open the doors we're on our way."

"Have your tickets ready, ladies," Grimaldi replied.

CAPTAIN YUN CROUCHED in the shadows, his eyes fixed on the American team. He had worked his way across the site, moving from section to section, clutching an AK in his bleeding, raw hands. The havoc wreaked by the American combat helicopter had left Yun shaken and bruised. His uniform was torn, filthy from smoke and wet from the rain. Though not badly hurt, he was bleeding from scratches caused by flying debris.

More than that he was consumed by an anger that

grew stronger with each passing moment. That rage was directed toward the invading Americans who had dared and won. The devastating power of the black helicopter had driven his soldiers back every time he had ordered them to attack. No amount of screaming at them made any difference. They were defenseless against the superior and awesome firepower of the aircraft. Yun had seen his men fall, bodies destroyed by the relentless cannon fire, and his instinct told him there was no way of defeating the helicopter.

With his force scattered and the site looking more like a battleground, Yun had taken cover in the shadow of the main complex building. Crouching there, he had witnessed the appearance of the two Americans coming up the ramp, using the helicopter as cover. His curiosity had gotten the better of him as the Americans had moved around to the north side of the complex, and he had followed.

He had witnessed the confrontation with Chin and the American team. The destruction of Chin's escape helicopter. The final indignity had come when member of the American team had recovered the computer disks from Chin's crushed body.

The black helicopter had swept in to pick up the team, and as they started to make their way toward it Yun received another surprise.

At the rear of the group, still clad in his work clothing, was Yun's blond-haired American prisoner.

The Korean had stared at the figure, almost disbelieving what his eyes were seeing. He might have asked himself how the man had survived during his escape and how he had found the other Americans.

Yun asked none of them, because the only thing that did matter was the chance he was getting. If nothing else came out of this whole affair, he could at least make good his promise.

That if the American did escape from the camp, Yun would find and kill him.

He checked the AK, making certain the magazine was loaded and the weapon was cocked. He glanced at the hovering helicopter. He would have to move within its position to reach his quarry. It might have been possible for Yun to have fired from where he crouched. The range was a little far in the poor visibility, and there was also the fact he wanted the American to see him before he died. Killing the man from cover wouldn't achieve Yun's full desire. He slipped from cover, keeping the wall at his left side as he edged toward his man. Rain stung his eyes, and he shook his head to clear them. It was only now he realized just how cold it was. The temperature had dropped severely again. The cold was making it difficult for him to maintain his grip on the weapon.

Yun had almost reached the point where he was directly in line with his target.

At that moment the downed AS365 burst into flame as the spilled fuel ignited. There was a soft explosion, the flames billowing up around the machine.

The resultant glare lit up the immediate area. Yun found himself exposed in the light, his form standing out against the concrete wall of the complex. There was nowhere to hide. Yun was in the open, his shadow black against the wall at his back.

Any further hope of concealment was gone. Surprise had been lost.

Yun stepped away from the wall, tracking his AK on the figure of his prisoner.

CARL LYONS HAD GLIMPSED movement off to his right as the leaked fuel illuminated the area. He half turned, saw Yun and the autorifle in his hands.

There was a frozen moment in Lyons's mind as he set eyes on the Korean. Images flashed up: the labor camp. Its shambling inmates; Chuck Rinaldi and his unnecessary death and the violent outcome of the incident that had followed; the suffering and the deprivation following Lyons's capture. They were still powerful in his memory, too strong to have lessened in their impact. They fueled his reaction at seeing Yun.

Lyons threw himself forward and down, hitting the hard ground. He pushed the muzzle of his AK up at Yun, triggering the powerful autorifle.

Yun's single shot passed over Lyons's prone body.

Then the stream of autofire from Lyons's weapon cut into Yun's body. The angle of fire drove the rounds up into the Korean's torso and chest cavity. He held the trigger back until the magazine was empty. Yun's body was reduced to bloody shreds, his uniform glistening with red. He fell back against the wall of the complex, slithering down to slump at its base. He fell sideways, his face pressing against the hard earth, his blood pouring from the open wounds in his body.

Lyons pushed to his feet, dropping the empty AK.

He reached Dragon Slayer and leaned against the open hatch, his remaining strength draining from his weary body. He was too tired to even climb into the cabin.

Two pairs of hands reached out to grab him. Lyons was lifted bodily into the compartment. He was pushed into one of the seats and when he glanced up he saw Blancanales and Schwarz leaning over him. They were staring at him with awkward grins on their faces.

Lyons felt Dragon Slayer lift, heard the hatch slide shut and lock tight. He looked at his partners and saw they were still staring at him.

"Son of a bitch," Schwarz said.

"We thought you were gone."

Lyons shifted on his seat. "First one of you who hugs me is dead."

Schwarz dropped into a seat next to Lyons. "There we were thinking he had a bad time."

"We come all this way and he threatens us," Blancanales agreed.

He looked back at Lyons. The Ironman had slumped back in his seat, eyes closed, his arms drawn across his chest in the position he had adopted during his captivity. Blancanales studied Lyons's appearance and knew he would never be able to understand what had happened to him, or what might be going on inside his head.

MCCARTER HAD SHRUGGED out of his combat harness before joining Grimaldi in the copilot seat. The

Briton stretched his long frame into the body-form comfort of the seat.

"How's it goin', buddy?" Grimaldi asked.

"A lot bloody better now than five minutes ago."

"Yeah."

Grimaldi completed his information feed into Dragon Slayer's computer. He held the course as he locked on to the distant signal coming from the carrier waiting for them out in the waters of the Sea of Japan.

"Any sign of interception?" McCarter asked.

Grimaldi shook his head. "I guess we took them by surprise. And knocking out the communication center back there didn't give them any chance to call in the Korean cavalry."

"You get what you went for?"

McCarter unzipped his pocket and pulled out the plastic box. He opened it and showed Grimaldi the pair of shiny disks.

"That's what all this has been about?"

"Too right," McCarter said.

"They run Slingshot from those?"

"So they tell me."

"I hope they lock 'em up good and tight this time," Grimaldi said.

"If they don't, mate, they'll have me to answer to. And I kid you not."

Grimaldi established a satellite link with Stony Man. He passed the handset to McCarter.

"Hi, David," Barbara Price said. "You feel like giving me an update?"

"We're all fine and thanks for asking, ma'am," McCarter said.

"Don't give me a hard time, mister. We've all been worrying like crazy back here. You think it's easy waiting around for news about you guys?"

"Miss Barbara, I do declare you require to chill out, child," McCarter drawled in an exaggerated Southern drawl. "Lordy, you will bust if you don't."

McCarter heard someone chuckling in the background and realized Price must have put the call on the speakers.

"David, just tell me you are all okay."

"All present and accounted for. Able Team is now three again. Cuts and bruises all around but no major damage."

"Where are you?"

"On our way back to meet the Navy."

"Objective achieved?"

"In my hand at this very moment. Intact."

"Boss man will be happy to hear that."

"Tell the Bear to run a satellite scan over the site. I think he'll like what he sees."

"Will do. Take care. All of you."

McCarter closed the connection. He put away the handset. Grimaldi was grinning at the interplay between the Briton and Price.

"One day you'll go too far with her."

"I know," McCarter said.

"So why do it?"

"Bloody hell, Jack, because I want to be there the day she blows her stack. It'll be nothing less than spectacular."

"It could also be your last day on Earth."

"True. But what a way to go."

Someone tapped McCarter on the shoulder. It was James.

"You were busy at the time," he said. "We didn't have time to bring you up to speed."

"What?"

"We couldn't just leave him, could we?"

James moved to one side so that McCarter was able to see into the rear compartment. He looked beyond Able and Phoenix to where Jerome Berkoff squatted against the bulkhead. The German looked frightened. He was just realizing what he had almost lost.

"I have a feeling he might regret being brought on board," McCarter said. "Once we hand him over, he's going to have a lot of explaining to do."

"When you're ready," James said, "I'll take a look at that leg of yours."

"Leg?" McCarter nodded. "I'd forgotten about that."

Grimaldi fed more power to Dragon Slayer's engines, feeling the helicopter surge forward. He checked his monitors. They were on course and they would be over the water soon. He was flying a direct course for the sea. Once clear of the Korean landmass he could make a run that would take them out beyond the territorial exclusion zone. Once they were in international waters the Koreans would have less of an excuse to follow them. It would also mean Grimaldi could call on the carrier to send aid if he found they were being threatened.

He put a satellite call through to Stony Man, getting Kurtzman on the line.

"Okay. We're homeward bound. I need anything you can get me on possible interception."

"I have you on the screen," Kurtzman said. "Nothing near you. Apart from you, the zone is empty."

"I'm flying low. Using the terrain tracking. If we can stay on this course and low altitude, I can maybe stay off their radar."

"No sweat."

"You had contact with the carrier?"

"They know you're on your way. Right now they're coming about and heading up toward where you should clear the exclusion zone."

"That's fine. If the situation changes, give me a call."

"You got it, pal," Kurtzman said.

"I think we're okay," Grimaldi called over his shoulder.

"About time," Blancanales said. "Now can we break out those damn flasks of coffee?"

"Knock yourselves out," Grimaldi said.

He just wished he had something other than coffee. They deserved better than that.

## EPILOGUE

*Stony Man Farm, Virginia*

"Talk about catching the flak," Brognola said.

He was in his shirtsleeves, stubbled, and looked as if he hadn't had any sleep for the duration.

"I thought the President was pleased," Price said. "He has his Slingshot disks back, and the Korean missile site has been put out of action."

"Pleased?" McCarter repeated. "He should be doing bloody back flips."

"Don't get me wrong," Brognola said, addressing the assembled teams. "He was ready to give you guys medals. But I told him you wouldn't hear of it. Same as when I refused his offer of pay raises."

There was a brief silence until Blancanales said, "He almost had me there. Hal, you been taking advice from David on how to jerk us around?"

Brognola waved a hand in surrender as he sat down.

"The grief is coming in from the North Koreans, the Chinese. Even the Russians."

"About?"

"They all figure we've been pushing people around again. The Russians blame us for the death of Nikolai Gagarin. The Chinese say we destroyed one of their helicopters and caused the deaths of a team of advisers who were at the Korean processing plant."

"Processing?" Manning said. "Processing what?"

"They claim it was some kind of water-purification facility."

"My ass," James muttered.

"And I suppose Jerome Berkoff was there to retune their TV sets?" McCarter said.

"They are all playing the victim in this," Brognola said. "It's all bluff because they know why we were there. They got their butts kicked, and they have to make the gestures to save face."

"This is all bull," Carl Lyons said. "Let's not forget I was right in the middle of this damn charade. There was no water plant. It was a missile site. They stole our defense data, and they were going to use it against us." He leaned forward and stared at Brognola. "Tell me our diplomatic pussyfoots didn't even mention I had been taken to Korea and kicked around like some football."

"You weren't mentioned, Carl. You're right. As far as the diplomatic community is concerned, you weren't there. They don't even have a labor camp. The Koreans haven't mentioned you and they won't. This is all shadow play now. Negotiations. Smoothing-over-the-cracks time. Making nice with the enemy. And before you say it I know it stinks. Hey, it isn't the first time it's happened and it won't be the last. We can't stand up to be counted because we're not supposed to exist.''

Brognola knew how his people felt. He had expressed his feelings to the President during their debriefing. His words hadn't fallen on deaf ears. The President was aware. But he had to play the game. He had made it known to the North Koreans that their project to kill Slingshot wouldn't be forgotten. His meeting with the North Korean representative had been icy, making the man fully aware of the U.S. government's feelings over the whole affair. His defiant stand had left the Korean in no doubt that the American administration would be watching them very closely.

''The President asked me to tell you *he* won't forget what you did. And I believe him for what it's worth.''

Lyons shrugged and slumped back in his seat. He gazed at a corner of the room, almost as if he were somewhere else. Although his wounds had been tended to and he had shaved off the ragged beard, he still looked gaunt. His face bore the marks of his time in Korea and the exposure to the harsh climate. Even Blancanales and Schwarz had noticed the change in his manner. He was slowly returning to his normal self, but there were moments when he drifted away to another place. Time was the only healer for his condition.

''After all the missions we've run, I don't suppose we should expect any other result,'' Katz said.

"You mean we should be used to it?" Manning said.

"What happens to Berkoff?" Schwarz asked.

"Good question," Brognola said. "He's claiming he did nothing wrong. Just took on a contract for an old customer. He says the U.S. can't accuse him of anything because he's not a citizen. He was living in Europe and just because he was working for the Chinese doesn't give us the right to harass him." The big Fed shrugged. "Maybe he's right. The legal departments can sort it out. Berkoff also says he didn't actually touch the disks. He was still setting up his equipment when Chin forced him to leave."

"He'll probably walk free," Katz said, "and then sue for wrongful arrest."

"Quo Lam Sun won't walk free," James said. "He died trying to help us. It doesn't add up somehow."

"Don't forget Chuck Rinaldi," Lyons said. "Everybody else did. Poor bastard didn't even know what year it was."

It was crazy, Lyons thought. People could be lost. They could die in some godforsaken place thousands of miles from home and nobody gave a damn. All the fuss centered around two plastic disks. Rinaldi was gone, his body buried in some unmarked grave, and in the main he would be forgotten. Lyons knew he could just as easily have ended up the same.

Dead, buried and forgotten.

But he had been lucky. He had been saved by a little old Korean who had pulled him out of the cold and revived him. Two strangers from diverse cultures, they had shared a little time together. Bound by similar experiences, unable to speak because of different languages, they had ignored the politics that said they were enemies.

Lyons didn't even know the Korean's name.

But he was damn sure he was going to find out what *Annyŏnghi kaseyo* meant.

# James Axler
# Outlanders®

# FAR
# EMPIRE

Waging a covert war that ranges from a subterranean complex
in the desert to a forgotten colony on the moon, former magistrate
Kane, brother-in-arms Grant and archivist-turned-warrior
Brigid Baptiste find themselves pawns in a stunning strategy of
evil. A beautiful hybrid carries an unborn child—a blueprint for
hope in a dark world. She seeks Kane's help, unwittingly leading
them into a trap from which there may be no escape....

*In the Outlands, the shocking truth is humanity's last hope.*

# DEATH LANDS®

JAMES AXLER

# DEATH LANDS

### Destiny's Truth

## Destiny's Truth

*Available in*
*December 2002*
*at your favorite retail outlet.*

Emerging from a gateway in New England, Ryan Cawdor and his band of wayfaring survivalists ally themselves with a group of women warriors who join their quest to locate the Illuminated Ones, a mysterious pre-dark sect who may possess secret knowledge of Deathlands. Yet their pursuit becomes treacherous, for their quarry has unleashed a deadly plague in a twisted plot to cleanse the earth. As Ryan's group falls victim, time is running out—for the intrepid survivors…and for humanity itself.